THE
DEEP END

A gripping crime thriller, packed with suspense

DENVER MURPHY

THE
BOOK
FOLKS

Published by The Book Folks

London, 2019

ISBN 978-1-0813-4376-7

www.thebookfolks.com

This book is dedicated to my son.
Dreams do come true.

Chapter One

'Detective Constable Ruby Knight,' she whispered to herself in an effort to combat the growing sense, prompted by the familiar surroundings, that she'd taken a step back in her life. She drove past the King Harry estate, following the same bus route she had taken countless times as a teenager. The infrequent gaps in the trees gave her a view of Verulamium Park on her left and the imposing sight of St. Albans Abbey just beyond.

An adult now, she was better able to appreciate the attractiveness of the area, but there still remained that longing to be somewhere more gritty; more exciting. Now sat in queuing traffic at the bottom of Holywell Hill, Ruby regarded the commuters entering the Abbey Station on her right with a hint of jealousy, knowing that they were most likely heading to Watford and then on to London.

Joining the Metropolitan Police had been an easy decision and she had spent the first four years of her adult life in England's capital city. Challenging as it had been, she had loved every minute of it.

Ruby's impatience in joining the force at the earliest opportunity, rather than waiting until after she had gone to university, was matched by her ambition to progress as quickly as possible. The price of becoming one of the youngest detectives in the country was leaving her beloved

London and returning to leafy Hertfordshire. But just like moving back in with her parents was meant to be a temporary measure, for convenience, she only planned staying at St. Albans Police Station to build up her experience before joining a CID in a major city.

She heard the ping of an incoming text and, stopped at a pedestrian crossing, quickly retrieved her mobile phone from her handbag.

> *Good luck investigating missing wheelie bins and who nicked the tombola money at the Spring Fete. x*

Ruby knew this was Emma's way of wishing her well on her first day, and typical of her former house-mate's sense of humour. She would save replying for later, especially because she couldn't think of a suitably witty response that wouldn't show the good-natured jibe had struck close to the bone.

The reality was more likely to be that she was in for a week of boring induction. Not only was she in a new role but she was also in a new police force; meaning hours of being shown the ropes.

Reaching the top of the hill and making the turn into Victoria Street, with the police station only just ahead, she consoled herself that it meant her day was likely to keep to normal office hours. Ruby had spent the weekend being more attentive to her various social media accounts, and not just to combat the boredom of being back in her childhood home. Some of it had been hope that others' excitement at her promotion may help her own doubts to recede, and making her news more widespread would cause it to be harder to slink back to London if she decided she couldn't hack the relative peace and tranquillity of a middle-class commuter town like St. Albans. One upside of her greater online presence had been Sally, an old school friend, inviting her to some farewell drinks for Zara, a girl she barely remembered. Ruby had found it odd that these would be held on a week night and had failed to respond to the invitation, but perhaps it could provide a useful tonic to what was bound to be a boring day and may see her start to regrow some roots in the area.

* * *

'It's DC Knight,' she said into the crackly intercom by the staff entrance to the station. She was pleased that she had managed to remember her new title this time, unlike when she had arrived at the barrier to the secure car park. In the door's mirrored glass, she looked herself up and down and was satisfied with her appearance. It was a simple grey trouser suit, classy but not too expensive, and the same as she had worn to interview. Ruby had a number of matching shirts but would wait until she saw what others in the CID here wore before committing to buy more suits. Similarly, she had elected to pull her hair back into a simple ponytail and her application of make-up was so light as to be almost imperceptible.

Ruby was far from conceited but knew that the combination of her West Indian father and Irish mother had blessed her with striking features, not least her combination of emerald green eyes and light brown skin. Whilst she was not embarrassed to admit that she had sometimes used them to her advantage, it was times like this when she feared it may cause people to underestimate her other capabilities. With her body no longer hidden under the standard police uniform, she would know very shortly whether she had done enough to give herself an air of professionalism.

'Know where you're going?' The duty sergeant at the front desk asked as soon as she entered.

'Of course,' Ruby replied with false confidence, briefly flicking her eyes to the sign on the far wall to check if her recollection from her interview had been correct. She breathed a short sigh of relief when she found herself in the stairwell used by CID and waited patiently for the door to be opened, fixing a warm smile that belied the butterflies in her stomach. She consoled herself with the knowledge that the next time she was in this exact spot she should have the door code. The door opened.

'Morning, have you come to fix the photocopier?'

'Piss off, Jamie,' interjected a woman, shoving the man out of the way. 'Hi, guv told us to meet you. I'm Louise Christie and this bell-end is James Dorkins.'

'Ruby Knight,' she replied, shaking Christie's hand. If Dorkins had been offended by the introduction, he didn't show it as he enthusiastically pumped Ruby's arm when it was his turn. His eyes never leaving hers provided some confirmation that she hadn't been unwise to leave a couple of her shirt buttons undone.

'I'd suggest we grab a cup of coffee first, but Monday briefing starts in a couple of minutes and I'm sure you don't want to be stood at the back on your first day,' Christie continued, leading them to a conference room at the far end of the open-plan office.

Dorkins' decision to stop to speak to those still milling outside didn't offend Ruby and she took a seat next to Christie, relieved at having successfully navigated the first hurdle of her new job.

'You worked here long?' Ruby asked, instantly wincing at how pathetic an attempt at small talk it sounded.

'Just over two years,' Christie replied enthusiastically. 'Up until this morning I was the newest fish here, so it's nice to be able to hand on the baton. I understand you worked in London; what brings you to St. Albans?'

'I grew up around here.'

'Oh, really? That's awesome and should certainly be an advantage as you settle in. I'm from Kent, so everything was new to me when I first arrived.'

In the short time they'd been chatting, Ruby had barely noticed the room fill. She didn't get time to cement her bond with Christie any further because in swept a person she recognised.

'Right, folks, let's get started,' announced Detective Chief Inspector Adam Nelson as he made his way to the front. He waited whilst the final few people found some space to loiter at the back of the rectangular room.

DCI Nelson may not have been the most senior of the three people who had interviewed her, but with Detective Superintendent Robson announcing he was based in nearby Hatfield, it was clear that Nelson was the one with the most invested interest in the appointment. Ruby didn't get the time to speak to him on a personal level but there was something about DCI Nelson that had served to dampen her concerns about moving somewhere more provincial. As intimidating as she had found his initial question about why she was looking to swap the hustle and bustle of London for leafy Hertfordshire, she had admired its potency, as well as the knowing smile that had accompanied its delivery; implying that he already understood why.

'Okay then, we thankfully had a fairly quiet weekend and, other than me needing to speak to DC Dorkins and DC Smith at the end of this, our caseloads are largely as we left them on Friday afternoon. Having said that, there are a few things happening in the area over the next couple of weeks I want you to be aware of. However, before we get on to that, I would like to begin by welcoming somebody.'

Ruby could already feel her cheeks beginning to flush and took a deep breath to calm herself.

'Some of you may have clocked that we have a guest among us this morning but, don't worry, we haven't started accepting requests for work-experience places from one of our local schools.'

Ruby looked up at DCI Nelson in shock, but he was surveying the room and soaking up the smattering of laughter that his comment had provoked. Her cheeks continued to redden but now with anger at such a cheap gag. In that moment Ruby was sure she would be further embarrassed by next having to stand and wave at her new colleagues; perhaps even perform some pathetic initiation like singing a song or telling them her favourite joke.

'Guv, I need to speak to you,' came an urgent voice from the doorway; instantly ceasing all other noise in the room.

'This had better be good,' Nelson responded, marching past all the faces; necks craned in the hope they might be able to determine the cause of this inopportune interruption.

'Don't sweat it, it's just guv's way of introducing you,' Christie whispered, apparently sensing Ruby's annoyance.

'Don't worry, I'm used to the office banter,' she responded, yet in a tone that implied she was anything but.

'No, you don't understand. The DCI likes to address the elephant in the room. This would have been his way of tackling what some people were thinking head-on. When he comes back, he'll probably tell everyone how suitably qualified you are and that your experience in uniform makes you more than ready.'

'Hmm,' replied Ruby, unconvinced.

Regardless, neither of them had the opportunity to find out what Nelson's original intention had been because his demeanour had changed entirely upon his return. 'Right, listen up, there's been an acid attack in Marshalswick–'

'Jesus, guv, on a Monday morning?'

Nelson shot a vicious glance at whoever had interrupted him, but his eyes then softened slightly. 'Yeah, pretty screwed up but at least it's not going to be a random thing. Uniform are at the scene and the victim's on the way to hospital.'

'Peters! Are you and Anderson still on the GBH?'

'Yes, guv, we've been waiting for some extra forensics that should be through this morning,' a guy near the front replied.

'Okay then, how about you, Jenkins?' The sound this elicited from the back of the room was more of a growl than coherent speech. 'You got a partner at the moment?'

'Cooper is on leave. I believe you signed his request,' came a voice so gravelly that it sounded as though he'd been gargling with engine oil.

'So I did. I guess that means you need a new one then, doesn't it?' Nelson continued, with the same knowing smile from the interview, made all the more recognisable because he was now looking directly at Ruby. 'Well how about it, DC Knight? Fancy foregoing all that induction nonsense and jumping straight in at the deep end?'

If Christie had been right, this was probably, albeit improvised, another one of the DCI's tests. Even if Ruby hadn't been keen to get to the heart of the action, she wouldn't have given him the satisfaction of seeing her apprehension.

'Absolutely, guv,' she replied, standing to emphasise that she was willing and ready.

'That's settled then. I'm sure you'll find working with DI Jenkins a unique experience.' Even if it hadn't been for the sniggers that greeted Nelson's comment, the dishevelled appearance of her new partner topping up his Styrofoam cup from the percolator in the corner would have given clue as to what she had to look forward to. Jenkins' unkempt hair was matched by the state of his beard; both heavily streaked with grey. His creased suit was at least two sizes too large for his slender frame and Ruby would have placed money on him wearing the same dark tie to work each day.

'Pleased to meet you, I'm Ruby,' she said in her most charming of voices, as he followed her out of the conference room. 'How would you prefer I address you? Is it sir, or guv, or—'

'Jenkins will do fine,' he growled, stepping past her outstretched hand.

'Certainly,' she responded, ignoring the shun and following him across the office. 'Let's get straight to it then. Perhaps on the way I can give you a rundown of my training and the sort of experience I gained whilst working for The Met.'

Jenkins' lolloping pace didn't slow but Ruby was on a roll.

'Am I right to assume you've worked here a while? It doesn't really matter because being a Detective Inspector you must have been in CID for some time, whether here or somewhere else.' Ruby took the smallest of breaths before continuing, 'I grew up in nearby Hemel Hempstead, but we came into St. Albans lots of times when I was young, and I know the area fairly well; at least the more central sections. Do I detect from your accent you're not from round these parts?'

Jenkins stopped and turned around. Ruby tried to replay the last couple of sentences she'd uttered to give clue as to what had finally sparked his interest.

'Are you planning on following me all the way into the toilet?' His even tone was as simple as if asking her if she took milk in her coffee.

'Oh, gosh, no. Of course not,' she replied, scanning her surroundings and realising that the short corridor they had just come down had led them to a door marked *Men*. 'It's just that I'm new to the station and I–'

'Good,' he interrupted, before holding out his Styrofoam cup. 'Could you take this for me then?'

'Er, okay, sure,' she replied with an awkward giggle.

Jenkins then pushed through the door but stuck his head back round before it closed. 'Perhaps you might like to wait back in the office until I'm finished.'

'Oh, yes, certainly,' Ruby responded, feeling her cheeks flush for the second time that morning. 'Wouldn't make a good impression on my first day if you and I came out of the…'

With Jenkins now gone she understood that she was only talking to herself and made her way gingerly back along the corridor.

* * *

With the briefing over, the office was a hive of activity. Some people were already at their desks and others were moving back and forth gathering whatever they needed for the day. No-one even glanced in her direction and that was fine as far as she was concerned; not having been allocated a desk made her feel like the only single person at a disco and she was happy to remain anonymous. To kill some time she took out her mobile to reply to Emma's text. It might not have been the most comfortable of starts but at least she could say that her first job was something big.

> *LMAO. Actually, my first case has come in and it's an acid attack – a big one. Hope things are quiet on your beat today and you don't have too many tourists asking for directions. Ruby x*

She would have liked to have been more specific about the investigation but felt it was professional to keep the details vague, at least until she next spoke to Emma. This way it wouldn't come across as her being defensive and she was rather proud of her little comeback about what Emma would be doing today.

'Don't just stand there, we need to get going,' Jenkins growled, walking past her without bothering to retrieve his cup.

Chapter Two

'Do I need to remind you not to touch anything?' Jenkins asked as he switched off the car's engine.

Ruby wouldn't dignify this insult with a response. Besides, it had only been a couple of minutes into their journey when she had given up trying to engage her partner in conversation, and she'd be damned if she was going to break her silence for this.

Stepping out of the unmarked Ford Mondeo into the fresh air and surveying the scene around her helped brighten her mood. Ignorant partner or not, this was exactly the sort of thing she had signed up for and she could feel her senses heighten. If it was not for what was directly in front of her, this street could be one like any other in the surrounding districts of St. Albans. The semi-detached houses were fairly uniform in design and screamed 1970s thanks to their white plastic cladding. With the residents either keeping their front gardens neat or simply tarmacking them to add more parking, the properties were similar to her parents' own house but likely to be worth twice as much because of their more desirable location.

Any sense of suburban tranquillity was shattered by the specific one they had come to visit. No doubt helped by Jenkins' delay in getting them there, the boundary to the property had already been cordoned off and the forensic team was currently erecting a white tent over the front doorway, indicating where the attack had occurred. The large gap between the two hastily parked police cars suggested that the paramedics had been first to arrive at the scene and the victim had already been taken to hospital.

As Jenkins led the way, Ruby fumbled inside her jacket for her warrant card, but the officer ensuring the few gathered members of the public kept their distance, had already lifted the cordon. The deferential way he nodded at her as she stepped under the plastic tape sent a small shiver of excitement up her spine. Emma could mock all she wanted, DCI Jenkins could make as many remarks as he liked about her age, and could continue to be unwelcoming, but that simple gesture by a uniformed officer – a rank she had held until a few days ago – told her that it was all worth it.

Any excitement was soon sucked out of Ruby when the full impact of what she had come to investigate hit her. Any sense that the horror of what had occurred had been taken away with the victim, was dispelled as soon as they stepped through the zipped opening to the forensic tent. The puddle on the floor in the entrance hall, marked by a plastic *1* for photographic purposes, was the single most gruesome thing she had ever seen. The outer edges of it were still the clear liquid of the acid, that had stopped eating away at the laminate flooring, but the middle was a mixture of varying shades of pink and red. Ruby could feel her gorge rising but couldn't tear her eyes away from it, as though she might be able to identify the specific parts of the victim's face that had been melted away.

'Perhaps we had better step through,' Jenkins announced, the softness in his tone was enough to break whatever spell Ruby had been under. However, what met them in the living room and through to the open plan kitchen/diner was somehow worse for the shocking contrast it provided. It was a scene replicated in countless homes up and down the country on a weekday: the television was still on, with the volume low, showing a modern cartoon that Ruby didn't recognise. The way the cushions on the sofa were scattered, unlike those neatly arranged on the armchairs, suggested that it was where the children had been watching their favourite programmes whilst their parents prepared breakfast. Moving through to look at the dining table, Ruby assumed they were both still of primary school age given the selection of sugary spreads that accompanied the half-eaten toast on their plates. But what she found most heart breaking was the two lunchboxes on the kitchen work surfaces, abandoned in the process of being filled presumably when the doorbell sounded. Such a mundane scene but one that marked the end of innocence for the entire family.

More than anything, Ruby wanted to ask Jenkins what he thought had happened to the children, for presumably they had not been allowed to accompany their father in the ambulance. And what sort of a state would their mother have been in, so concerned for her husband and yet having to worry about who was going to look after them? Much as she didn't want it to, Ruby's mind imagined what those initial few minutes must have been like. With their mother occupied in the kitchen, would one of the children have been the first to respond to their father's screams of agony? Did they find him slumped in the hallway, hands to his face, with pink liquid already oozing between his fingers? The wife would have needed to get them out of the way before calling for help, knowing that it was a race against time as the acid consumed flesh and muscle.

Ruby looked around; surely she would have brought him into the kitchen to try and dilute the acid, if not through sheer instinct but following the instructions she would have received over the phone. But there were no signs of that, and the sink was empty, aside from some water pooled at the bottom, presumably from where she had earlier filled the kettle.

'Has anyone been upstairs yet?' she called to the man in the white boiler suit, who was crouched on the living room floor and putting down one of the plastic numbers next to a footprint on the rug.

'Not yet, why?'

'She took him upstairs,' she replied, walking past him and steeling herself for what awaited. The droplets on the dark carpet as she ascended were confirmation enough even before what awaited her in the bathroom. Here was a panorama of devastation where all the various toiletries, that Ruby was in no doubt an hour ago had been neatly arranged, were scattered on the floor as the woman dragged her blinded husband to the bathtub. She had the foresight to use the shower attachment rather than try and splash water onto his face and risk injury herself. Although the water sprayed around the bathroom meant it was not quite such an intensely visceral sight as with the puddle downstairs, it still looked like a scene from a horror film.

'Are you okay?' Jenkins asked from behind her.

'Don't worry, I'm not going to touch anything,' Ruby replied bitterly, feeling not at all guilty at taking out her feelings, chief among them anger, on her partner. How could someone do this? This was far worse than any of the stabbings or even murders she had attended in London. Whatever the motive behind the attack, Ruby could think of nothing that could cause someone to use such a vile and evil method. And to do so in front of the man's wife and children, ensuring that his intended victim wasn't the only person to come out of this with life-shattering injuries.

'Nasty, isn't it?' Jenkins said, apparently untroubled by her outburst.

Despite everything, Ruby couldn't prevent a shrill laugh escaping her at this massive understatement. 'Promise me we'll get him,' she whispered, not caring that this may come across as exactly the sort of naïve thing he would expect her to say.

Jenkins shrugged. 'It's more than likely they know who he is,' he replied evenly.

'Well, what are we waiting for?' Ruby said, heading back down the stairs and huffing irritably at the forensics guy impeding her progress, finally marking up the spots on the carpet.

Chapter Three

'What are you doing?' Ruby called impatiently, leaning back into the car. It had taken them the best part of half an hour to get to the hospital, thanks to a combination of Jenkins' unwillingness to break the speed limit and the nearest A&E being Hemel Hempstead since the one at St. Albans Hospital closed in the early '90s. But whatever frustration Ruby had felt on the way over was tempered by imagining how much worse it must have been for the Robins.

'I didn't get a chance to fill in my notebook back at the house,' Jenkins grumbled.

'That's because we were in a hurry to get here, which, if you don't mind my saying so, is pointless if we spend the next ten minutes sitting in the car park.' She didn't wait for a response and started marching to the entrance, only slowing her pace slightly once inside to give him a chance to catch up.

Unsurprisingly, they were told that Mr Robins was still in theatre, but his wife was waiting in the room that had been prepared for him to go into afterwards.

'Perhaps I should handle this?' Ruby said as they approached the door. She took Jenkins' arched eyebrow as an invitation to qualify her request but knew tact might be the better part of valour. 'She might be more willing to open up to another woman.'

'If you like,' he said, offering a similar shrug.

'Maybe you could get us a coffee or something in the meantime,' Ruby said. She was nervous enough as it was, without the thought of him standing over them growling and grunting at anything he didn't like the sound of.

With Jenkins safely pottering down the corridor, Ruby took a deep breath before entering the room. 'Hello, Mrs Robins, I'm DC Knight,' she said in as calm a voice as possible – the situation taking all the thrill out of being able to use her new title for the first time in public.

'Have you got any news on Michael?' Mrs Robins asked, looking up with hollow eyes.

'I'm afraid he's still in theatre,' Ruby replied, pulling up a chair to sit beside her. 'I was terribly sorry to hear about… what happened… to your husband.'

Mrs Robins shook her head, not in contradiction Ruby assumed, but in disbelief at the situation.

'I know that going through it now is probably the last thing you want to do, and we'll take a more comprehensive statement later, but I need to ask you a few questions to help our investigation.' Ruby waited for Mrs Robins' nod of consent. 'Did you see the person who did this?' she asked, posing the question she hoped would lead them directly to the culprit.

'No, it was Michael who answered the door and then… and then I heard him screaming and I ran to him… I didn't know what had happened, but he was holding his face and just… just screaming.' To Mrs Robins' credit, the tears that had begun streaming down her face hadn't managed to prevent her from getting her words out.

'I take it, then, that you didn't see anyone running away…?'

'No, I just wanted to know what was wrong with Michael, and I was begging him to show me what had happened to his face… and I managed to pull his arms away and then I saw… then I saw…' Mrs Robins could keep her composure no longer and Ruby could feel her own tears form in the corner of her eyes. She quickly blinked them away, more glad than ever that she had convinced DI Jenkins to stay outside.

Having waited for what she deemed an appropriate length of time, and with Mrs Robins bringing her sobs under control, Ruby continued. 'Do you have any idea who might have done this to your husband?'

'I just told you, I didn't see him. I was too busy trying to help Michael and then I had to keep the kids away whilst I phoned 999.'

Ruby hadn't sought to interrupt Mrs Robins' misinterpretation of her question. 'But can you think of anyone who might have wanted to cause your husband any harm? Anyone with a grudge, for example?'

'No, of course not,' she replied, adding to her protestation a look of pure fury as though it were being suggested that her husband had somehow provoked the attack.

Again, Ruby didn't allow herself to be offended by Mrs Robin's reaction, sure that if in a similar circumstance herself, she too would be looking to lash out. 'Anyone at work, that sort of thing?'

'He's a fucking estate agent. People who don't manage to sell their house as quickly as they would like hardly go around throwing acid in people's faces!'

'Would you mind giving me the address of where he works?' she said, maintaining a false calmness.

* * *

'How did you get on?' Jenkins asked when she finally found him outside the entrance to the hospital. If he had gone to get coffee, he hadn't decided to save her any.

'As well as could be expected,' she replied, trying to mask any defensiveness in her tone.

'I guessed as much,' he responded, walking in the direction of the car. 'So where to now?'

'He's a partner in a small, independent estate agent, just off the high street.'

'As good a place to start as any, I suppose,' came the unexpectedly positive reaction.

Chapter Four

Pulling up on a double yellow line in the heart of St. Albans' city centre didn't feel as deliciously naughty as Ruby would have expected. 'Don't you need to leave a sign in here or something, in case the traffic wardens come along?'

'Nah, they can ticket us all they like. As soon as the registration number goes into the system it gets wiped.' Ruby smiled at this response because it was the longest answer he had yet provided her and, given how mundane the question had been, she took it as a sign that he might finally be warming to her.

Her bubble was soon burst. 'Perhaps I should handle this one,' he said, and without waiting for Ruby's reaction, entered the estate agents.

'How can I help you?' asked a dark-haired woman in her late twenties, standing up from one of the three computer terminals.

'I'm DI Jenkins and this is DC Knight,' he replied in his typically gruff voice.

'Perhaps we ought to sit down,' Ruby added, having observed the colour drain from the woman's cheeks, and assuming that Jenkins wouldn't think to offer such a courtesy. That he didn't shoot her a look of admonishment suggested that, despite his claim to want to lead, he wasn't irritated by her interjection. 'And who are you?'

'I'm… I'm Samie,' she stuttered, retaking her seat.

'You got a last name, Samie?' Jenkins asked.

'Yes,' she replied, before sensing the awkwardness of the pause that followed. 'It's Wright… as in Samie Wright,' she added, looking down in embarrassment.

'And does anyone else work here, Miss Wright?' Prompted Jenkins.

'Yes, there's Jake and Michael… I mean Jake Hubbard and Michael Robins,' she corrected herself. 'Look, if it's something about the business, really you should be speaking to one of them. I just work as their personal assistant, answering the phone, dealing with the clients when they're out, that sort of thing. In fact, Jake should be back from an appointment soon and Michael… well, er, I'm not sure what he's up to this morning; he usually pops in first thing no matter how busy he–'

'It's Mr Robins that we've come to see you about,' Ruby said, wondering if Jenkins would have elected to stop the woman's rambling at any stage.

'Oh, Jesus. Is he okay? Like I said he usually–'

'He suffered an attack at his home this morning, Miss Wright,' Jenkins interrupted.

'An attack? What, like a heart attack? But how could that be, he's only in his–'

'No,' he said, his voice firmer this time. 'He was attacked this morning. At his house. We're not at liberty to give you the details at this stage but he was taken to hospital where his injuries are currently being treated.'

This time there was no verbal response and Samie slumped back in her chair in stunned silence.

'I appreciate this is a lot for you to take in,' Ruby said soothingly. 'But we need your help in trying to work out who may have done this to him.'

'I… I don't understand.'

'The nature of the attack gives us reason to believe he would have known his assailant and we want to establish whether it had anything to do with his work.' Jenkins continued, causing Ruby to wonder whether she would sound similarly dispassionate once she had been in CID as long as him.

'I can get you the files of all his clients,' Samie responded, moving to get up from her chair.

Ruby held her hand up. 'In a moment. First, can you think of anyone who might wish to see Mr Robins come to harm?'

'Oh, Jesus, no! Michael is a good guy, wouldn't hurt a fly.'

'No disgruntled clients, someone who was unhappy with the service he provided?'

'No, no-one. Everybody likes Michael. It's largely thanks to him that we're able to compete with all the chain estate agents. He... and Jake of course, pride themselves on providing a more personal service and they do everything they can to help our clients. It's our USP and the reason why he decided to set up his own business. Of course some people want to market their property at well above the going rate but if they don't like our honest valuation they just go elsewhere.'

It was clear that Samie was proud to work there and Ruby wanted to take advantage of how she had begun to open up to them. 'And how long have you been here?'

'About a year now. I arrived as a temp to get them through a busy period. Jake had joined the year before and they were thinking about bringing in another partner but then I, er... they decided to take me on full time instead.'

'They must have been impressed with your work,' Ruby responded as earnestly as she could.

'Right, about those files then...' Jenkins said impatiently, clearly having grown tired of the conversation.

'Oh... er... yes, if you'd like to follow me out the back. Jake says we should just keep everything on computer, but

Michael likes us to have a physical copy to hand. You know, just in case the system was to go down or something and we needed to retrieve a client's details.'

Ruby allowed a smile to escape her as she zoned out Samie's chatter, all the while hoping that she would continue to babble on, in the knowledge that it would be driving Jenkins mad. Having got up to look at the properties displayed in the window and quickly becoming depressed by how far out of her budget even the flats were, she soon plonked herself down in Samie's chair. She had neglected to lock her computer and Ruby resisted the temptation to open some of her files; instead staring at the desktop with the business' corporate logo and trying to digest all that had happened so far that morning.

Much as it had been a source of irritation earlier, she wondered whether she should get herself a small leather notebook, similar to Jenkins'. She considered what she would write in it based on their investigation so far and realised that she would barely be able to fill a single page. Although, in some respects, that was preferable to what would surely follow once they left here. Armed with the details of all their clients, which she could hear being photocopied out the back, all she could look forward to this afternoon was trawling through them one-by-one.

So caught up was she in thoughts about whether Jenkins would leave her with the lion's share of the work or if, for some bizarre reason, this was the sort of thing that floated his boat, the blaring of the car stereo out the front barely registered. It was only when she heard the driver's door slam shut that she looked up to see a man in sunglasses stood by an Audi convertible with the estate agent's logo on the side.

As soon as he finished checking something on his phone, he entered the shop. 'Well good morning gorgeous, you're not going to believe the property I've managed to…' The words died in his throat and Ruby had to suppress a smile at the exaggerated way he took off his sunglasses and peered forward. 'You're… you're not Samie…'

'I'm guessing you must be Jake,' she replied flatly, choosing not to address him more formally. Already she had decided that he was the stereotypical estate agent – all flash and flannel – and she was looking forward to seeing how he attempted to smarm his way out of this.

'Er yes, where's Samie? She's not meant to leave the front unattended.' He paused, composing himself, before flashing a smile that was all pristine white teeth. 'Is there something I can help you with? Are you buying or selling?'

It seemed to be confusion rather than guilt that still lingered in his eyes, but Ruby's next sentence was designed to make certain. 'I'm DC Knight and your PA is currently helping my colleague, DI Jenkins, with something.'

'Oh,' he said, sitting down. 'Is Samie okay?' The look that accompanied this suggested a more pertinent question would have been asking what she had done wrong, but Ruby was touched by his concern and, more significantly, believed he wasn't hiding anything illegal himself. Moreover, the reality of having to deliver the same bad news, made her feel bad for judging him so quickly, misplaced and misogynist greeting or not.

'Are you okay out there?' Jenkins' gravelly voice called from the back. Ruby winced at how paternalistic it sounded but if Jake noticed, his face, which had remained one of concern, didn't show it.

'I'm just informing Mr Hubbard,' she replied, hoping that this would bring an end to the exchange but, equally, knowing that Jenkins may choose to join her. Much as she wasn't looking forward to having to explain what had happened to Jake's partner, she would be outraged if Jenkins stormed back through and took over. First day and her superior or not, she would be having strong words with him when they returned to the car.

But after an anxious pause she heard another filing cabinet being opened and she took a deep breath. 'I'm sorry to have to tell you this but Mr Robins was attacked at his home this morning.'

This time there was no confusion as to her choice of words, which she chalked up as a victory over Jenkins. 'Holy shit, is he okay?'

'I'm afraid I don't have his current status, but he was seriously injured.'

'Oh my God… who… why?'

Ruby was convinced by the sincerity of his response but knew she would be remiss not to seek assurance. 'That's what we are trying to find out. I'm hoping you may be able to help us with that but, for the record, do you mind telling me where you were at approximately 8.05am this morning?'

'I was at a viewing,' he responded without showing the slightest offence at the implication of the question. 'A lot of our clients work during office hours and like to see places first thing in the morning, as well as later in the afternoon. Michael enjoys taking his kids to school, so I tend to do the earlier ones.' He dropped his eyes and Ruby wondered whether he was thinking about the impact on the children. 'It was at his home you said?'

'Yes.'

'Shit,' he murmured. 'Am I right in thinking it wasn't a break in?'

'Why do you say that?'

'Well, it's just the timing seems wrong.'

'Indeed, Mr Hubbard, and we have reason to suspect that the attacker was known to Mr Robins.' She could see Jake open his mouth to speak and raised her hand to silence him. 'I'm afraid I can't go into the details but is there anyone, anyone at all, you can think of who might have held a grudge against Mr Robins?'

'No, no-one.'

The same response as Samie had given.

'If not through work but, perhaps socially?'

'Michael and I don't really see each other outside of work. He has a wife and kids and tends to just do family stuff in the evenings and at weekends.'

'I see you're married too,' Ruby said, glancing down at Jake's ring.

'Oh yeah, but we don't have any kids. Well, not yet anyway. We still like to go out and stuff.'

'I think we're about done here,' Jenkins said, re-emerging and offering Jake the merest nod of greeting. 'Any joy?'

Mortified by his turn of phrase but deciding that it would be best not to amplify it by addressing it, Ruby simply turned back to Jake. 'Thank you for your time, Mr Hubbard. We're likely to come back and see you at some point but, in the meantime, if you think of anything, do let us know.' This would have been the ideal time to have a business card to offer him but she wasn't going to give Jenkins the satisfaction of asking for one of his. Just another thing, along with being allocated a desk, she would have to sort once she got back to the station.

Chapter Five

'So, what do you make of it then?' Ruby asked, after suffering the first part of their journey in silence.

'Make of what?' Jenkins responded without taking his eyes off the road.

'About the chances of the next local elections leading to the Conservatives regaining control. What do you think I meant?' Ruby was frustrated, she was irritable and, most of all, she was hungry.

'The estate agents, then,' he replied, without a trace of offence in his voice. 'It would appear that there is no direct link.'

'Appear?'

'Well, until we work through those files we won't know for sure, but I assume your guy was as clueless as that girl.'

'Miss Wright you mean,' she corrected, wondering if he would even pick up how condescending his turn of phrase was.

'Yes, that's right,' he said flatly.

'Is that what we're going to do now? Work through those files, I mean.' She still wasn't looking forward to it but at least she would have the chance to pick up some lunch back at the station.

'We need to go and see his parents first. They live locally, and they can give us a steer on where to look in terms of his personal life.'

'Oh,' Ruby replied, knowing that telling them what had happened would be many times worse than what they had gone through at the estate agents.

'Don't worry, uniform will have already been to inform them.'

'I wasn't,' Ruby lied, annoyed that he was able to read her thoughts so easily. 'I was just wondering why we need to ask them when we could just ask his wife.'

'Yeah, we could go back to the hospital if you like,' he said, suddenly craning his neck to look for a place to turn the car around.

'Wait a…' Ruby started to protest but then saw the trace of a smile on Jenkins' face. It was as unusual as it was unexpected. 'You're just messing with me.'

'If you say so, but let's stop for a coffee first.'

'If you like,' Ruby replied, delighted that she would get the chance to grab something to keep her going.

* * *

Perhaps it was because they sat facing each other but Ruby found herself able to engage Jenkins properly for the first time that morning. He still kept his answers short, and seemed far more interested in consuming his Americano and bacon panino but she steadily built up a vague picture of who this awkward and somewhat reluctant person was before her. She would have liked to have probed deeper, to gain an understanding why he just seemed to be going through the motions in a career that must have spanned thirty years but didn't want to spoil the mood by being intrusive. Not that she would have expected to get anything deep out of him anyway. Certainly, if he had been selected by DCI Nelson to act as a mentor, it had been an odd choice. In reality, the more she thought about it, the more she wondered whether this was another of his tests.

Was Nelson waiting for her to return to the station, expecting her to complain that she couldn't work with this man and demand that she be given a new partner; someone like DC Christie?

Irrespective of what Christie had claimed Nelson's intentions to be in the briefing, she was determined to not only withstand any pressure put on her, but also appear to thrive under it. Much as she was still unsure about Jenkins, she would make this partnership work one way or another, and just hope that Nelson was satisfied enough with her performance that he switched her over to someone more appropriate once Jenkins' usual partner returned from holiday.

'Right then,' she said, downing the rest of her skinny latte. 'We'd better get back to it.'

* * *

Michael Robins' parents lived in Wheathampstead, a village to the north of St. Albans, and the sight of a Volvo estate parked on the gravel drive triggered a thought in Ruby. 'Do you think the children are here?'

'I assume so,' Jenkins replied.

'You could have told me that before.' But Ruby didn't need to wait for his bland reply to know that he didn't think it was important. She, however, did; if nothing else because it magnified the apprehension within her. Would she be able to tell from their eyes the full extent of the horrors they had witnessed?

'Yes, we were told to expect you. I'm Susan and my husband is Peter,' Mrs Robins senior responded to their introduction at the door. 'The boys are upstairs playing, and I would appreciate it if we kept the noise down. They've only really just settled and I don't want anything else upsetting them.'

'Of course,' Ruby responded in little more than a whisper.

'Can I get you a drink?' Peter asked as they entered the sitting room.

'No, we've just–'

'Coffee. Black, no sugar,' Jenkins called over her shoulder.

Peter happily tottered off into the kitchen and, for the briefest of moments, Ruby wondered whether Jenkins' rude interruption had been in order to give them an opportunity to talk to Susan alone.

As they sat down, Jenkins gave her a look to enquire whether she would like to lead on this. She hoped the sparkle in her eyes that accompanied the gentle incline of her head did enough to tell him that she was looking forward to learning from the supposed expert.

Whether his failure to start off with offering his condolences was down to his typical lack of sensitivity, or further indication that he wanted to get to the crux of the matter before Peter returned with their refreshments, Ruby couldn't tell. 'Unfortunately, your son's wife didn't get a look at the attacker and we are trying to establish possible motive.'

'Go on,' Susan responded warily.

'Can you tell us the nature of their relationship?'

'They're husband and wife. I thought you knew that,' she replied acerbically.

'And how would you describe their marriage?' he continued, ignoring any sense of provocation.

'Look, what is this?' Susan countered loudly, clearly ignoring her own request that their conversation was kept quiet. 'My son is in hospital with… with God knows what having happened to him and you want me to sit here and discuss the intimacies of his marriage?'

'Has he been under any stress recently? Fallen out with anyone, perhaps?'

'Are you suggesting he somehow brought this on himself?'

Ruby didn't like the similar accusation that had been levelled at her by his wife and could see that, irrespective of Jenkins' apparent calmness, this conversation was only heading one way; as illustrated by the anxious glances she could see Peter casting from the kitchen.

'Look, Mrs Robins, I'm sorry that we have to ask you these questions, especially at such an awful time,' Ruby said in as soothing a voice as possible. She took the switch in Susan's focus, accompanied by a slight softening of her glare, as a sign that her intervention might not prove unhelpful. 'I can only begin to imagine what you, what all of you,' she continued, with a glance to the ceiling for effect, 'must be going through right now. I want to assure you that we are desperate to find the person responsible for this… this atrocity, but in order to do so we need your help.'

'But there's… there's no-one who doesn't like Michael. He's always been such a nice person, ever since he was a boy.'

'I get that, Mrs Robins, really I do, and that's what we keep hearing. But this attack… the very nature of it… does not suggest a random act; it was something pre-meditated. In the absence of any obvious grudge against your son, we need to dig deep to find out who possibly could have wanted to cause him harm. And in so doing we may ask some questions that might otherwise appear inappropriate.'

'I understand,' Susan said, bowing her head before looking up again. 'And I'm sorry for being… well, you know…'

'I know,' Ruby responded, noticing that Susan hadn't looked in Jenkins' direction when uttering her apology. 'We've got the details of all his clients at work and we need you to give us an insight into what he's like outside of the office.'

Susan paused, giving the request some thought. 'I don't know what to say, really. He's still in touch with a couple of old school friends…'

'If you could give us their names…'

'Sure. They all grew up in the same area, I knew their mums and I can tell you that they're all decent people. None of them would do anything like… like that. But, other than them, he just spends time with the family. He says that being an estate agent is a sociable job and so he likes to unwind with his wife and children.'

* * *

'So, what do you make of it then?' Ruby asked, repeating her question from earlier, now that they were back in the car. What she really wanted to know was Jenkins' reaction to how she managed to turn the conversation around, and she was fully aware that if she wanted anything approaching a compliment then she was going to have to graft for it.

'Well,' he said slowly. 'I think that if we are to have any hope, any hope at all…'

'Yes?'

'…of the Tories not regaining control of the local council then either the Lib Dems or Labour will have to up their game.'

Ruby looked at him stunned, but then that smile broke out again, this time much fuller and completely transforming his face from the grumpy, tired, disillusioned detective into a glimpse of what he might have been like once upon a time.

Chapter Six

'Well, this is where the hard work begins,' Jenkins said as they made their way back up to CID. 'It's not all glamour, you know.'

'You call this morning glamorous?' Ruby scoffed, paying close attention to him punching in the code and committing it to memory. 'So, what we've just done is as good as it gets?'

'Pretty much,' he said, pulling open the door.

'So why don't you just retire then? You look old enough.'

'And do what instead?' Jenkins shrugged, making a beeline for the kitchenette.

Ruby didn't get the opportunity to become exasperated, nor did Jenkins manage to get his umpteenth coffee of the day, because DCI Nelson stuck his head out of his office.

'Good, I'm glad you two finally made it back. In you come,' he said before ducking back inside again.

'Guv.' Ruby nodded as they walked in. She was going to wait to be invited to sit down but when Jenkins took the first of the two chairs opposite Nelson's desk, she decided to follow suit.

'So, how's it going?' Nelson asked, steepling his fingers. He may have been looking at Ruby as he said it but, not least because she didn't understand the full nature of the question, she decided now would be a good time to show deference to her more senior partner. 'That good, was it?' he said with a knowing smile, after a few seconds of silence passed.

'We've made some progress with the investigation,' Ruby responded, keen not to allow Nelson's thoughts to dwell on her relationship with Jenkins any longer.

'Anyone in custody yet?'

'Well, no, it's not been as simple as that, has it, Jenkins?' She looked to the side of her, willing him to speak up. She knew their lack of any concrete lead would be much better coming from him.

'In what way?' Nelson said, never taking his eyes off her.

'We've spoken to his wife, we then went to his place of work, and we have just got back from his parents' house.'

'And?'

'And we've got the names of all his clients and his closest friends.' Ruby sincerely hoped her tone was not coming across as defensive.

'And?' Nelson prompted once more.

'And we're going to work our way through them now.'

'Is that it? No-one sticking out?'

'Well, er, no. Everyone we spoke to keeps going on about what a nice guy he is, and how everyone likes him.'

'What, so someone just decides to chuck a cup of acid in this nice guy's face, is that it?' Nelson said, shaking his head in frustration. 'Do you realise what it'll be like if people think there's some lunatic running around attacking people at random?'

'Listen, guv,' Jenkins said, leaning forward. 'It's exactly as she described it. Wife didn't get a look, and no-one can think of anyone who holds the slightest grudge against the man. We're just going to have to do the grind and play this one out.'

'Okay, fine,' Nelson said, standing. 'But I want no stone left unturned with this one. Now get to it.'

Jenkins stood up, but Ruby remained where she was. 'Guv, is this a good time to ask where my desk is?'

Chapter Seven

The afternoon had been tedious and passed far slower than the first half of the day. Ruby did get her new desk, one tucked over in the far corner near the photocopier, and she had to cross the whole office if she wanted to speak to Jenkins about anything.

Having called the three names given to them by the victim's mother, and with each of them expressing both shock and surprise that anyone would want to hurt their friend, as well as providing concrete alibis for their whereabouts that morning, she moved onto the stack of client folders that Jenkins had divvied up between them. This was an even slower process: they sorted them into piles based on previous convictions and the time that had elapsed since concluding their business with the estate agents. Although they found a couple of people they wished to follow up immediately, Jenkins agreed with Ruby's belief that none of the files would lead them to the attacker.

'What are you doing?' she asked, less out of genuine curiosity and more because he seemed engrossed in filling in a small notebook when it should have been knocking off time.

'Although I use it to keep a record over the course of an investigation, I never like to leave without having first caught up on the events of the day.' Jenkins must have taken her quizzical look as a cue to continue. 'That way I can park my work in the knowledge I have written down what needs to be done in the morning.'

'Did you write *more boring phone calls*?' Ruby said in a gently mocking tone.

'No, I think we should start off by visiting some of his neighbours. I thought about doing it this afternoon, but I'd rather catch them at a similar time to when the attack occurred. May help to jog their memory more than what uniform managed to gather,' he said, waving the write ups from the initial door-to-door enquiries.

'Are you saying uniform won't have done a good job?' Ruby asked haughtily.

'No,' he replied mildly. 'Except they don't have the benefit of a wider understanding of the facts of the case, like we do. Based on our investigations so far, we are able to ask more pertinent questions.'

Ruby gave a grudging shrug.

'For example, we know that he wasn't very sociable…'

'Takes one to know one,' she muttered to herself.

'…so anyone noticing an unfamiliar car parked outside recently holds more significance for us than it would have to uniform. I'll give you another example…'

But Ruby was done with having the obvious stated to her, even if she were somewhat grateful that he seemed more willing to discuss things than earlier. 'Anything about me in there?' she teased, gesturing back to the notebook.

'Take the piss all you like, but any good detective will tell you that it's essential to find a way of parking up your investigations at the end of the day. Some people visit the gym after work, others take the dog out for a walk as soon as they get home…'

'And you?'

'I don't have a dog and I'm not much interested in going to the gym so I happily fill in this little notebook and then lock it away in my drawer until morning. Like I said, each to his own.'

'*Their* own,' she corrected gently. 'But I think I'll stick to a nice glass of wine for now,' she added, barely noticing the brief snort of derision her comment had provoked, because it put her in mind of Sally's Facebook message about Zara's farewell drinks. She had dismissed the idea, especially because it would mean travelling all the way home to Hemel, only to come back into St. Albans again. Fair enough, the pubs around where they had gone to school were more your typical English boozer rather than the snazzy wine bars around here, but it would be a hassle nonetheless.

However, it wasn't just the lure of a glass of wine that was causing Ruby to reconsider going. No matter how much she reminded her parents that her move back home was out of necessity and only temporary, they failed to appreciate she was an independent adult now. Dinner would be prepared for her and, in return they would be expecting a detailed account of her day, just like when she used to return from school.

So, attending the farewell drinks for a girl she barely remembered might not be such a bad thing after all. Another plus side was that attending in her work clothes would mean it wouldn't seem off if she decided to stay only for one drink. By the time she got home her parents would be heavily into the soap operas they resolutely refused to miss, and she might be allowed to get away with a quick summary of her first day of being a detective during one of the ad breaks.

'Well, I think I'll head off then,' she said, realising she was still standing at Jenkins' desk and he had gone back to whatever it was he was writing. She found his grunt of a reply a fitting end to how their day together had begun and headed for the stairs contemplating where she was going to eat before-hand; keen to make up for not having a proper lunch.

* * *

Ruby arrived at the bar, just off the high street, twenty minutes earlier than they were due to meet. Her meal at one of those chain Italians hadn't taken nearly as long as she had expected. It was the first time she had dined in a restaurant on her own and, without company, she worked her way through her starter and main courses far quicker than if she had been chatting away. At least it gave her the excuse to order a desert and, feeling suitably guilty but passing off her excesses as a one-off to celebrate making it through her first day as detective, she had little regret about her choices.

Not sure when the others would arrive, Ruby opted for a small glass of white wine, reasoning that she could afford to order another later and still be fit to drive. However, with most of the contents drained she considered just finishing up and heading home. She hadn't had a huge amount of sleep the night before and, with her stomach full of carbs, spending the rest of the evening in front of the television with her parents suddenly didn't seem so bad. But much as she dared herself to simply get up and walk out, it was fear that she may bump into one of her school friends as she departed that caused her to stay.

The welcome she received as the six of them arrived in dribs and drabs was warm, particularly from Sally, and, even though she hadn't seen many of them for years, and whilst it was clear that they had remained a fairly tight-knit group ever since school, she soon settled. In fact, the only person she didn't really connect with was Zara, supposedly the very reason for her being there; not that she was bothered, what with her due to be half-way around the world in a matter of days.

Zara aside, Ruby's relative comfort within the setting was somewhat short lived as it became clear that the group was treating the evening as though it were the weekend. None of the others were driving and a couple had even booked the morning off the next day so that they could enjoy themselves without fear of regretting it too much. With her second small glass of wine consumed, and having been forced to move onto Diet Coke, Ruby found herself less and less interested in the increasingly raucous conversation. In fact, she was about to make her apologies and leave when someone she recognised arrived at the table.

'I'm sorry I'm so late, girls, I was at a conference in Guildford and the traffic on the M25 was a nightmare,' said Danny, a lad who had been in Ruby's year at school. Ruby was wondering why he hadn't used it as an excuse to miss the whole evening altogether when he suddenly turned in her direction. Narrowing his eyes slightly, his face transformed into one of recognition. 'Oh my God, it's you!' he virtually shouted. With barely a glance at Sally, he squeezed into the gap on the bench between her and Ruby. 'Look, I'll get everyone a drink in a minute but first let me find out how on earth you managed to find this one,' he declared, giving her the broadest smile.

Ruby's initial discomfort about being given near-celebrity status by someone whom she must have spoken to less than a dozen times at school, was tempered by the knowledge that to leave without at least talking to him for a while would appear rude. Perhaps it was the fact that he was also driving but she no longer felt in such a rush to leave. Striking the perfect balance between sharing his own story with asking plenty of questions about hers, it was only when Zara suggested they all move on to a place with a dance floor that Ruby realised it had got late.

Whether he sensed her reluctance to go with them or just felt it time to retire after a long day, he asked her where she was parked, and having established that his was nearby, offered to walk her to her car.

Walking along the moonlit street with a guy she barely knew, seemed a fittingly odd end to what had been a bizarre day, but Ruby did feel a slight thrill. However, the excitement soon turned to anxiety as they entered the car park. Not that it had been a date, or anything approximating one, but she always felt nervous when saying goodbye to a guy. She supposed it wouldn't be too weird if he tried to give her a kiss on the cheek.

But she need not have worried. As soon as he clocked her VW Up! GTI, with its vivid red paintwork gleaming under the car park's sodium lights, he seemed more interested in it than her. Knowing that she would need her own transport when leaving London, she had decided to splash out on a something sporty, in an effort to balance out the disappointment she felt at having to move back in with her parents.

Ruby took Danny's various compliments about the car graciously, trying to hide the pang of jealousy she felt at him seeming more interested in it than her.

Chapter Eight

The tingle of excitement from the night before had long worn off by the time Ruby got to work the next morning. The relief at having made it through her first day, which had been partly responsible for her decision to meet her school friends at the bar, was replaced by the fear that DCI Nelson would accost her again at any moment, demanding the sort of progress that she and DI Jenkins had been unable to deliver. As she trudged over to her desk, far more offended by its sub-par location than she had been yesterday, she saw that not only was Jenkins not at his own, superior desk, but there were no signs that he had yet arrived.

'Anyone seen Jenkins?' she called loudly to no-one in particular, glancing at her watch in frustration. So much for visiting Michael Robins' neighbours at the same time as the attack had occurred.

'He's in his usual spot,' replied a guy she remembered Nelson referring to as Smith in the previous day's briefing. She stood there, hands on hips, to illustrate that this was a less than adequate answer. 'You'll find him in the kitchenette,' he continued, lowering his voice. 'But I wouldn't even think about disturbing him until he's finished his second cup of coffee.'

Fuck that, thought Ruby, marching straight over to the small room that contained little more than a few cupboards, a fridge that was in dire need of cleaning out, a kettle, and a sink that was already half full of dirty mugs. 'You ever thought of saving some of that for the rest of us?' she said grumpily, nodding in the direction of the percolator that Jenkins was shielding with his body, like a wild animal protecting its freshly caught kill.

'I always re-fill it if I take the last cup,' he replied matter-of-factly, keeping up his ability not to rise to any of Ruby's jibes.

'Whatever. I thought we were meant to be heading out to Marshalswick first thing?'

'Yep,' he said, topping up his Styrofoam cup. 'I'd be there now if I hadn't been waiting for you to get here.'

'What the…?' Ruby stopped herself finishing her outburst. She could swear she saw that faint glimmer of a smile again as he walked past.

* * *

'Let's try the wife again,' Ruby said a couple of hours later. They had followed up all the neighbours whom uniform had spoken to and, in their desperation, knocked on some more doors further down the street. They gained nothing more than was already in the notes, with everyone understandably busy at that time of the morning and, with the road being used as a rat-run during rush hour, they had failed to notice any unusual cars passing through. And with regards to the more specific questions they were able to ask, anyone who knew the Robins' offered similar answers to what they had been given the day before. To all intents and purposes, they were a nice family who seemed to get on well with everybody.

'I thought you said that your chat with her yesterday went as well as could be expected.'

'It did,' Ruby replied defensively, her mood having not been helped by their false start to the day. 'But I gave her some things to consider and I'm expecting that she might be thinking a little clearer today.'

'I see,' he responded enigmatically, and in a way that made Ruby suspect he knew the truth beneath her claim; that she wanted another crack at talking to her today in the hope that she might be able to approach it better.

'Perhaps we might pick up a coffee on the way.' She smiled, realising from the suspicious look Jenkins offered her that this was far too quick a turnaround in demeanour to appear convincing.

'And you say I'm obsessed by caffeine,' he said, but only after he had turned away towards the car.

* * *

'What are you doing?' Ruby asked as Jenkins started veering off their route to the room that housed Michael Robins.

'I need to pick up the photos.'

'What photos?'

'You'll see,' he replied, continuing on his way.

Shaking her head, Ruby paused by the door and drew in a deep breath before opening it. What met her inside was both haunting and strangely comforting. Lying in the bed, and with his face covered in bandages like some modern-day Egyptian mummy, was Michael Robins. Having spent most of the past twenty-four hours talking about him, it seemed strange that this was the first time she was meeting him. Not that she could actually see any of him. With only his arms outside the blanket, and with his hands as well protected as his face, no doubt having suffered the same kind of horrific injuries as he desperately tried to claw away the corrosive acid, she couldn't see a single patch of flesh. She welcomed the sterility of the situation, having no desire whatsoever to witness the horrors that lay beneath the bandages, and satisfied that the steady beeping of the heart monitor and slow movement of the respirator meant that Michael was doing as well as could be expected.

In the same chair as Ruby had found her in yesterday was Mrs Robins, but this time she was asleep, as illustrated by the faint snores struggling to compete with the sounds of the medical equipment. It wasn't cowardice that prevented Ruby from seeking to wake her. She could only imagine what this woman had been through since yesterday morning and was content to allow her a few more minutes of blissful ignorance before she woke up again to the dreadfulness of her situation.

Ruby was considering leaving and tracking down Jenkins when the door opened. It was him, and the way he gently eased it shut behind him suggested he had quickly appraised the situation. 'What have you got there?' she whispered, pointing to the paper folder in his hands, as much to break the awkwardness of the silence as anything.

'The photos I told you about,' he said, reaching inside.

'Photos of what?' But no sooner had she asked the question than she realised the answer. Despite now knowing they were pictures of Michael's injuries, she was powerless to stop herself taking them from Jenkins and studying them.

'Jesus fucking Christ,' she said under her breath. Much as she hadn't wanted it to, her imagination had tried to depict what the acid must have done to Michael's face since they had first heard of the attack. But the reality was far, far worse. Her initial thought was that it would no longer resemble a face but, in many respects, that would have made easier viewing. Being able to make out his eye sockets, the remnants of his nose, and where his lips had once been, only made the devastation wreaked by the acid all the more potent. How he was still alive after all that was a complete mystery to Ruby.

Finally breaking the spell, but knowing that those horrific images would remain with her for the rest of her life, she thrust them back in Jenkins' direction. 'When did they... why did they take them?' she stuttered.

'In situations like this, they always take photos before operating. It helps us with the prosecution.' Jenkins must have interpreted her look of revulsion as a sign that he needed to expand on his claim. 'You know, for the judge as well as the jury, so they're less inclined to impose a soft sentence on the attacker.'

'Only if we find him,' she responded sourly. 'Perhaps we should come back another...'

The sound of Mrs Robins stirring stopped Ruby from finishing her suggestion. Wondering whether they could slip out before she opened her eyes, instead she quickly helped Jenkins slide the photos back in the file. Ruby hoped that Mrs Robins would see them one day, but only when she was sat in a courtroom and the man responsible was stood in the dock.

'Hello, Mrs Robins,' she said gently, once she was awake and looking blankly in their direction. 'I'm DC Knight, I was here yesterday. I don't believe you met my colleague, DI Jenkins.'

'I'm sorry,' Mrs Robins croaked, repositioning herself in her chair.

'I said that I'm DC Knight and this is—'

'No,' she said, shaking her head and with her eyes blinking all the time. 'I wanted to apologize for yesterday.'

'Oh,' responded Ruby, taken aback and glancing quickly in Jenkins' direction. 'Really, think nothing of it. How are you today?'

'The nurse convinced me to go home last night to try and get some sleep, but I guess it was only being back here with him that allowed me to finally rest.'

'Home?' Ruby said, unable to hide the shock in her voice.

'No, sorry,' Mrs Robins replied, shaking her head again. 'I meant back with the kids, at their grandparents' house. They said you came around to speak to them yesterday.'

'They did?' Ruby asked nervously, hoping that Susan hadn't shared with her how offended she had been by Jenkins' line of questioning. If she had, it might make the job of getting Mrs Robins to open up all the more difficult.

'Yes, she said you seemed thoroughly determined to catch whoever… whoever… you know…' Tears began to fall down her cheeks and Ruby found herself wondering how many more she would inevitably shed before her life took on a semblance of normality again. Not that it necessarily ever would. She reached for a box of tissues by the bed. 'And that's why I wanted to apologise for being off with you yesterday,' she continued.

'Please Mrs Robins, there's no need,' Ruby responded, feeling the prick of her own tears beginning to form. Her overriding emotion was guilt. Instead of gorging on Italian food last night, killing time before meeting with people she had little interest in seeing, she could have still been at the station working to alleviate a little of this woman's pain. As she had walked along the moonlit streets with Danny, she hadn't once thought of where Mrs Robins might be and how she might be feeling. Most of all, she felt guilty for so readily accepting Jenkins' claim that it's important to separate work and outside life. How, just by filling in his stupid notebook, he could switch of his feelings was beyond her. No, she wouldn't allow herself to become detached like that; only concerning herself with the wicked deeds done by those they were chasing as long as they fell within office hours.

'I could do with stretching my legs,' Mrs Robins said, getting up. 'Fancy a coffee?'

'You two go ahead,' replied Jenkins.

'I hope you don't mind my saying so, but you seem quite young to be a detective,' Mrs Robins said as she led Ruby down the corridor.

'Wise beyond my years,' Ruby responded, not wanting to divulge how very new to the job she was.

'I take it you haven't found out anything of use so far,' Mrs Robins said, more seriously this time.

So much for taking it steady. 'No firm leads as yet,' she replied. 'But we're following all lines of enquiry,' she continued in a vain attempt to sound reassuring.

'I thought as much, and so you're hoping I may be of more use than I was yesterday.' More of a statement than a question. 'Do you smoke, DC Knight?'

'What?' Ruby blurted out, taken aback by the sudden change in direction. 'No, I don't.'

'Shame, it must be ten years since I last had a fag, but I feel like I really could do with one now. Do you mind if we skip the coffee and go outside? I might be able to bum one off a visitor and, if not, the fresh air would probably do me more good.'

Ruby stood awkwardly as Mrs Robins choked and spluttered her way through the cigarette. Had the person who donated it to her not been stubbing out her own as they approached her, Ruby would have thought that Mrs Robins' determination to finish it was down to not wanting to appear ungrateful. The upshot of Mrs Robins' struggle with the cigarette was that she was delaying each subsequent inhalation by appearing quite chatty.

Not that anything Ruby was able to find out was especially helpful. Despite being able to probe her far more than she could yesterday, it seemed there really wasn't anyone Mrs Robins was aware of who disliked her husband, even slightly.

* * *

'I don't want to go back to the station,' Ruby confessed when she and Jenkins were back in the car. The cautious nature of his driving now seemed an advantage.

'Let's not then,' he said in a tone that could almost be described as cheery. 'I'm sure the DCI will radio in if he gets desperate for an update.'

'Where are we going then? It's a little early to stop off for some lunch,' she said, her stomach making a little growl of protest at the claim.

'We'll go and visit some of his friends. Shouldn't take long.'

Ruby gave a quick snort of laughter at this, even though she doubted it was a deliberate attempt to be funny.

* * *

Jenkins had been right, it hadn't taken long and, after a disappointingly quick stop-off to grab a sandwich, Ruby found herself being taken back to the station. Michael Robins' friends were as they had appeared on paper; decent respectable people and nothing like the type Ruby would consider capable of committing such an appalling act. And, like with everyone else, they couldn't think of a single thing he could have done to provoke it. If Ruby hadn't been quite so concerned about how all of this was going to sound to Nelson, she might have noticed that some of the awkwardness between her and Jenkins had faded. Whereas yesterday they just seemed to be tripping over each other when trying to talk to people, and any positive interventions had been borne out of a concern that the other person was messing things up, they had started to find something of an equilibrium. Not exactly a good cop/bad cop routine, but Jenkins seemed to know when to back off and allow Ruby to contribute. It seemed he was learning to appreciate her tact and sensitivity, whilst she relied on him when the situation called for something more succinct.

'Seriously though, what now?' she asked, punching in the number to CID and opening the door.

'I guess we just have to be patient.'

'Patient about what?! We should just hope that the attacker might have a fit of conscience and stroll in downstairs to hand himself in?' Ruby glowered, daring Jenkins to give his typical shrug of the shoulders.

She didn't get to see any kind of response. 'Ah, the gruesome twosome has returned, no doubt anxious to appraise me of their outstanding progress so far today,' Nelson called from his position beside one of the detectives' desk.

Ruby looked round the open-plan office to see if she could read on anyone's face if they shared her thoughts that Nelson seemed to just be a dick. What a contrast to the man she had met at interview. His unspoken reassurance that her move here wasn't like going to the back of the beyond may have been true given what she was investigating, but that didn't mean she didn't feel cheated all the same. She had thought she saw the same drive and determination in him that she possessed, and she would be able to grow under his tutelage. But really, he was just another guy who thought it was acceptable to use his position of authority to lash out under pressure. Ruby knew that she could be a little fiery and hot-headed on occasion, but trusted that by the time she had as much experience as he had, she would have learned to control it and remain professional throughout.

'Don't leave it so long to pipe up this time,' she hissed at Jenkins as they made their way into the DCI's office.

'Look, I'm not even going to ask you how it's going because I can tell from your faces,' Nelson said once they were all sat down. 'And equally I'm certain that, if I did, you would be keen to reassure me that you are following up every possible angle. Is that about the size of it?' Ruby didn't bother nodding and, from what she could tell, nor did Jenkins. 'Okay, so let me just share with you where I am with this at the moment; strictly for the purpose of keeping you appraised of the whole situation. Call it professional development, if you like,' he added, fixing Ruby with a condescending smile. 'Tomorrow morning at 10am,' he paused to look at his watch. 'Approximately eighteen hours from now, I am going to be walking into a press conference where I will be required to give details about what happened to… to…'

'Michael Robins,' Jenkins said flatly, and Ruby had to bring her hand to her mouth to stifle a smile at the look of reproach Nelson shot him.

'Yes,' he said, waving his hand dismissively. 'But what they really want to know is if we haven't already got a suspect in custody, then we are very close. If I can't give them that kind of reassurance, then they are likely to think all manner of things; first and foremost that we have a crazed acid attacker on the loose. Now this has already gained a bit of national interest but imagine what a field day they will have with this if I arrive tomorrow morning to admit that we are no closer to catching someone than when we started.' Nelson sighed and massaged his temples. 'Look, like I said before, I'm sure you're doing everything right. Steve, you and I have known each other for many years…'

Ruby looked up in confusion before realising that he was referring to Jenkins. In different circumstances she might have found it amusing how quickly she forgot that her partner had a first name and, if she came to think of it, he had never used hers either.

'…and I wouldn't have put you on this case, Miss Knight, if I didn't believe you could make good on the promise you showed at your interview.' Still a dick or not, she couldn't help but feel heartened by this praise. 'I just need you to do your very upmost to give me something, *something*, to take into that press conference tomorrow so I am not entirely perjuring myself when I offer the sort of reassurance the public require.'

'Don't worry, guv, we're on it,' Jenkins said, standing up. Ruby followed suit and was relieved to see that Nelson seemed content with such a meagre response to his plea.

'So, what now?' Ruby said once they were outside his office, already sick of asking the question so many times.

And it wasn't just that, however better their meeting with Nelson might have ended in comparison to the start, she now felt compelled to pull an all-nighter to try and find him what he wanted.

'Like I said before, we just need to be patient,' he replied, heading in the direction of the kitchenette.

Ruby's shock at such a flippant response caused him to pull out a few metres lead over her but she dashed forward and overtook him before he could get to the percolator. 'No way, don't you dare even think about coffee until you tell me what you mean by that.'

'I need one because I didn't get to have one whilst we were at the hospital.'

'What? What has that got to do with anything, and besides, we didn't go to the cafeteria we…' She stopped, irritated with herself that she had started to dignify his ridiculous statement with a justification. But there was also something else. She couldn't pinpoint what exactly, but there was something in his expression that suggested he had more to say.

'Instead of getting one myself, I caught the doctor whilst he was doing his rounds.'

'And?' she prompted impatiently.

'After all we've heard from people, do you now believe that the attack must have been random?'

'Er, no… no I don't,' Ruby replied, curiosity now replacing her anger.

'No, me neither,' he replied conversationally and leaving enough of a pause that Ruby had opened her mouth to speak again. 'And the doctor told me that they are going to be bringing Michael out of his coma in the morning.'

'Oh, shit,' she whispered, understanding the implication of this news. However, the excitement she felt didn't last long and she was scowling at Jenkins again. 'How come you didn't tell me this earlier?'

'You never asked.'

Chapter Nine

Ruby made a show of gathering some files to take home with her, just in case Nelson viewed her leaving at a reasonable time as a sign that she was not taking his predicament seriously enough. Not that she had any intention of removing them from her car's boot. There would be no point; their only hope in cracking this investigation wouldn't be available until the morning, and Jenkins didn't make a similar pretence. As with the day before, he just wrote whatever he needed to in his little notebook, before locking it in his desk drawer.

In a gesture that implied he wasn't oblivious to Ruby's situation, he suggested that they meet up at the hospital rather than come into the office first thing. Even if it were not for her desire to avoid DCI Nelson until they had something worth sharing, she welcomed not having to travel in from Hemel Hempstead, only to then drive back out there again.

The day's events and her tiredness from the night before conspired to make Ruby happy to return home in time for dinner with her parents. Tonight she found something reassuring about being in a situation so familiar to her, and she maintained a positive demeanour, whilst lying her way through their questions about how much she was enjoying her new job.

'I know you can't give us any details, but surely it wouldn't be wrong for you to provide us with a clue?' her mother pleaded. This was the third time her mother had attempted to rephrase what was essentially the same request.

'Okay,' Ruby said with mock exasperation, secretly enjoying the way her mother's enthusiasm was starting to rub off on her. 'As you say, I can't give you many details, but you might be interested in a press conference due to air tomorrow at 10am. It'll probably only be on the local news, but it might provide you with the sort of information you are looking for.'

'Oh my goodness, it isn't… is it?' her mother virtually squealed in excitement. 'Did you hear that Frank?' she continued, slapping her husband hard on the arm. 'I told you they would put her on it. You said no. You said they wouldn't have someone new on something so big. I told you that they would; that they would see how talented she is and know that she is one smart cookie. You were wrong to say they would leave it for more experienced detectives.'

As harsh as her mother's remonstrations sounded, they were delivered with such delight that it would be hard not to forgive her getting carried away. Certainly Ruby's father didn't seem the slightest bit offended. He just nodded in that slow way he always did when she was nagging him.

'But, Mum, you're not to tell anyone, okay?' Ruby was far from convinced by the look of hurt that crossed her mother's face. 'Don't come over all coy with me; if I didn't say it, you'd be on the phone to Auntie Margret in Galway as soon as I went upstairs.'

Ruby's mother opened her mouth to protest but then shut it, offering Ruby a guilty smile instead.

'I'm serious, Mum,' she added. 'Promise me you won't.'

'Okay, fine,' her mother said huffily, but unable to stay down for long. 'Did you hear that, Frank? If this is what our daughter is doing in her first week in the job, imagine what she'll be working on this time next year?!'

Ruby, if for no other reason than to try and provide some support for her father, continued to suffer Fiona's incessant chatter for a while longer, in the hope that when EastEnders started, it might give them some respite. When it didn't, Ruby excused herself, offering an apologetic glance at Frank as she headed upstairs.

Although she was feeling tired and probably could have gone to sleep there and then, she knew that this couldn't be the pattern she set out for herself each evening. What she really needed was to gain herself more of a social life around these parts. Ruby got out her phone and went onto Facebook. There was a thread about the previous night, with some accompanying photographs. With most of them having been taken at the venue where the others moved on to, and showing the girls in various stages of drunkenness, Ruby was glad she had made her exit when she did.

With Danny.

Danny had posted on the thread that he was pleased they had such a good night, which had prompted many of them to confess they were suffering from it today. Ruby wanted to add something witty, to somehow get involved in the conversation, despite it being many hours old by now, but couldn't think of anything. Instead she decided to send Danny a friend request. To prove to herself that it was just part of the process of building up a larger circle of acquaintances, she did the same for the rest of the group. With the exception of Zara.

Having finished doing that she was about to put her phone down when a notification flashed up on the screen. She had a message through Facebook. It was from Danny.

Hi

The initial thrill of being contacted so soon was tempered by the simplicity of its contents.

Hi, she typed back but left her finger hovering over the send button. It just seemed like a pointless reply; one sent purely for the sake of it. She would need to add something but anything that came into her head either seemed similarly vacuous or too desperate for attention.

Thanks for walking me back to my car last night.

You're welcome. I had a good time.

Ruby smiled contentedly and hoped this was a direct reference to their time alone, rather than one about the evening in general. She willed herself to leave it at that.

Me too. She quickly typed, promising herself that this was it, but remaining in Facebook all the same.

Would you like to join me for a drink on Friday?

His message was immediate, and Ruby knew that she couldn't delay replying too long, because that would give the impression she was having to think about it too much.

Sure, who else is going?

Ruby was anxious to know if she was reading more into this than Danny intended.

No-one, but I can invite the others if you'd like.

No, that's fine. Message me the details later on in the week.

Ruby closed the app, satisfied that being the one to end the conversation balanced out her decision to meet alone. She wondered if he was feeling the same thrill of anticipation that she was. One thing was for certain, if he had found her sufficiently attractive to ask her on a date, when all she had been wearing was her conservative work clothes and subtle make up, she intended making his jaw drop the moment she walked into whichever venue he selected. Just a little harmless fun and she would make sure he had to work a little harder than he'd needed to this evening.

With her mind full of outfits, some of them owned and others she could buy if she had sufficient time between now and Friday, and matching them to the different places he might take her for their date, she didn't realise that she was gradually drifting off to sleep.

Chapter Ten

Embarrassed that her parents might see that she had slept in her suit, Ruby got changed into her pyjamas before heading to the bathroom the next morning. She wasn't sure whether it was the benefit of a good night's rest, the anticipation of Friday's date with Danny, or the hope that she was about to get the breakthrough in her case she so desperately needed, but she had a spring in her step.

Despite feeling better able to deal with her mother's babble that morning, she was keen to get to the hospital as quickly as possible. Parking up a good twenty minutes before she was due to meet Jenkins, she was surprised to find him already there and leaning against the car's bonnet, soaking up the sun's early rays. Even before he spoke, she could tell there was something different about him this morning, and not just because he was waiting for her. She had never contemplated his bathing habits but his hair and beard, whilst still unfashionably shaggy, had a certain sheen to them and his skin was less sallow.

'Morning, guv,' she called cheerfully, interested to see if he noticed her unusual show of deference.

If he did, he didn't acknowledge it. 'Shall we go in then?' Jenkins said, already heading toward the entrance.

It came as a surprise to neither of them that Michael Robins had yet to wake; the lead nurse hadn't given them a set time but they had assumed the anaesthetic would have worn off by now.

'Shall we go for a coffee and wait?' Ruby asked.

'If you like.'

Jenkins shrugged, and she couldn't work out whether his apparent ambivalence to caffeine that morning was genuine or put on. Certainly he didn't sup it in the greedy way she had observed him before but maybe, like her, he was just trying to kill some time knowing that they would shortly need to phone DCI Nelson.

Having dragged things out until 9am, they made one final return to the ward. With the nurse occupied somewhere else, Ruby turned to Jenkins. 'Do you think we should just go into the room anyway?' Despite needing him to understand the implication of what she was suggesting, she couldn't bring herself to be specific about what she was proposing.

'Mrs Robins is bound to be in there,' he replied, clearly catching her drift.

'She might have some more information she wishes to share with me,' Ruby added hopefully.

'Well, I guess we should then, you know, just in case she has something it would be worth Nelson knowing prior to the press conference.'

Ruby smiled at the conspiratorial tone Jenkins had adopted. She was a long way from liking her partner, but he was proving to be far less of a drain than she had believed him to be on their first day.

The slight buzz of excitement their plan had given her quickly faded as they entered the room to find Mrs Robins in her usual chair. Thankfully she wasn't asleep this time but her haggard look was enough to indicate she had got little rest during the night.

'I was hoping he would have woken up by now,' Mrs Robins said. Ruby found the confirmation of her own thoughts, although unwitting, somewhat unsettling.

'Perhaps you might like to get some fresh air before he does,' Ruby responded, hoping she had added enough inflection to the way she said *fresh air* to awaken the nicotine receptors in Mrs Robins' brain.

'I want to be here when he does,' she said flatly.

Ruby shot a look of desperation at Jenkins.

'I hope you don't take this the wrong way,' he said in a soft tone that was alien to Ruby's ears. 'But you might like to use the opportunity to freshen up before he does. You're going to need to be as strong as you can for him, and anything you can do to reduce his concern for how you are coping, will enable him to concentrate on dealing with what has happened. I'm sure DC Knight and I can spare a few minutes to wait with Michael whilst you attend to yourself.'

Even though Jenkins had put his suggestion far more tactfully than she would have ever thought him capable of doing, Ruby still winced at the expected reaction from Mrs Robins.

'I guess you're right,' she said, hauling herself up from her seat. 'When I told his parents I wouldn't be coming back to see the kids last night, Peter insisted on driving over to drop off a few bits for me.' She picked up a small holdall from beside the bed. 'It would be nice to just brush my teeth, splash some water on my face and maybe do something to sort out my hair. Just promise me you'll come and get me if he starts to stir.'

'Jesus, are we really going to do this?' Ruby asked once they were alone, appreciating the irony of her question given she was the one who had suggested it in the first place.

'It's for them that we're doing this,' Jenkins replied, approaching the head of the bed. Under other circumstances Ruby might have been offended by him assuming the lead in this, but here she was grateful to merely be an observer. *An accomplice*, corrected an unwelcome voice in her head.

If Jenkins had any similar doubts he chose neither to voice them nor convey them through his actions. Instead he confidently placed his hands upon Michael's shoulders and rocked them, almost imperceptibly gently at first but then firmer and more determined. Ruby wanted to call out for him to stop but, with them already having crossed the line, it seemed foolish for them to attempt to return. So she approached Michael from the other side of the bed, figuring that waking to her tones would be far more preferable than Jenkins' gravelly delivery.

'Mr Robins, it's time to open your eyes now,' she said soothingly, fighting how foolish she felt. 'Everything is okay. You're safe in hospital but you need to stop sleeping for a moment.'

From the mound of bandages came a short groan. Ruby put her hand on Jenkins', but a shake of his head indicated that they couldn't afford to stop now and risk Michael slipping back under.

'That's it, Mr Robins, you're doing a great job,' she continued uncertainly. 'You just need to wake up properly now, so we can check you're okay.'

Another groan, a little louder this time and followed by indistinct sound. She put her head close to the bandages to try and make it out. 'Water,' came the incredibly dry croak. Ruby chastised herself for not thinking of that before and having some ready. Her hand was shaking so much as she tried to pour out a glass that that she sloshed water onto the table.

'Let me do it,' Jenkins instructed gently, no doubt influenced by the way the glass was clinking audibly against the ring Ruby wore on her right hand, as she continued to shake.

With the delicacy of a surgeon Jenkins tipped little more than a few drops through the small gap in Michael's dressings that had been left for the respirator to poke through. The accompanying smacking sound as Michael tried to move the water around his parched mouth was as tragic as it was encouraging. A little more from Jenkins, just enough to create some lubrication and a horrible sight caused Ruby to recoil. From the gap in the pristine white bandages poked a pink tongue, searching for more water. This time Jenkins was generous, to the point that she feared Michael may begin to splutter but the steady gulping sound confirmed that the flow was both consistent and manageable.

'There will be more in a moment, Mr Robins,' Jenkins said once the glass was drained. 'But first we need to see how well you keep that down. Tell me, do you remember that you have been in an accident?

'Yes.' Still a croak but more easily understandable now. Ruby knew where this was leading and she couldn't help but glance anxiously at the door. It was irrational to think that Mrs Robins would be coming back already but that didn't stop the skin prickling on her arms. She tried to settle herself with the knowledge that finding them now would be better than when Jenkins had been shaking her husband awake.

'Do you know exactly what happened to you?' Still as soothing as you were likely to get from a man like Jenkins but delivered with a hint more urgency.

The pause that followed was long enough for Ruby to consider whether Michael had fallen unconscious again. 'Yes,' came the eventual reply. Despite having never spoken to this man before and without the clues offered by facial expression, the full meaning in that simple three-letter word was clear. The hurt contained within his answer removed any concerns that he may not remember the attack. Ruby's satisfaction at this was heavily tempered by understanding how awful it must be for him. Whilst he would have to live with the consequences of what had happened for the rest of his days, encountering unimaginable challenges both physical and mental along the way, perhaps being spared the memory of the moment his life changed for ever would have been something of a blessing.

Except that it could prevent him gaining what little comfort he may be able to draw from seeing the person responsible brought to justice.

'Who did this to you?' Jenkins asked, now with a fierceness to his tone that Ruby found almost as uncharacteristic as when he had been gentle. This passion, this intensity, was how she felt towards the job and she realised in that moment that Jenkins had once had it too. But it was not lost, just hidden, and, as well as catching whoever had caused them to be in this hospital room, she was determined to find a way of unearthing it entirely.

She was so caught up in her thoughts, and how her mother would chide her for always seeking to take on the problems of others, that she nearly missed Michael's response. A quick glance at her partner confirmed that Jenkins had failed to understand it too.

'Say that again, Mr Robins,' he requested, more forcefully now.

They heard Michael swallow in an attempt to clear his throat for his second go. But still neither of them could make anything out except that it sounded like it began with an S. As Ruby leaned in closer, she wracked her brains to remember which names of the dozens of clients they sifted through had either first names or surnames that started with that letter. Michael's third attempt was similarly unsuccessful and, worse of all, Ruby could tell from his strained delivery that he was losing what little strength he possessed. She pressed her head so close to the bandages that she could feel his rapid breathing on her ear. It caused her to shudder but nowhere near as much as when the sound came out of his mouth again.

'Stranger.'

She looked up at Jenkins in horror.

Chapter Eleven

The wait until Mrs Robins returned was far worse than when they had worried she might disturb their attempts to wake her husband. But at least working out what they were going to say to her provided something of a distraction from having to face up to the reality of the situation they were in.

'What if he tells her about it when he next wakes?' Ruby hissed.

'And what difference will that make?' Jenkins retorted. 'Unless we tell her the truth about us questioning him and failing to come and find her, it all amounts to the same thing.'

'So we just tell her he hasn't stirred and hope for the best?'

'Not in so many words. Tell you what, why don't you leave this one to me?'

'If you insist,' she replied, hiding how content she was with the offer.

They didn't speak for the remainder of the time and listened out for footsteps coming up the corridor. When, finally, one set didn't keep on going Ruby was almost pleased that the tension would at last be broken.

Jenkins was fishing his mobile out of his suit jacket. 'It's the office needing us to call in,' he said loudly to Ruby, with his back to the opening door. 'Oh, Mrs Robins, you do look much… better,' he said, turning around. 'I hope you don't mind if we leave you to it, we've got to…' Trusting the wave of the phone was enough, he was already easing past her and out into the corridor.

'We'll see you soon,' Ruby added uncertainly, keen not to get left behind and considering whether, in her current state of shock, Mrs Robins would be alarmed by the swiftness of their departure.

'Best to avoid having to tell a lie,' Jenkins whispered.

'Well, apart from that bit about needing to check in,' Ruby said, wondering why she was choosing to be petty.

'That wasn't a lie. It's past 9am now and the DCI will roast us alive if we don't update him before he goes into the press conference.'

'Shit!' Ruby murmured. 'What are you going to tell him?' She felt slightly guilty for not saying *we*.

'The truth of course. He's not going to like it, but he needs to know.'

Ruby accepted that Jenkins was right but that didn't stop her feeling incredibly uncomfortable. 'Do you think you can hold off for a few minutes? Give us a chance to think this through?'

'Okay,' he shrugged, indicating that, although willing, he didn't necessarily see the point.

'Maybe it's too soon to take what Michael told us as being what actually happened,' she said as they stepped out of the entrance and into the cool morning air. 'You know, maybe his memory hasn't caught up with him yet and so, whilst he might have remembered what had happened to him, he isn't able to place the face.' She could tell by the blank look on Jenkins' face that he was as unconvinced with this line of argument as she was. 'Or perhaps he's scared to tell us who did it in case… in case it endangers his family or something.'

'Well I suppose that is a possibility,' Jenkins conceded. 'But it doesn't really change anything at the moment. We still have to tell Nelson that we haven't got anything.'

Ruby sighed, admitting defeat. 'Best get it over and done with.'

'I'll put it on speakerphone, so you can hear his reaction,' Jenkins said without a trace of humour, placing his mobile on the Mondeo's bonnet once he had punched in the number.

'Jenkins is that you?' barked Nelson after barely a couple of rings.

'Yes, guv, we're at the hospital.'

'I was just about to call you.' To Ruby it sounded like Nelson was a little short of breath. Anger can do that to a person.

'They started to bring him out of his coma last night and we were hoping that we might be able to speak to him and get a name.'

'And?' The impatience was clear.

'Well he had only just woken up and he wasn't able to…'

'Shit!' The venom in Nelson's delivery of the curse was enough to cause Ruby to wince. 'But never mind that now, there's been another attack.'

'What did you say, guv?' The shock in Jenkins' voice was reflected in his expression and when he looked at Ruby she mouthed the words *What the fuck?*

'I'm going to have to postpone the press conference for an hour or so until it is clear what the implication of this is.'

'Can you be more specific?' Jenkins requested firmly.

'Look, I just told you, there's been another attack!'

'An acid attack, guv?' Ruby chipped in, unable to contain herself.

'Is that you, Knight? Yes, that's what I said. I have to go but you get yourselves back here straight away, you hear?'

Ruby punched Jenkins on the arm so he would turn to her before replying. 'No,' she whispered.

'Guv, give us the address and we'll go to the scene.'

'No, I have Smith and Dorkins.'

'Call them back,' Jenkins' tone was forceful, perhaps bordering on insubordinate. But even though the seconds of silence that followed were oppressive, Ruby was thankful, irrespective of the outcome. Even before the phone call Jenkins had proven himself a useful partner this morning, and someone she could look to learn from. But having the courage to contradict the DCI wasn't due to his obstinate personality, but came from whatever credit he had gained over his years of experience.

'Fine,' Nelson responded eventually. 'But I want a full report from both of you as soon as you have finished. Dispatch will give you the address.' The line went dead.

Ruby wanted to thank Jenkins but needed to tackle something else. 'I think it might be better if you jump in with me,' she said nervously.

'Not a chance,' Jenkins said, already pulling open his car door. 'But you can come with me if you like. I'll drop you back here later.

Ruby sighed. 'Can we at least go at the speed limit this time?'

Jenkins laughed; full, hearty and all the more noticeable because it was the first time she had heard him genuinely amused. 'Grab what's on the back seat,' he said, starting the engine. Ruby stretched behind her and saw an emergency light on a sucker pad. She didn't need any further instruction to know what he wanted and, having reached through her window to attach it to the roof, Jenkins flicked a switch on the dash she hadn't noticed before. Even in the sunshine she could make out the pulse of blue above her, accompanied by lights discretely hidden in the front grill. 'You might want to put on your seatbelt,' he joked as he pulled out of the parking space.

Ruby had been in marked police cars countless times attending crime scenes, but Jenkins' driving was something else. So mesmerised by the tremendous speed with which he piloted their exit from Hemel Hempstead, delivered with such smoothness and confident, controlled inputs of steering, it took a while for Ruby to start to contemplate the implication of DCI Nelson's revelation. It was only then that she realised they hadn't even called for the address and, not wanting to disturb her partner's concentration, she phoned it through.

'Repeat that, over,' she instructed but knew it was just her brain failing to contextualise quickly enough what she had been told.

'57 Verulam Road,' came back the monotone voice. 'Address is for…'

'Platinum Estate Agents,' she whispered at exactly the same time as it was said over the radio.

'Victim's name is…' Ruby found herself wishing that what followed wasn't going to be female. '…Jacob Hubbard.' She instantly regretted how relieved she was to find that it wasn't Samie Wright.

'Thank you, out,' she said, ending the transmission and turning to Jenkins. His face didn't betray any emotion but the slight drop in his speed implied that he had found news of their destination something of a shock too. 'Is it okay to talk to you?'

'Go ahead,' he replied evenly.

'Well, er… I…' Ruby didn't really know what to say.

'Perhaps it would be best not to think about it too much before we get there.'

Even with there being plenty of traffic to navigate, Jenkins had them at the premises in under ten minutes. They didn't know the exact time of the attack, but the presence of the ambulance and two paramedic cars suggested that their conversation with Nelson could only have been a couple of minutes after the emergency call had come through. With the location being in the centre of town, this time there were far more onlookers gathered and the uniformed officers were in the process of ushering them back to establish a cordon.

'What's the matter with you?' Ruby hissed at a woman busy trying to take a selfie with the scene in the background. Ruby didn't wait for a response and pushed past her more firmly than was strictly necessary. The bunching of the paramedics was an instant indication that Jake was receiving treatment on the pavement outside the shop. Ruby was powerless to stop herself peering over the top of them but wasn't disappointed to find that his face was already covered in dressings.

'See this?' Jenkins whispered to her, pointing at the car parked next to them. Even if it wasn't for the company logo on the door, Ruby would have recognised the Audi convertible from the last time they were there. But there was something more specific that Jenkins was trying to show her. The gleaming black metallic paint was spoiled at the rear quarter by a splatter of what could only have been the corrosive acid used to attack Jake. It might only have given them the angle of attack, but it was a start.

With a single nod Jenkins then stepped into the premises.

'Passers-by?' Ruby called in the direction of a uniform stood next to two people she didn't recognise, sat in the corner. She could tell from the horror on their faces they had either witnessed the attack or had attended Jake whilst they waited for the emergency services to arrive. 'There's a kettle out back. Make them a cup of tea whilst DI Jenkins speaks to them.'

As keen as Ruby was to hear what they had seen, her immediate concern was for Samie. She was with another officer, sat at her usual desk. 'Perhaps you could help your colleague with the teas,' Ruby said, not failing to notice the look of resentment on the copper's face, no doubt prompted by the fact that he must have been at least ten years her senior.

'I'm so sorry,' Ruby said, taking her own seat and trying to maintain her composure in the face of Samie's tears. If finding out Michael had been attacked had not been distressing enough, she could only imagine what it must have been like for this one to have happened in front of her. 'That must have been awful for you.'

'His… his face, it was just… just gone,' she managed to get out in between sobs. Ruby shuddered at the thought; seeing the photographs of Michael taken before his surgery had been bad enough.

'Is there anyone I can call to come and look after you? A boyfriend perhaps?'

'No,' she sniffed, shaking her head. 'I don't have a boyfriend.'

Ruby was going to suggest someone else, but she wanted to get to the real reason why she needed to talk to her. 'Tell me what happened,' she said softly. The question she wanted to ask was who did it, but she felt the need to be as gentle as possible. From what she could hear over her shoulder, Jenkins was taking a more direct approach with his witnesses.

'I heard this screaming, it was dreadful, and so I dashed out to see what had happened.'

'Were you the first person to get to Jake?'

'Yes, I think so. Another man was there a couple of seconds later and the other one,' she nodded in Jenkins' direction. 'The other one was there a few moments after that.'

'What did you see when you first looked out the window?'

'Jake was holding his face but… but by the time I had got outside he had fallen to the ground.'

'And did you see anyone else? Anyone running away?' Ruby could feel her heart rate rising in anticipation of the answer to her question.

'No,' Samie replied, shaking her head. 'I was just concentrating on Jake.' Her tone was apologetic.

Shit, thought Ruby. She couldn't bear the idea of having to leave here without something of a description. 'Er, what about sound? Did you hear footsteps running away?'

'No, I was just… I was focusing on Jake.' Her sobs, which had largely come under control, began again in earnest. But sympathy wasn't the only thing Ruby felt this time. She also felt anger, but what disturbed her most was that it wasn't entirely directed at this mystery attacker. Samie had been sat at her desk, with the massive window in front of her. Even if she hadn't looked up until she heard Jake's screams, surely she would have got a glimpse of whoever was running away. It wasn't as though Jake's body was to one side, he was slap bang in the middle of her eye-line, exactly where he had chosen to park his car the last time Ruby had been here.

'Didn't you hear him pull up?'

'Who?' Samie asked, reaching for another tissue from a box in the drawer.

'Jake,' Ruby replied, trying to force as much patience into her tone as possible.

'No, why?'

Ruby ignored the question because to answer it would come across as unnecessarily harsh. 'But even if you didn't hear it, surely you would have seen it, even just out of the corner of your eye?'

'Well, er… we get a lot of traffic passing at this time of the morning and Jake usually pulls up there. I used to tell him he'd get a ticket from a traffic warden but whenever one came along he would always dash–'

'What about his music then?'

'How… how do you mean?'

'The last time we were here it was blasting out of the car and I see he has his roof down again.'

'I… I don't know,' Samie whispered with her head down, before bringing her eyes up to meet Ruby's. 'Look, what do you want from me? I already told you what I saw.' She was nearly shouting now.

Ruby opened her mouth to speak again; to tell her she needed to quit being so defensive when all she was doing was trying to catch the person responsible for both of her employers suffering from about as horrific an attack as she could imagine. But a strong hand had been placed on her shoulder. She wanted to cast it off, but she knew what it signified. She was overstepping the mark and Jenkins was trying to prevent her going too far. And yet she was unable to entirely bury her fury as she turned up to look at him.

'I've just about finished with my witnesses,' he said evenly. 'How are you getting on here?'

Ruby drew in a deep breath. 'I think we're about done too,' she said, standing up before facing Samie once more. 'Again, I'm very sorry you've had to go through this. If anything occurs to you before we return, then please don't hesitate to get in touch.' In her effort to sound calm and professional she knew that her tone came across as cold.

As soon as they were back outside Jenkins went over to talk to one of the paramedics, giving Ruby a few moments to calm down.

'What did she say?' Ruby asked when he returned.

'It's hard to tell but it sounds like, if anything, he got it worse than Michael did. They wanted to take him away sooner but were concerned that the acid would continue eating into… into him if they didn't keep attending to it there. Some ambulance crews in London have strong alkaline solutions for this very thing but they had to make do with what they could find. They reckon it's touch and go whether he will pull through.'

'Shit.' Ruby swore loudly enough to cause one of the uniform officers to spin briefly in their direction. She hadn't even considered that this might turn into a murder investigation.

Jenkins lifted the cordon, so she could crouch under, before turning to her. 'Was there a problem back there?' The mildness of his tone didn't disguise what he was referring to and Ruby was grateful that he hadn't phrased his question more judgementally, like *What got into you?*

'It's nothing, guv,' she replied sheepishly. 'I was just frustrated that Samie had nothing for us to go on. I guess your guys didn't have much to offer?'

'No, one of them only realised what had happened when he heard Samie shrieking over Jake's body and the other came around the corner and saw the three of them there.'

'It just feels like we're never going to catch this guy,' Ruby said, voicing her greatest concern.

'I must admit that I was starting to feel the same when we were in the hospital earlier, but this gives us far more to go on. We might be just out of the city centre's CCTV coverage, but someone could have seen what happened. Uniform will start going door to door and we'll put an appeal out for witnesses, just in case there was someone driving past who didn't realise what was going on until we give them a nudge.' Perhaps he could tell from the look on Ruby's face that she wasn't convinced because he added: 'But even without any of that we can be pretty certain it now has something to do with the business. It might mean having to go back through all those files again but this time we are more sure that the attacker is in there somewhere, and we have two dates and times we can cross reference them against.'

'And maybe that's why Michael couldn't give us a name. He can't be expected to remember the identity of every client, especially when he is just waking up from a coma.' She knew her words sounded hopeful, but anything was better than the despair that had prompted her into laying into Samie.

'Quite possibly,' he said with a kindly smile. Ruby didn't know what had got into Jenkins this morning but, if he carried on like this, she believed she might even come to like him one day. 'To be honest, much of the job is the grind. As unexciting as it sounds, most cases are cracked by just going through the available evidence again and again until something comes up.'

'We'd best get to it then,' she said, opening the car door. 'Just promise me that the DCI is going to see it that way too.'

Her reply was Jenkins' familiar shrug and, much as it still irked her, within this context she could understand it. In the short time she had known DCI Nelson it was clear that he was very much results driven, and had little time for anything he might consider an excuse.

Chapter Twelve

'No, don't bother with overtime,' Nelson barked. 'You've had the best part of three days since the second attack and a fresh approach over the weekend might yield some better results.'

In many respects Ruby felt she should be grateful that she was going to get some time off. Her first week in the job had been far tougher than she imagined and, with her and Jenkins having worked through the list of clients from scratch since Wednesday, she needed a break for her own sanity as much as anything else. But it was the implication that they had missed something, or just weren't good enough, that stung. A part of her would welcome someone else going through the evidence, if nothing else but to prove that their failure to come up with a single credible suspect was through no fault of their own.

Ruby knew that Jenkins was finding it tough too. Not that he had ever admitted it, but with all his experience, their lack of progress must have been hard to take. The different side to him that had been revealed on Wednesday had largely been masked again. In the mornings he had been especially quiet and withdrawn, causing Ruby to suspect that he was having trouble sleeping, not least because of the way he had reignited his obsession with caffeine. Not that she was having the unbroken eight hours a night that she had become accustomed to. She had found herself waking up from dreams that, to one degree or another, related to the case. On one such occasion she recalled dragging Samie outside the estate agents to see what the acid had done to Jake's car and, on another, she remembered shouting at her that if she didn't start thinking of a way to help them she would be next. More than anything Ruby had been concerned by the level of anger she had shown in her dreams and had to fight to keep her emotions under control during the daytime, especially when all her mother wanted to do was talk to her about the job.

So, yes, as pissed off as she was with Nelson, she would welcome a chance to recharge her batteries, starting with her date with Danny that evening. To say she had barely given it a second thought, except when he had texted her with the name of the venue, would be a lie but she felt far less prepared than she had ever been when going out with a man before. Whereas Ruby's reaction to him selecting a bar rather than a restaurant had been one of disappointment, because it implied he was viewing a date with her more casually than her ego liked, she was now glad of the opportunity to have a few drinks. To save herself time and money she would drive and get a cab home afterwards, perhaps using the journey in to collect her car the next day as a chance to do some retail therapy.

'Is that it then, guv?' she asked Nelson, doing little to hide the petulance in her tone.

'Just close the door on your way out,' he said, motioning them to get up.

'You shouldn't be so hard on him,' Jenkins said once they were outside.

'I suppose,' she conceded. 'Do you think he might fail my probation?' A few days ago she could think of nothing more terrifying but a small part of her, the exhausted and pissed off part, almost welcomed the thought of being forced into switching careers.

'No,' said Jenkins, giving another of his rare laughs. 'Nelson is a good man and he'll see you right. Which is why I think you should go a little easier on him.'

'I don't understand.'

'Of course you don't, but he and I have worked together for many years. Let's just say that if this case were not putting a lot of pressure on him, on us all, you would see a completely different side to him.'

'Okay,' she responded, sounding far from convinced despite having seen a glimpse at interview of what Jenkins must have been referring to. 'I guess I'll save my judgement of him for another time, and hope he does the same with me.'

'That's the spirit,' Jenkins said warmly.

Ruby regarded him with a quizzical look. 'What's got into you? You've been miserable as sin these past few days and now that Nelson has chewed us up again you seem in a better mood. Didn't you hear what he was saying about getting others to work on our case over the weekend?'

'So what?' Jenkins said, with a knack of delivering what could be considered as a provocative phrase without the slightest hint of unpleasantness.

'Don't you mind his insinuation that others could do it better than us?'

'No,' he replied simply.

'Why the hell not?'

'They won't find anything because we have done our job properly.' The surety of Jenkins' claim was enough to disarm Ruby. 'And meanwhile we shall get some much-needed R and R. Surely a youngster like you has plans for the weekend?'

'Well, er… yes… yes I do,' she responded, feeling uncomfortable despite knowing that there precisely zero chance Jenkins would follow this admission up with an enquiry as to what she was specifically doing, if nothing else but for the fact that every attempt she had made to engage him in conversation about his life outside of work had entirely failed.

'So, there you go then,' he smiled, pulling his notebook out of his jacket, and heading to his desk to fill it in. Ruby still didn't subscribe to Jenkins' belief that it was essential to find a way to leave the job behind at the end of the day, but envied the contented way he sat there writing his notes. Not that she would ever give him the satisfaction of doing something similar, but she decided to tidy her desk, so she wasn't met with an unruly mess when she returned to it on Monday morning.

Chapter Thirteen

Ruby's friends in London would have laughed to see her arrive early to an engagement twice in the space of a week. It wasn't that she found time management hard but, until moving back in with her parents, she'd had little incentive to rush getting ready. Not that anyone who saw her that evening could have accused her of failing to make an effort. She might not have found time to shop but the top and jeans combination was a perfect match for both the destination, and not wanting to seem like she had gone to too much trouble. Yet it was the details that set it off. The top was sufficiently low slung to expose some cleavage, but not so it looked like she was doing so deliberately. Similarly, the decision to wear jeans may have appeared casual but they were an expensive, tight fitting pair that accentuated her long legs. And then there was the application of her makeup. People had often commented how naturally pretty she was, but Ruby knew how to emphasise the vivid green of her eyes and her fulsome lips.

Danny was in for a treat and she would know from the moment he clapped eyes on her how shocked he would be with the subtle transformation from Monday. But much as she welcomed the thrill of anticipation, helped by the first sips of alcohol already working their way into her system, it wasn't proving the complete distraction from the case that she had hoped. She knew Jenkins was right when he had tried to reassure her that they had done everything properly, but she still couldn't prevent her mind going over things in a vain attempt to find gaps. Most disappointing of all was when they had gone back to the hospital to see Michael yesterday. Her initial relief at seeming to have got away with their actions of trying to bring him round on their previous visit, was soon met by him once again denying he knew the identity of his attacker.

Yet, she had tried to take the positives from it and worked on the theory that the client must have been better known to his partner, Jake Hubbard. Although they didn't want to discount anybody, it did allow them to focus on those Jake had been dealing with more directly. However, with their trawl through the list still failing to provide a potential suspect, and with Jake likely to remain in a coma for much longer than Michael had, the week had ended in frustration.

So deep was Ruby in reliving the frustrations of the past few days that she had taken her eyes off the main entrance to the pub and only became aware of someone approaching her table at the last moment. She stood up to greet him. 'Well hello,' she called. But, although the man turned in her direction, it wasn't Danny. She could feel her cheeks instantly blush. 'Oh, sorry, wrong person,' she said, plonking herself back down and taking little satisfaction from the look of disappointment on the guy's face.

She took a large swig of her wine to calm herself. The last thing she wanted was for the real Danny to arrive and misinterpret her appearance as nerves, which she would only serve to reinforce if she explained the case of mistaken identity. She tried to reassure herself that the guy, who thankfully had now walked off, did at least bear a passing resemblance to Danny and, in the heat of the moment, it was perfectly understandable that she might mistake the two, especially because she had only seen Danny once in the past four years.

Yet her mind wouldn't stop whirring and she was considering whether she should go outside to get some fresh air in the hope that the chill might remove the flush from her face, but then it suddenly ceased.

Mistaken identity.

Heat of the moment.

Despite the victim's screams no one had seen the attacker because he had been so keen to make a quick getaway. What if the reason why she and Jenkins had been unable to find a suspect who linked with both Michael and Jake was because there was no link? She knew that it was a fanciful notion, desperate even, but that didn't stop what they knew so far fitting.

From the very beginning it seemed preposterous that someone would commit such an abominable act because of something to do with an estate agents. They had checked the books and there was no suggestion that the business was in any kind of financial trouble. But Michael's relative lack of a social life and no one having a bad word to say about him only seemed to point to it having to be something to do with work. Ruby was convinced that if she and Jenkins were guilty of anything, it was failing to explore Jake's personal life in as much detail. Naturally they would delve deeper into it, but they had been understandably blinded by the link with work.

'I've got to go,' she murmured to herself, lifting her glass to drain it but, at the last moment, thinking better of it. It would be bad enough that someone might see her at the station dressed as she was, without making matters worse by stinking of alcohol.

She had almost made it to the door when Danny pushed through from the other side. 'Ruby, what's going on?' he asked, clearly alarmed by her demeanour, if not her direction of travel.

'Oh Jesus, I'm really sorry. Something's come up at work that I have to respond to.'

'Oh, okay,' he replied, crestfallen.

'I promise I'll make it up to you,' she said and, fearing that it sounded a weak farewell, kissed him on the cheek in an action she hoped he would see as a sign of her continuing interest.

Normally so confident when walking in high heels, she had to slow her pace back to the car for fear that she might topple over. Kicking them off and throwing them in the passenger footwell, she resolved that she would have to enter the police station in bare feet and just hope that she could slip past whoever was in the duty area unnoticed.

Whilst it might still have been relatively early in the evening, it was a Friday night and downstairs was busy. Fortunately, that served to see everyone preoccupied and she was similarly relieved to find CID empty, with the couple of people on duty presumably preferring to be out in the car.

Her first action when sitting at her desk was to phone DI Jenkins. She hadn't needed to call him before and she had trouble finding the scrap of paper he had written his number down on in her neatly arranged piles. She met its eventual switch to voicemail with a touch of relief, having not worked out what to say to him without sounding like she had gone mad. Leaving as calm and polite a message as she could muster, she hung up.

Ruby sat motionless for a few moments; without Jenkins' guidance she didn't know where to begin. What motivated her now as much as anything was a desire to ensure that when Jenkins did return her call, she was able to provide more of a basis for her theory than *well, I was in this bar waiting for a guy to meet me…*

With nothing more useful springing to mind, she logged onto her desktop to read back through her write up of her visit to Megan, Jake's wife. It wasn't so much

Jenkins' notebook that had caused her to be more thorough with her recording of events, more that she wanted to gather the evidence to suggest she had done an adequate job, should Nelson choose to call into question her capability. But it was exactly as she had remembered it; Megan had been in too much of a state of shock to prove useful. She hadn't been hostile like Mrs Robins; rather, she was still failing to comprehend what had happened. Ruby wished that they had gone back to see her today, even if continuing to go through the client files had seemed a far better use of their time.

'Sod it,' she murmured to herself. She wouldn't wait until morning. Even if it meant nipping into the 24-hour Tesco's at Jarman Park on the way to the hospital to pick up a jumper and a cheap pair of flat shoes, she was going to speak to Jake's wife tonight. Perhaps then she could go home and get some rest and revisit things in the morning. But going to see her without at least trying to get hold of Jenkins again felt wrong. Perhaps he had simply missed her call and hadn't spotted the answer-machine symbol pop up on his phone. Even if she couldn't convince him to abandon whatever he was up to this evening, she would feel better for having left him a message explaining what she was doing. Sure enough, the phone rang through to voicemail and she left a similarly breezy recording as before.

About to depart, Ruby realised it would just about top off a thoroughly dissatisfying week to go all the way over to the hospital to find that Megan had gone home to get a few hours' sleep.

A quick call to the duty nurse revealed that Megan hadn't been seen at any point during her shift. Ruby's frustrated response had been due to realising that visiting Megan's house at this time of night would appear far less casual. Added to this was the considerable detour venturing out to the large Jersey Farm housing estate would mean. And yet Ruby wasn't to be dissuaded.

Even with the aid of her car's satellite navigation, Ruby found herself needing to retrace her steps a couple of times, having become lost in the rabbit warren of side roads and not helped by few of the houses choosing to illuminate their door numbers.

When she was eventually sure she had found the right property, a simple but pleasant two-up, two-down semi, she noticed that the car on the driveway was a decade old Vauxhall Corsa and a world away from the flash Audi convertible her husband had been cruising around in. Yet, as uncharitable as she found the observation, considering what had happened to him, she couldn't help but remember the cocky swagger and smarmy way he had addressed her when he'd entered the estate agents.

Taking a deep breath as she walked up the short path to the front door, she gave a confident knock and prayed that she hadn't disturbed Megan's sleep. Even if she hadn't heard the footsteps coming from the hallway, rather than the stairs, the sight of a whisky tumbler in Megan's hand was enough to reassure her. Judging by the glassy look in her eyes, this wasn't her first either.

'Can I help you?' Megan prompted. 'If you've come here to offer your condolences then I appreciate it, but it's really getting quite late now.'

'Oh, gosh, no,' Ruby said, realising that Megan didn't recognise her and chastising herself for leaving her handbag with her warrant card back in the car. But then something about Megan's now perturbed look, caused her to replay what she'd just said. 'Oh, Jesus, I didn't mean it like that. Of course I hope Jake is doing...' She paused in an effort to finally compose herself. 'Perhaps I should start again. I'm DC Knight, we met at the hospital on Wednesday.'

'Of course, I'm sorry,' Megan said, before looking her up and down. 'Is there something the matter?'

Ruby gave a nervous laugh that she hoped wouldn't be taken as her making light of the situation. 'No, not at all, and I apologise for the… unusual timing of my visit. I wanted to follow up some questions as part of our investigation.'

'Erm, okay,' Megan shrugged, not so much inviting Ruby in, more heading back inside and failing to close the door behind her. 'I'd offer you something, but I think I've finished the last of the bottle,' she called over her shoulder, without a trace of humour in her tone.

'No, I'm fine thanks. Drinking on duty and all that,' she responded, hastily kicking off her shoes as she entered. By the time she made it into the ample sized kitchen-diner, Megan was already sat at the table, staring wistfully at her near-empty glass. A mean voice in Ruby's head dared her to ask to be made a coffee. 'Well I don't want to take up too much of your time,' she said instead. 'I just need to see if you've had any further thoughts on who might have done this to your husband.'

'No closer to catching the bastard who did this then.' More of a statement than an accusation, and yet not something Ruby was willing to admit to.

'We're following up all possible leads,' Ruby responded in a voice she knew sounded more perfunctory than reassuring, before reminding herself that it was empathy that got Mrs Robins to finally open up. 'I can only imagine how awful this must be for you,' she offered with genuine sincerity.

'Yeah, it's like… like I'm living in a dream. I know what's supposed to have happened to him, but the… the person lying in that bed just doesn't seem to be my Jake. Perhaps if they would allow me in there when they change his bandages…'

Ruby shuddered at the thought, and was glad that Megan was spared the horror of what she had seen in the photographs of Michael. 'I understand,' she said, wanting to move the conversation on. 'Naturally with what happened to his business partner we have been focusing on anyone associated with the estate agents but I'm keen for us to explore every possible angle. When I spoke to you at the hospital you said you couldn't think of anyone who would want to harm Jake.'

'Yes, why?'

'Well, it's easy to be...' Ruby paused, desperate under the circumstances to find a more appropriate word than *blinded* '...influenced by how serious the attack is. But who knows what drives these sick individuals to do what they do? It could be the result of a very minor disagreement.' She knew that she was starting to waffle and regretted not having the benefit of Jenkins' more direct style along with her. 'So, if there is anyone, anyone at all, who you think might have something against your husband, then I need to know.'

Megan shook her head slowly. 'There's no one,' she replied, almost absentmindedly.

Ruby could feel the frustration rising within her and knew that it meant anger wouldn't be far in its wake. As hard as she had found it to believe with Michael Robins, she had come to accept that he was the thoroughly all-round nice guy that everyone made him out to be. But two in a row? Even if she hadn't met Jake, weren't all estate agents meant to be cocky little shits?

Fighting her emotions and hoping that, in her mild intoxication, Megan would fail to be able to read her expression correctly, Ruby decided on a change of tack. Perhaps a more subtle approach would get her to open up more. 'Tell me a little about your husband.'

'Like what?' came the dull reply.

'I don't know, where the two of you met, what you like to do, anything really.' Regarding the mildly quizzical look her request received, she added: 'It helps in an investigation to build up as broad a picture as possible.'

What Ruby hadn't anticipated was the blow by blow account of their life together since they had first met. It wasn't so much that it was long, more that it all sounded sanitised, not helped by Megan's monotone delivery. 'And how would you describe Jake as a husband?' She interjected at a point she felt wouldn't be entirely inappropriate.

'Oh, he's a great husband. He's very attentive and kind.' Again, delivered without any real feeling.

Ruby swallowed hard. Much as she was concerned by the dispassionate responses, her next question was liable to entirely rouse Megan from her slumber of indifference. 'Any marital issues?'

'Marital issues?' Her confusion sounded legitimate.

'In the couple of years you've been married have you encountered any… problems? You know, like with other women?' Ruby wasn't sure why she was trying to provoke this poor person, but she was desperate to find some dirt on Jake. She was absolutely convinced there was no way he was squeaky clean because, if he was, she would have to admit that this whole evening had been a wild goose chase and, instead of trying to enjoy her weekend like a normal person, she was running around clutching at straws.

'He would never look at another woman,' Megan stated.

Ruby regarded her with suspicious eyes. Had it not been for the way Jake had entered the estate agents on Monday, she might have failed to notice the hint of menace in her tone. She wanted to challenge her claim; she needed to, but she knew she was close to crossing the line again and this time she didn't have Jenkins to lay a firm hand on her shoulder.

There it was, a darkness in Megan's eyes, only perceptible because it was now gone again. If Ruby didn't do something right away, she was going to lose any impetus she had gained. She steeled herself with the reminder that she wasn't here because of any fear for her job or because she wanted to prove something to DCI Nelson. The real reason why she had sacrificed her date with Danny was because she wanted to crack this case, and she wanted to do so because of the moral purpose that had caused her to take a different path than her school friends; most of whom had gone on to university. She had trained in London to be closest to the action and her main concern with moving back out to Hertfordshire had been that she would be wasting her talents on petty crime. And yet on her first day she had been given the most heinous of attacks to investigate and she was determined to find the culprit, not for herself, for Jenkins or for DCI Nelson, but for all the people out there who were now scared that something like that might happen to them. It was her job to protect the public and to make them feel protected. But most of all she was doing this for Michael, Jake, and their families who were going through hell because of one individual's selfish actions. And, as a consequence, she would be damned if she was going to let fear of causing this woman offence stand in the way of giving her what she really wanted – justice.

'Now, we both know that's not true, don't we Megan?'

The horror that swept across her face was far worse than Ruby had feared. She felt compelled to apologise, to try and soften her harsh words; explain that it had been a long week and she was being over-zealous in her desire to catch the man responsible. But she knew that in doing so, she would be doing her instincts a disservice. Megan was hiding something and, although it may have nothing whatsoever to do with the case, she wanted to know what it was. Having ruled it out she might then find herself able to go home and get the rest her body was now craving.

'How, how did you know?'

Know what? Ruby opened her mouth to say, before deciding that Megan was more likely to divulge the details if she remained of the belief that Ruby knew whatever it was she was trying to hide.

'But it was just a fling, it ended months ago. Who told you? Was it *her*?' Ruby had to fight to stifle a smug smile. So, she had been correct; all this time she had felt guilty about judging a man in a hospital bed with half his face eaten away so easily. 'Who is she?' Megan demanded, all of her previous vacantness now long gone.

'What? You don't know?' Ruby had blurted this out before she had time to think about it.

'He never told me,' she said, hanging her head in a shame she did not deserve. 'I… I found the messages on his phone and assumed it must have been a client. I was going to leave him but…'

'Megan,' Ruby said firmly, reaching across the table to put a hand on her arm. 'You don't have to justify yourself to me.'

'I know, but I need to explain. I wanted to leave him, I really did, but he begged me to stay. He promised that it was a one off and he would end it. He told me I could check his phone if I didn't believe him. I did… but only secretly because I was worried that I might end up pushing him away, convincing myself that, having agreed to stay, I owed it to him to start trusting him again.'

'And? When you checked his phone, I mean?'

'Nothing. The calls and messages stopped when he said it did.' Perhaps Megan could see the sceptical look on Ruby's face because she added: 'I can show you, if you like. I took his things home from the hospital.'

'I think that might be useful,' Ruby said, trying to sound professional, whilst wondering if her interest in doing so was more out of curiosity than anything to do with the case. She waited awkwardly whilst Megan went upstairs, listening to her rummaging in the bedroom above her.

'Here,' she said, thrusting the phone at Ruby, almost in a gesture of defiance. And she was right; the messages had stopped, with the last one more than three months ago. Ruby hoped, for Megan's sake, that what Jake had told her was true, but already she had her doubts. None of the messages on either side were signed with even an initial and Jake had entered the person's contact details as a road name. This didn't seem to suggest the work of someone who had stumbled into a fling, however one did that, but a confident and competent adulterer.

Ruby had to fight to stifle that smile again. Within a matter of minutes of being back at the station she could work out who this mystery woman was. She didn't have a house number for her to use in the police database but a quick flick through the client folders should tell her what she needed.

'I just have to ask you one more question and I'll leave you in peace,' Ruby said. 'I hope you don't mind but, seeing as you weren't exactly upfront with me earlier, I find myself having to ask you again whether there is anything else you think I should know. Anything Jake has got himself caught up in or a friend or someone he has recently had a disagreement with?'

'No, I promise you that's it,' she said, and the pleading tone of her voice caused Ruby to be even more glad that she was now leaving.

The overriding emotion Ruby felt as she started her car and programmed her sat nav for the station was one of vindication. Irrespective of whether this led anywhere, and the likelihood was that, if Jake had been telling his wife the truth about the affair ending months ago, it wouldn't, she was right to have delved into his personal life. She reached into her handbag to try and get hold of Jenkins again but thought better of it. Once she had the details of the person behind the mystery messages she would leave him a far more urgent voicemail than her gentle ones of earlier.

Chapter Fourteen

Now that Ruby had a true sense of purpose, she barely paid any attention to whether the uniformed officers in the duty area noticed her, and much less what they made of her appearance. Racing with excitement across CID to her desk, the hatred she had developed for the client folders over the past few days had evaporated. Now looking for something specific it was like she was seeing them in a new light, and she furiously flicked through them to find the street name in question. There, she had it. A Mr and Mrs Hill. Her finger tingled with excitement to think that maybe, just maybe, she was holding the details of the attacker. She had considered whether their unspoken assumption all the way along that it been a man was wrong, but it didn't make sense for it to be the woman Jake had scorned by breaking up the affair. Unless Michael had also cracked on with her, which seemed highly unlikely given everything she'd been told about him, then it wouldn't make sense for her to be responsible. No, it was far more likely that the husband had found out about the affair and decided to wreak his revenge. Perhaps he had assumed it was Michael because he was the estate agent they first met and then, when he discovered he had got the wrong guy, he went back to finish the job.

Much as all this sounded plausible to Ruby, she wasn't quite ready to call Jenkins again. She would feel much more comfortable once she had pulled the couple's records off the main system. Neither of them would have any previous convictions, otherwise they would have come up in their searches before, but Ruby felt that just seeing their faces might give her more confidence in her theory. She knew it was wrong to judge people by their looks, not least because of the assumptions that had been made about her over the years, but she wanted to know what it would be like to stare into the eyes of such evil.

Logging onto the central database, having first reminding herself that she really should commit her password to memory and not be relying on finding the tatty post-it note each time she required access, Ruby had to have three goes at typing *Hill* such was the effect of the adrenaline running through her veins.

'No, it can't be,' she whispered, double checking she had selected the right people from the long list of the same surname, by virtue of their address. She tried to calm herself by considering that these might be the new residents at the property and that it was the old owners who were involved in this, but they had lived there for more than a decade. She switched back to the file and could see that their house was still for sale, and had been on the market with the estate agents for the past six months. Not that Ruby was even remotely interested, but she could see why they were struggling to shift it. She didn't know the going rate for one of these Edwardian townhouses but the dated décor, and bathroom suites from the last century would certainly put her off as a prospective buyer. But then, being in their sixties, perhaps they weren't into the neutral colours and minimalist design of modern interiors.

Ruby felt close to tears. She knew she had an active imagination but even her mind couldn't comprehend Jake having an affair with this woman. It was another dead end. 'Unless…' she shouted into the empty office, having locked onto a glimmer of hope.

She began rummaging through the files again. It wasn't a street she recognised but it was perfectly conceivable that the estate agents marketed more than one property there. Wasn't that the whole point of having those boards outside; to advertise their services and, if there was a quick sale, encourage other residents to sign up with them? It may not have worked in the case of the Hills but that wasn't to say…

Ruby had reached the bottom of the pile. She started going through it again but knew she hadn't missed any out. The retired couple were the only people in the street to have used Platinum Estate Agents. Now the tears did come. If anyone else were there she would have fought them back, determined not to show them any sign of weakness, but alone, she could give in to the mix of emotions coursing through her; all of them bad.

With the flow of tears abating, but her misery as deep as ever, she began rearranging her desk to how she had left it that evening. Not that anyone was likely to notice anything out of place, but she wanted to cover her tracks as best she could. She reminded herself that she was no worse off than when she had left here whilst Jenkins was still completing his notes. If she went home, got some sleep and then checked with Danny in the morning that he wasn't too sore about her running out on him, then maybe she could come in on Monday morning as though nothing had happened. But she knew that was shit too. The whole reason why she had been so distracted whilst waiting for her date to arrive was because she was unhappy with the way the week had gone. She would dread coming in on Monday, and having to start again the pointless trawl through everything they had done already.

'Fuck!' Ruby cursed loudly. She had forgotten her calls to Jenkins. The messages she had left might have sounded casual, but he was bound to be suspicious, even if it was just that she had chosen to call him in the first place. She would need to think of something suitable to tell him. Naturally she would look to hide the lengths she had gone to in order to get the information, and she certainly wouldn't share how convinced she had become that she had found the culprit of the attacks, but the fact was she had found out something that hadn't been revealed to them before. Jake Hubbard had been having an affair.

Acknowledgement of this discovery did make Ruby feel a little better about things. If she stripped away her over-zealousness this evening, which, if she was feeling more charitable towards herself, she might be able to put down to the exuberance of wanting to prove herself in a new role, she wasn't left with nothing. There was still an angle for them to work on. She still didn't like how the lengths Jake had gone to in covering his tracks were preventing her identifying his mistress, but that might point to something else. The reality was, as careful as he had been, Megan had still found out. What if he had ended it, as he had promised her, but had simply moved on to another woman? Ruby had been sensible enough to have a quick scan through the recent messages from his other contacts when Megan had handed her his mobile, but surely someone as conceited as him would be wise enough to find an alternate means of communication; perhaps something as simple as a burner phone.

Feeling decidedly better, although with far more questions than actual answers, Ruby logged off and made her way back to the car park. She would begin on Monday by having his car checked. She figured it was a bit like when men removed their wedding ring as soon as they left the house, it made sense to her that he would keep his alternate mobile safely tucked away in the glove box.

If she needed an indication of how late it now was, there was only a trickle of revellers tottering along Victoria Street and, as she made the left turn onto Holywell Hill, she could see that most of the bars were shut. It made her wonder what Danny had done after she had left. Much as she was saddened to think he had simply returned home, disappointed, she would rather that than him deciding to stay out and find someone else. But there was no point pulling over and texting him now. She would have to wait until tomorrow to find out whether she had blown her chance.

Twenty minutes later and without consciously thinking about it, Ruby took the turn off that veered away from her parents' house and in the direction of the hospital. There was every chance Mrs Robins had gone home to spend the night with her kids, but Ruby would not phone ahead. It was just a twenty-minute detour and if Jake was the serial adulterer Ruby believed he might be, then Michael must be aware and, given the strength of their relationship, so too would be his wife.

It hadn't even occurred to Ruby that the senior nurse would be unwilling to admit her to the ward and it was only thanks to the confirmation that Mrs Robins had decided to stay the night, and it was she that Ruby had come to see, not their patient, that finally saw her entry granted.

Nevertheless, her relief at not ultimately being turned away was replaced with concern when she found, perhaps unsurprisingly, both Mr and Mrs Robins asleep in his room. Ruby was touched to find that the nurses had erected a small camp bed for Mrs Robins to sleep on.

'What? What's wrong?' Mrs Robins said, immediately trying to sit up, no doubt startled by Ruby's appearance as well as the unusual hour.

'It's nothing. Please, don't get up,' she said, placing a soothing hand on her shoulder. 'I hope you don't mind, but I wanted to come and see you about something.'

'What is it?' Mrs Robins replied, rubbing the sleep from her eyes. 'Have you made a breakthrough?'

'No,' replied Ruby guiltily. 'But there is something I need to ask you. I don't know how much of this I'm allowed to tell you so please don't repeat this to anybody, but are you aware of any… issues Jake and Megan Hubbard might have been going through?'

'Issues? I don't understand.'

'Any problems in their marriage?'

'Er, no, I don't think so. Why?'

Ruby drew in a deep breath. 'Are you aware that Jake was having an affair?'

Mrs Robins was wide awake now. 'Oh shit, poor Megan.' This response was far more convincing than any denial she might have offered. 'I mean, we only met a few times, but she seemed a nice enough woman. I always found Jake a bit smarmy but thought that was part of his… well, I wouldn't say charm but certainly his personality. I never thought he would actually, you know, do anything.' She paused for a moment in thought before looking back at Ruby with an intense stare. 'This hasn't got anything to do with what… what happened, has it?'

'I don't know,' replied Ruby honestly. 'It's just something I need to follow up.'

Mrs Robins' head started nodding slowly but stopped abruptly. 'But what has that got to do with Michael?'

In that instant Ruby knew she should have anticipated that question and, equally, understood that she couldn't share her theory. As mad as it would sound to Jenkins, Mrs Robins would rightfully find it ludicrous. She needed to be spared the pain of believing her family's life had been ruined by mistake, at least until Ruby had a shred of evidence to suggest it was the case. 'Are you sure you can't think of anyone Jake was close to at work, even if you hadn't believed him to be… romantically involved with them?' She winced at the shrillness of her voice, a certain giveaway that she was trying to deflect Mrs Robins.

'No, I told you,' she said firmly. 'And you still haven't answered my question!'

This was very much the woman Ruby had met the first time at the hospital and, much as their relationship had improved over the course of the week, any sense of cordiality on her part was only because she was relying on Ruby catching the person who did this to Michael.

A groan from the bed shook them both from what had turned into a confrontation. Mrs Robins shot Ruby a glance of retribution for having disturbed her husband. She moved over to whisper to him with a tenderness that was almost heart breaking. 'It's okay love, I'm here. Do you need me to get the nurse to give you another dose of pain killer?'

'No,' he croaked. 'Please.'

'Shhh, don't worry, my love. It's okay, I won't do anything you don't want me to.'

'No,' he repeated, louder this time and causing a look of worry to cross Mrs Robin's face. 'P-lease.'

'Please, what?' she responded, the distress in her voice evident. 'I can't understand you, Mike.'

There followed another groan and Ruby could see the sheets above his chest deflate as he attempted to try again. 'Po–' more of a deliberate pause this time '–lease.'

Both Mrs Robins and Ruby must have grasped the meaning at the same time because their eyes locked. 'The police, honey? Is that what you're trying to tell me?' The grunt that followed unmistakably sounded positive. 'Yes, the police are here. Is that what you wanted to know?'

'No,' came the familiar response. 'Po-lease. Jake. Samie.' Mrs Robins continued to look puzzled, but Ruby understood.

'Thank you, Mr Robins, please get some rest,' she called out, standing.

'Where the hell are you going?' Mrs Robins demanded. 'What's going on?' Her head was switching back and forth from Ruby to her husband's bandaged form, in a manner that might have been comic under different circumstances.

'I'm sorry, I have to go,' Ruby said firmly, already pulling open the door. 'Please reassure your husband that everything is in hand and I'll see you both soon.'

She didn't wait for a response and winced as she marched down the hallway, expecting Mrs Robins to follow her at any moment. But she didn't and, having offered the senior nurse a brief nod of thanks as she left the ward, she was soon alone with her thoughts in the hospital car park.

Her head was swimming, but in a far more productive way than in the helplessness of earlier. She needed to think this through but first she wanted to try and get hold of Jenkins again. 'For fuck's sake!' she cursed loudly as her call continued to ring and ring as before. 'Guv, it's me again,' she said as soon as it went to voicemail. 'I really need to speak to you. I've found out that Jake Hubbard has been having an affair. It's with Samie, the receptionist… the PA or whatever the hell she is. I want to find out what's going on. I'm heading back to the station to get her home address. Please call me when you get this!'

Ruby felt a huge sense of relief at finally verbalising what she had been up to that evening. There was no going back now; there was no returning home to pretend she had attended her date as planned and then walking back into CID on Monday morning as though nothing had happened. All this time she had been fearing that she had been acting unprofessionally; that she was allowing her emotions to cloud her judgement. But she had been right to press Megan and now, it transpired, she was similarly correct to have been frustrated by Samie's uselessness after the attack on Jake. Some people might have put her behaviour down to the shock of what happened, especially if they knew that she and Jake were closer than employer and employee, but Ruby would swear she was holding something back. It might be only small and have nothing whatsoever to do with the identity of the attacker, but she was going to find out; and take no small amount of pleasure in calling her a liar in doing so.

With her thoughts competing with the concentration of driving whilst tired, it came as a shock when the late-night radio station she was listening to suddenly switched to the hard tone of her mobile ringing.

'Jenkins?'

'Yeah, it's me,' came back a low growl. 'What do you want?'

Ruby decided that now wasn't the time to play games and point out that he was the one phoning. 'Where have you been? I've been trying to get hold of you all night.'

'I must have been asleep or something,' he replied, still sounding like he had been gargling with a packet of razor blades. 'Can't it wait until Monday?'

'You didn't listen to my messages?' Ruby wondered where the hurt in her voice stemmed from.

'I listened to the first and couldn't be arsed to work through the others. Look, just spit it out so I can get back to sleep.'

* * *

'Don't go around there, I mean it!' Jenkins' impatience at Ruby's long and garbled recounting of events that evening was clear.

'But I need to,' she protested. 'I need to find out what the hell is going on.'

'Listen,' he sighed. 'Although I still think you could have left this until Monday, there's no point going around there now. If you're right and she is trying to hide something, then you arriving in the middle of the night is only going to arouse her suspicions.'

Ruby could see his point but that didn't mean she had to like it. 'What, just let her get away with it?' she responded petulantly.

Another sigh from the other end of the line but different this time, reminding Ruby of how her father reacted when he knew she was being over-indulgent with a request. 'I'm not saying that. Let's just wait until the morning when we can speak to her at the estate agents. It'll seem more… normal.'

'We, guv?'

'Yes,' he groaned. 'I'll meet you there at 9am, now promise me you'll go home and get some rest.' The line went dead.

Ruby let out a little squeal, and didn't notice that she had cut up a taxi driver with her sudden swing into the right-hand lane, so she could do a U-turn at the approaching roundabout. She didn't know what she was excited about and surmised that it was more relief than anything. Jenkins may not exactly have been thrilled by what she had told him, but he hadn't called her mad. What's more, he was prepared to help her get to the bottom of it, which provided some form of vindication for her actions that night and she welcomed that she wouldn't have to keep blundering around alone. She still hadn't made her mind up whether Jenkins was actually any good as a detective but even just his presence would serve to curb her exuberant tendencies.

As she tiptoed up to bed she was adamant that she wouldn't be able to get a wink of sleep, such was the extent that her mind was continuing to race, but for the second time that week she managed to drift off before she even had the chance to change her clothes.

Chapter Fifteen

Whether her parents had been aware of the hour she finally arrived home, Ruby didn't know, but they must have assumed she would be having a lie-in that morning, because their bedroom door was still shut as she crept to the bathroom. Partly not wanting to waste this opportunity to escape the house undetected, and mainly because her efforts last night had left her ravenous, she decided to forgo her usual bowl of cereal in favour of a drive-thru McDonald's breakfast.

Having devoured her double sausage and egg McMuffin meal in the car park, she felt embarrassed re-joining the cars queuing up to place their order. However, she figured that picking up Jenkins a coffee was the least she could do to thank him for being willing to humour her, on what was supposed to be his day off.

As with Wednesday's trip to the hospital he was there before her and, judging by the state of him resting on the corner of the Mondeo's bonnet, he could do with all the caffeine he could get. 'Thanks,' he growled, taking the cup and swallowing half of its now tepid contents.

'Rough night was it?' she said, hoping that the quip wouldn't provoke him into berating her for waking him up.

'Something like that,' he muttered, draining the remainder of the coffee.

Although Jenkins didn't show a reluctance to be there, he seemed to have largely returned to his old self; rebuffing all Ruby's attempts at small talk as they waited for Samie to come and open up the premises. She wasn't overly bothered, acknowledging that, had she stayed out with Danny, she would be nursing her own hangover right about now.

'I can't believe she'd be late like this,' Ruby said, finally giving in to the irritation that had been steadily building since she had first parked up. 'I mean, you'd think she'd actually be in early, what with having to hold the fort while her bosses are in hospital.'

'Perhaps she figured that there was little point coming in at all,' Jenkins responded, shrugging.

'Well that's fine because I'm not hanging around any longer anyway,' Ruby said, giving the door to the estate agents one last futile tug before stalking back to her car. 'Are you going to follow me or what?' Jenkins hadn't moved his position an inch.

Offering the same sigh as when on the phone last night, he clambered back into his Mondeo. To punish him Ruby considered speeding off before he started his engine, but she guessed he would require little provocation to make him consider returning to the comfort of his own bed.

Fleetville is one of the less salubrious areas of St. Albans but the property Ruby pulled up at looked decent enough; appearing to be well looked after, with a newly painted front door and an attractive trellis between it and the downstairs window, with some form of ivy being trained up it. Even the rent on such a house would take up the lion's share of Samie's salary, but she was the only registered occupant. Keen as Ruby had been to go around there immediately after talking to Michael at the hospital, she still felt anxious as she pushed the doorbell.

Such was the delay in the door being opened that Ruby had started to believe that the house must be empty. 'Oh, it's you,' Samie said, dressed in clothes that suggested she had no intention of going into work. Ruby could forgive her unwelcoming tone because they hadn't exactly parted on the best of terms when she had last seen her.

'We have some follow up questions from the other day.'

'Okay,' she replied, folding her arms across her chest.

'We went to the business first, but you weren't there.'

Samie rolled her eyes as if to say *well, obviously not* and Ruby could feel the anger rising again. In many respects she welcomed it. 'Are you going to invite us in then?' she asked, her voice dripping with sarcasm.

'Look, what is it?' Samie demanded, not budging. 'I told you all I know when you came to the shop on Thursday. Perhaps this can wait until I'm back in on Monday.'

Ruby felt Jenkins' hand on her shoulder. *So soon, but I'm only getting started?* she thought to herself, before realising that he was gently trying to move her out of the way. 'Enough of this bullshit,' he growled. 'Unless we can sit down and have a nice chat, I'll arrange for you to be pulled in for questioning.'

The defiance remained in Samie's eyes and Ruby imagined she was going to spout off about knowing her rights in the manner people often did, but something about Jenkins' grim expression must have caused her to change her mind. 'Fine,' she huffed, leading them inside.

'Nice place you've got here. Live alone, do you?' Ruby commented conversationally, unsurprised her question received little more than a *yep* in response.

'Fancy making us a cup of coffee?' Jenkins ventured once they had arrived in the small sitting room.

'I'd rather just get this over and done with,' she replied in a low voice, causing Ruby to shoot her partner a glance as if to say, *what the hell's got into this woman?* It appeared that any compliance that had been generated by Jenkins' threat had only been temporary. His shrug in response conveyed the message, *don't ask me.*

'Fine, well let's get to it then, shall we? Tell me a little about Jake.'

'Jake? Like… like what?' Ruby took pleasure in seeing the uncertainty creep into Samie's, previously stony-cold, features.

'Erm, let's see,' Ruby replied in mock thought. 'You told us on Monday how well you got on with Mr Robins. How would you describe your relationship with Mr Hubbard?'

'Yeah, he's a good boss really. He's quite considerate.' Ruby raised her eyebrow in a gesture that she hoped would be taken as meaning, *I just bet he is.* 'I guess that's about it,' she added, crossing her arms once more.

'Is that what made you sleep with him?' Ruby could sense that Samie wasn't the only person in the room shocked by the bluntness of the question.

'What? How dare you!' Samie roared, standing up.

'Oh, I'll tell you how I dare,' Ruby countered, also rising and swatting away Jenkins' outstretched hand. 'I was prepared to put down your failure to share with me that vital bit of information on Thursday to you being in a state of shock, and the fact that I hadn't asked you directly. But now I know you're lying to me and I want to know why!'

'It's not a crime, is it?' Samie said, her eyes glowering.

'Well, that depends how this all plays out. Let's see now; how about you didn't like it when his wife found out and he decided to break the affair off? You've been hounding him these past few months to start up again and when he finally moved on to someone else, you couldn't accept it. You decided that if you couldn't have him then you'd make sure no one else would want him.' Ruby quickly turned to regard Jenkins, his mouth open, aghast, and gave him a wink that she prayed he'd interpret as being confirmation that she knew what she was doing, and he just needed to play along for the moment.

'No, fuck no, I couldn't…' Samie stammered.

'Then sit down, and stop messing us around,' Ruby hissed, taking a deep breath to compose herself whilst Samie's back was turned.

'Okay then,' she continued calmly, once they were all seated again. 'This is how it's going to work. I'm going to ask you some questions and if I think you're lying I'm going to arrest you on suspicion of attempted murder. I guess I'll have to spend the journey into the station figuring out why you decided to attack Michael as well, but we'll cross that bridge if we come to it,' she added, waving her hand dismissively. 'So, you and Jake had an affair. Yes?'

'Yes.' A simple and immediate response.

'And it ended around three months ago. Yes?'

'Er… yes.'

'There you go again, lying to me. But I'll let you off, this one last time if you show me your phone.'

'My phone?' Samie sounded genuinely confused.

'Yes, your phone,' Ruby responded, adopting the same tone as she might when talking to a small child. 'I haven't yet learned to trust you and so I would like to see for myself.'

Samie shifted awkwardly in her chair and fished her mobile out of her tracksuit bottoms. 'I've put in the passcode,' she said, handing the device over. Ruby offered her a smile that she hoped appeared warm rather than conveying the smug satisfaction she felt at the obvious show of compliance.

Judging by the number of different contacts messaging her, it was clear Samie had a wide circle of friends, but it didn't take long to scroll down and find the thread she was looking for. She had used the same street name as Jake had, and Ruby shuddered to think that the reason might be because they had used the property to carry out their sexual liaisons. But then, how could she do that if the couple who lived there were retired? The database would have said if they had emigrated or something, even if they were still waiting for their house to sell. No, it must be for the more obvious reason of simply trying to hide it. But as Ruby scrolled back up the list there was only one other contact that wasn't a person's name.

'How long ago did the affair stop?' Ruby asked casually, whilst still swiping through.

'Oh, like you said, a good couple of months ago.'

'Then how do you explain this?' she said, turning the phone to Samie. It seemed to be as she had suspected; the affair hadn't stopped, and communications had merely switched to a different phone. And what was it Jake had said to Ruby when he had mistaken her for Samie whilst she sat at the computer? *Morning gorgeous.* She had dismissed it at the time as the sort of misogynistic comment a flash prick like Jake would say, but it was hardly the kind of greeting you offered the person whom you were trying to keep at a distance, having broken off an affair with them. It must have been hard for her, knowing he had gone back to his wife and she didn't even have a boyfriend.

Samie was about to take the phone when something in her eyes caused Ruby to snatch it back. 'Sorry, just one more thing,' she tried to say as calmly as possible. She wasn't quite sure why she had done it but a voice in the back of her mind was telling her she was overlooking something. Was it to do with the poor attempt to cover her tracks, given she didn't have a multitude of other client contacts? No, but Ruby could sense it was something close.

'Hey, you asked if you could check it and now you have!' Samie's protest was more than sulky, there was a hint of desperation in it that matched the look in her eyes.

'How long did you say you have worked at the estate agents?' Jenkins enquired, his tone innocent.

Ruby wanted to concentrate on what she was doing but couldn't help thinking what an odd question this was; irrelevant in many respects. Fear that Jenkins was nowhere close to being on the same page as her, turned into belief that he knew exactly what he was doing. He was trying to distract Samie to allow Ruby to finish what she was looking into. She doubted he understood exactly what she was on to, not that she fully understood it herself, but he must have read something significant into the sudden change of mind regarding handing back the phone. His question might have been irrelevant, but it was a simple one that would deflect Samie from what she clearly considered an invasion of her privacy.

'I told you, about a year now. Why?' Her tone was more curious than hostile, but Ruby forced herself to zone out the conversation; she needed to use the opportunity to figure out what it was that was bothering her about the messages.

That's it! It took every ounce of Ruby's self-control to prevent her blurting this out instead of thinking it. Piss-poor or otherwise, why would Samie be looking to cover her tracks if she didn't have a boyfriend? She hovered around the top of the list and selected the first male name. She didn't need to read any further. *Why don't you pick up a bottle of wine on your way home x.*

Ruby looked up and, fortunately, Samie was still facing Jenkins, answering another of his simple questions. Why had she lied? Perhaps she hadn't wanted to come across as bad as Jake; she was just an innocent, impressionable receptionist, duped into believing her more mature boss actually felt something for her. But she had denied having a boyfriend when Ruby had asked if there was anyone she could call to come for her in the minutes following the attack on Jake. It made no sense to lie then, Ruby didn't know about the affair at that stage. Unless…

'You told me you were single,' she interrupted in as conversational a tone as she could manage, lowering her gaze to the screen, for fear that her expression may betray her.

'Er, that's right.' Samie replied, turning back from Jenkins.

Ruby couldn't resist raising her eyes. 'And you said you live alone, is that correct?'

'Yep, this place is all mine,' she responded, looking up and to the right. Ruby wracked her brains to try and remember whether that was where people glanced when they were lying or accessing a memory.

'Don't mind if I use the bathroom, do you?' Jenkins said, leaping to his feet with a speed that belied his age.

'Wait, no you…'

'I can find my own way,' he announced over her protests and, bizarre as his behaviour seemed, Ruby knew that, just as she believed he had trusted she might be onto something, she should now follow his lead. Samie was up too and Ruby, praying that she hadn't entirely misread the situation, dived forwards to stop her being able to block Jenkins' path. It was one thing to mistakenly assume that he could use the facilities but another one altogether for him to have to manhandle her out of the way when they didn't have a warrant to search the premises.

'What the fuck?' Samie cried as she bounced off Ruby's body. Ruby knew she would have to think of an excuse for her action, but that could wait until she found whether Jenkins was genuinely onto something. Her intervention had enabled him to exit the room and she could hear him running down the short hallway in the direction of the stairs.

Turning back in anticipation of what Samie might do next, Ruby was surprised to find that she wasn't looking at her but staring up again. In that moment, she realised that her failure to remember which side was meant to be the tell-tale sign of someone lying had been irrelevant. Samie hadn't been accessing a certain part of her brain but had been unconsciously looking up to one of the rooms above. Ruby didn't know how Jenkins could have cottoned onto it so quick, especially as he would have been viewing Samie at an acute angle, but she needed to warn him, just in case.

'Kyle, look out!' came the scream next to her. This prompted a scrambling noise from directly above, in contrast to the hammering of Jenkins' footsteps on the stairs.

The next few moments were somewhat surreal. Samie was now looking directly at Ruby but not with triumph or even defiance; it was fear. Whether for herself or whoever she had been hiding upstairs Ruby couldn't tell but she knew then that, whatever it was, it was serious enough to have to be linked to the attacks. Ruby's mind began replaying their conversations in the estate agents. She was in no doubt that the news of what had happened to Michael had come as a complete shock and, equally, she would be willing to bet she did not suspect her boyfriend to have any involvement. However, when she spoke to her again, following the attack on Jake, Ruby wasn't so sure. It would seem her frustration that Samie hadn't seen anything, despite facing the large window, outside which the attack had occurred, had been justified. There was every chance she had witnessed it and had seen that it was her boyfriend, finally getting his revenge on the man with whom Samie had been having an affair.

Ruby looked up again, this time in her own terror. What kind of a person was Jenkins running towards? Not only had he resorted to the most abominable of actions to satisfy his jealousy but had been so carefree in his approach to have not even bothered to make sure he had the right guy the first time around.

As if to confirm her fears, Jenkins' arrival in the bedroom was met by a series of crashes and bangs. Ruby was wracked with indecision. She wanted to go and help her partner but was scared of what might happen to her if she did. She hadn't yet decided the extent of Samie's culpability in all this but was sure she could beat her off if she needed to escape the house.

'Ruby, front door!' Although the shout from upstairs was muffled, she would recognise that gravelly voice anywhere. She didn't know if Jenkins was similarly concerned for her own safety but now wasn't the time to question orders. She dashed towards the hallway, her body tense in case it needed to react to Samie trying to stop her. But there were no hands impeding her progress and she threw open the front door before hearing more crashing from above, and this time sounding much clearer.

It was only when she heard the thump to the side of her and she swung her head in that direction, that she realised what had happened. For all the threat Samie's boyfriend had posed, he had chosen to escape through the window, and had attempted to use the trellis to descend safely. She didn't know how far he had got before the wood had snapped away from its mountings but, judging from the way the man was getting back to his feet, it was enough to prevent his fall being too severe.

This time there was no thought from Ruby. Even a moment's pause would have been enough to allow him to start running and, after that, it was anyone's guess whether she would have the pace to catch him. Instead she took a two-stride run up and dived at him, knocking him back off his feet in a manner described by a passing motorist in his statement to the police, as reminding him of a rugby player making a final, desperate tackle.

Instinctively she crawled onto his back, hoping that she might be able to pin him down, but he was already using his strength to flip her over. In complete contrast to her feelings from earlier, and with her now being the one on the ground, she wished that he would use this opportunity to flee. But he was now on top of her, expertly using his knees to pin her arms down. She couldn't make out the features of his face, such as it was silhouetted against the sun above, but she could see his right arm being raised back; his hand balled into a fist. She closed her eyes and turned her face for the impending impact. She had never been punched before in her life and wondered how much it would hurt.

Ruby felt the weight on her arms release before she heard the man's body hit the ground next to her. She looked up and saw Jenkins kneeling on his back and pulling his arms around, so he could cuff his wrists.

'I need to get myself a pair of those,' Ruby said, relief washing over her.

'Yeah, you could use them on Samie,' Jenkins said dryly, in between breaths, and causing Ruby to roll over in the direction of the house, concerned. But Samie wasn't trying to flee, she was just stood in the doorway, silent tears streaming down her face. Nor did she move as Ruby hauled herself to her feet and walked across the small patch of lawn. She simply nodded as Ruby read her the same rights as she had issued countless times as a uniformed officer, but the first as a detective. With Jenkins having done the same for her boyfriend, but still occupied with ensuring that, despite the handcuffs, he posed no threat, she put the call into the station for the marked cars to attend the scene.

Chapter Sixteen

It was a strange feeling driving back alone to the station. Even if the rear legroom in her little Up! GTI wasn't minimal, it would have been inappropriate for her to use her own personal vehicle to transport a suspect. If it wasn't for the aches already setting into her body, and the sight of the police cars in front, she could almost believe that she had imagined the whole thing. Now that the adrenaline was leaving her system, she was starting to feel the effects of having so few hours' sleep the night before. In making an arrest, what was meant to have been a couple of hours at most, was going to turn into a full day of interviews and paperwork.

Having parked up and now entering the station, Ruby was surprised by what awaited them. It hadn't been as though she expected their arrival to be met by applause from their gathered colleagues, but the scene somewhat eerie. With DCI Nelson still on his way in, having been disturbed from whatever activity he did on a Saturday morning, the only other people there, other than some uniform milling around, were the two detectives on duty. Given the look of confusion on their faces, Ruby understood that they must have been the ones tasked by

Nelson to review the case. The fleeting conversations she'd had with them over the course of the week hadn't given her any cause to dislike them, but she couldn't help but offer them a smug smile as she marched past. She was sure any sense of satisfaction she had derived would pale in comparison to seeing Nelson's reaction when he arrived.

With Samie and her boyfriend, whom it turned out had recently been released from prison following an eighteen-month stint for GBH, booked in and waiting in separate cells she joined Jenkins for a coffee in the downstairs staffroom. 'So, what made you do it?' she asked him whilst blowing the steam off the top of her mug.

'I guessed she didn't live alone.'

'How?' responded Ruby, genuinely interested.

'Well, it was just a hunch at first,' he said modestly.

'Go on,' she prompted.

'Aside from her taking a while to answer the door…'

'She might have been getting dressed...'

'But the shadow of movement as she approached the door suggested she had come from somewhere downstairs. Then she didn't want us to come in, nor did she want to leave the room to make us coffee.'

'What, in case we might follow her?'

'Maybe,' he replied simply. 'But then I saw the way two of the photo frames on the mantel piece had been moved, obscuring the middle two…'

'She might not have been a very tidy person…'

'…in a room that was otherwise neat and well ordered. I was going to try and take a look but then I noticed the DVD rack in the corner of the sitting room. It was carefully stacked filled with rom coms and the like, but on top, was dumped a small pile of action movies.'

'So?'

'So when you changed your mind about giving the phone back and I bought you enough time to do whatever it was you were doing, I guessed you were on to something when your next question was asking about her being single.'

'Okay, fine,' Ruby said, holding her hands up, but not unkindly. 'I submit to your powers of deduction.'

'Then her glance upstairs was rather obvious, wasn't it?' he added with a smile.

'Oh yeah, dead giveaway,' Ruby agreed, taking a swig of her coffee to prevent her expression suggesting it hadn't been quite as simple as that for her.

'DCI Nelson is looking for you,' a woman in uniform said as she came into the staffroom and headed towards the cupboards.

Ruby made sure she was ahead of Jenkins as they left, but she didn't immediately run into Nelson. 'He said he's up in his office,' the duty sergeant offered, not taking his eyes off the logbook he was filling in.

The short trip up to CID was enough to convince Ruby that she might have been premature in expecting them to be received with open arms and cries of congratulations. He had uncharacteristically left his door open and Ruby entered gingerly, unsure whether she would still have been expected to knock first.

'Wasn't our last conversation yesterday about you two not doing any overtime this weekend?' Nelson said, gesturing to the chairs in front of his desk.

'Yes, guv,' Ruby replied, deciding she would say as little as possible until he revealed more of his hand of cards.

'And yet here we all are, and with two people arrested downstairs.'

'Yes, guv,' she repeated.

'For the sake of being thorough, let's just assume I wasn't told anything when I got the call to come in and you just go through it from the top. DI Jenkins why don't you start?' Not a request but an order.

'DC Knight phoned me to say she had discovered that Jake Hubbard, the second victim, had recently been having an affair.'

'Is that correct?' Nelson said, turning towards Ruby.

'Yes, but I needed DI Jenkins' direction as to what we did with this information.'

'I see,' Nelson replied, steepling his fingers.

'Mrs Hubbard didn't know who the mistress was and so it seemed sensible to see if Jake's business partner was aware. Once Michael Robins identified the receptionist as the person with whom he had conducted the affair we decided to go and see her. We went to the estate agents first and when she hadn't…'

'And what made you both think this was somehow connected to the attack?'

Ruby paused, wondering whether Jenkins would feel he should speak at this point. With nothing forthcoming, she continued: 'Well, firstly we had been over and over those client files.' She wanted to make the point that Nelson's assumption about the quality of their work yesterday had been wrong, and emphasised it by failing to hide the edge of bitterness that had crept into her tone. 'There was also something not quite right about the way she was responding to my questions when we arrived at the second attack.' Again, hoping that Nelson would see that Jenkins' insistence that they be the ones to attend the scene first had been justified. 'I know she would have been in shock or whatever, but it just didn't add up. She had also claimed not to have a boyfriend but then when we went to the house…'

'Okay, I think I get it,' Nelson said, standing up. 'Listen, it all sounds to me like good detective work, but I'll save final judgement until after the interviews and if we have enough evidence to make a charge.'

'Fair enough, guv,' Ruby said, also getting up.

'You look… tired, Steve, are you sure you don't want someone else to handle this whilst you go home and get some kip?'

If Jenkins was offended by the offer, he didn't show it. 'No, guv, I want to see this through,' he said mildly.

'And you DC Knight?'

'Not a chance,' she added.

'As I expected,' he laughed, leading them out of the office and downstairs. 'Whilst Steve's conducting the interview, you can grab a drink and view the direct feed in the room next door.'

'Yeah, right,' she snorted but the way Jenkins had stopped walking made her turn and face the DCI. 'Jesus, guv, tell me you're actually joking here?'

'I understand how you feel, but I'd be crazy to let a rookie conduct such an important interview for their very first time.' The reasonableness of his tone only served to further enrage Ruby. 'Tell me I'm right, will you, Steve?'

Jenkins merely shrugged but she could see from that gesture that he agreed with what Nelson was saying. And why wouldn't he anyway? Even though her impetuousness had led them to a result, all she had done this week was show how hot-headed she could be. 'Please,' she said, looking at them both. 'I've earned this.' She paused, shaking her head. 'I've proven my detective skills, now let me prove that I can play the game too.'

'I don't know,' replied Nelson, rubbing his forehead. 'What do you think, Steve?'

The wait whilst Jenkins first studied Ruby and then looked back to Nelson was agonising. 'I trust her,' he said finally.

'Then I guess that's good enough for me,' the DCI responded, and started walking again.

Ruby wanted to thank Jenkins but she knew that the best way to reward his faith would be to sit back and play the silent partner in there unless he called on her to add something. They had started the week with him patronisingly reminding her not to touch anything in a crime scene and had ended it with him going out on a limb to reward her for providing the breakthrough in the case. She would not have minded if he now wanted to establish clear ground rules for the interview.

But he didn't.

'So, who should we start with first?' he asked as soon as they were stood in front of the duty sergeant. That she knew the answer didn't help settle her nerves. It wasn't just Jenkins who was risking his reputation by having her in there; any credit she had built up with him, and indeed Nelson, would be wiped out entirely if she messed this up.

'Definitely Samie. I don't know what incentive he would have to co-operate whereas I'm sure she'll spill the beans if she thinks it might reduce her own culpability. Armed with her information we might be able to force a confession out of him.'

'Agreed.' Jenkins nodded and motioned for Samie to be collected. 'Shall we grab a coffee before we start?' It was the knowing smile that accompanied the question, as much as the suggestion itself, that provoked a laugh from Ruby and washed away all her anxiety.

Chapter Seventeen

That afternoon had been the single most satisfying time of Ruby's career so far. She hadn't thought that it could be any better than the adrenaline rush of actually catching the guy, but ensuring they had enough to charge him was a deeper, more rewarding experience. It would be an exaggeration to suggest it had gone like clockwork but Ruby's assertion that Samie would crack had been an accurate one. Her affair with Jake had been long-running and had started as soon as she began work at the estate agents. Her claims that Jake had taken advantage of her seemed a little far-fetched to Ruby's ears, and certainly because she claimed not to have admitted to him that she had a boyfriend, but Ruby had decided to let it slide in an effort to maintain the compliant atmosphere.

The first she had known about Kyle's discovery of their relationship had been when she had seen him outside the estate agents. Ruby had asked why she hadn't told the police there and then, and ensure that she was protected until he could be arrested, but she claimed that he had winked at her through the window before running off. She said that the cold and dispassionate way he had done it, following such a brutal attack, made her scared that if she did say something he would seek to harm her family. Ruby didn't buy it and it certainly didn't explain the hostility they had experienced when visiting her house, but a gentle hand on her knee under the table told her that challenging this would be best left until after they had heard what Kyle had to say on the subject.

The fact was they had her on record saying she saw Kyle with the pot of acid in his hands standing over the body of Jake, and that he had later told her that he had attacked Michael first by mistake. That she had never mentioned Jake to him at all had led Kyle into believing that Platinum Estate Agents was effectively a one-man band. Kyle, as part of his confession, a pathetic grovelling affair full of excuses regarding his childhood and how he was brutalised in prison, no doubt only made because his solicitor's advice was that he could expect a lighter sentence by cooperating, explained that he realised his mistake when the messages from Samie's lover didn't stop after Monday morning.

Ruby couldn't help but ask him why he hadn't sought to punish Samie. His response was that the thought of her was the only thing that had kept him going in prison. He blamed himself for her seeking comfort in another man, but wanted to illustrate that it had to stop, and to ensure she would never consider doing such a thing again. His backing up of her assertion that the only reason why she had sought to protect him was through fear, Ruby believed was more because he hoped she would reward him by standing by him in prison again, rather than it actually being the truth. Nevertheless, and even with her limited experience, she doubted the Criminal Prosecution Service would think there was enough evidence to charge her.

* * *

'Can't you just write *job done*, or *case closed* in there?' Ruby said, gesturing to Jenkins' notebook, which he had been diligently filling in for the past ten minutes. It was late at night by the time they had finished all the mandatory paperwork and, much as Ruby was anxious to get home, she thought it would only be fitting if they walked out together. Not that anyone would notice; Nelson had gone as soon as Kyle had been charged. His congratulations might have been muted but she figured that unless she did something catastrophically wrong from this point, passing her probation should be a breeze.

'At risk of sounding like a broken record, you more than anyone should now understand the importance of…'

'Blah, blah, work/life balance and all that shit,' Ruby said, good-naturedly. She was tempted to add that it was her failure to park everything yesterday evening that had led them to this result, but she knew it didn't need saying. 'I reckon I'm long overdue a large glass of wine, but I think I might crash out as soon as I get home. How about you?'

'Yeah probably,' he replied quietly.

'Well I suppose you might as well take your time, seeing as we have nothing worthwhile to go home to,' she said, hoping he wouldn't be suspicious of her sudden lack of urgency.

Getting out her phone, and contemplating whether Danny not texting her was a sign that he was no longer interested, she started to think of what she should say. Her initial plan had been to send an apology, not too grovelling, and confidently enquire when they could reschedule. But now it was more than twenty-four hours later she felt it needed more than that. From her experience, guys didn't like to hear how busy at work she was, so she wouldn't go into too much detail about what had caused her to abandon him.

> *Hi Danny, I'm really sorry about last night. Can I make it up to you? Ruby x*

She wasn't wholly satisfied with it but, with the ball having been placed in his court, it should do the job. She was considering going back to geeing up Jenkins when her phone pinged. She could feel her heart beginning to race as she looked at the screen. The speed of his reply was either very good or very bad.

> *I was disappointed not to get to spend time with you, but I do understand. I'm guessing it's a bit late to get together tonight so how about tomorrow? Dan x*

'Are you ready then or what?' Jenkins called from across the office.

'Hold your horses!' she shouted back, quickly typing in her reply as she walked.

> *Great. Text me the details in the morning and I promise not to run out on you x.*

'Come on then! All work and no play makes Ruby a dull girl.'

They barely spoke as they made their way to the car park, but it was a comfortable silence and Ruby decided that she was starting to like working with DI Jenkins.

Chapter Eighteen

The drive into the station on Monday morning felt different to a week ago. The first day nerves had gone, along with any fears that she might have made the wrong decision in moving out from London. She'd even texted her friend, Emma from Wandsworth, a link to the new article about the acid attack, suggesting that she might find it *interesting reading*. None of the investigating officers had been named but it had been enough of a hint to elicit the response *Holy shit!!!* followed by a string of emojis.

Any fears Ruby had held about meeting Danny yesterday, and how it might lead to starting the week with a hangover, had been dispelled by his text that morning. He had suggested they meet for a picnic in Verulamium Park and insisted that he had everything covered, and she only need bring herself. Her optimism that this was a far more serious proposition than simply going out for a drink was matched by it being unseasonably warm and sunny weather.

They had sat on a blanket, sipping Prosecco, with Ruby trying to show moderation in the face of all the delicious food he had brought. That some of it had clearly been home-made, rather than picked up from M&S on his way down, said a lot to Ruby about his domestication. Even though they had chatted for quite a while at Zara's leaving party, she could tell he was a little nervous talking to her. At first, they spoke about school, but with them having few shared experiences there, and them starting to relax in each other's company, they soon moved onto more relevant topics. She admired the way he was keen to hear about her work, but was respectful enough not to ask any sensitive questions. And although he was clearly doing well himself, he didn't seek to boast about his own job and the fast start he had made in the short time since leaving university.

It was Ruby's suggestion that they go to The Waffle House, rather than end their date once the sun started to go down. Sat in the large heated gazebo outside, neither of them could resist the lure of the sweet treats they observed being brought out to the other customers. Sharing a banoffee waffle, which arrived accompanied by whipped cream and toffee sauce was as romantic an end to their date as she could imagine.

Although they had spaces in the same car park this time, Danny had insisted on waiting until she got in hers before returning to his own. Ruby felt none of the irrational pressure from last Monday and decided that, having technically met Danny on Friday, even if it had been only for a matter of seconds, her rule about not kissing on the first date didn't apply. It had been intentionally brief, but just enough for Ruby to get a sense of how much he fancied her, and to provide Danny with an incentive for him to continue to pursue her.

He didn't text her that evening but she wasn't too concerned. As much as she had welcomed his keenness to rearrange their date for as soon as possible, she would need to train him into accepting that her work meant she wouldn't always be able to be as attentive as he would like.

Cutting it so fine that she arrived at the station with only seconds to spare until the briefing was due to start, she headed immediately into the conference room. With just the briefest of nods at Jenkins, who had already taken up his position by the percolator at the back, and looking like he had got less rest than she'd had on their day off, she located DC Christie in the second row of chairs.

'Hey girl!' Christie called cheerfully, in what Ruby assumed was meant to approximate an American accent. 'I heard about your bust at the weekend. Congratulations!'

Much as Ruby wanted to tell her all about it, she figured that being modest would be the appropriate course of action. 'Yeah, it was pretty exciting.'

'I bet! I heard you put that sick fucker flat on his arse.'

'Well, sort of, but I couldn't have arrested him had it not been for Jenkins.'

'Oh, are you two getting along then?' The surprise in her tone was obvious.

'He's alright once you get to know him,' Ruby replied, hoping to strike a balance between sounding too keen and not paying Jenkins the respect he deserved.

'Shame Cooper is back then,' Christie said mischievously, nodding over Ruby's head and causing her to turn around to see someone she didn't recognise chatting animatedly to Jenkins. The pang of jealousy she felt was the same as if she had turned up at Verulamium Park yesterday to find Danny feeding strawberries to another woman on his picnic blanket. Why hadn't he told her that his usual partner would be back from holiday today? A few days ago she would have only been too delighted at the prospect, but now it seemed a betrayal.

'Morning, campers,' DCI Nelson said, announcing his arrival. 'I trust you are all fit and raring to go. Especially you, Cooper, although I suspect that tan has more to thank a bottle for than the actual sun.'

Ruby joined in with the laughter this comment provoked, but more out of spite towards the unwanted intruder.

'Although not everyone had quite as relaxing a weekend as they may have planned. I'm sure many of you have already heard this, but, the acid case, yes the one that seemed inexplicably to be going nowhere,' Nelson paused to look in Ruby's direction but this week she wouldn't let herself be rattled by his so-called sense of humour, 'has led to a result. Picture, if you will, DI Jenkins dashing up the stairs, claiming to be busting for a wee, and DC Knight waiting outside for their suspect to come falling out of the window, and you have pretty much got the gist of it. Am I right detectives?'

'Pretty much,' Ruby repeated as sarcastically as she could, after Jenkins had offered little more than a grunt.

'Good. Well, regardless of the details, this was an important collar and we can hope that this week might see the return of our typical cases.' Ruby wondered whether she could detect a tinge of regret to Nelson's tone. 'Speaking of returning to normal, I assume Steve that you're going to want to partner up with Cooper again; if for no other reason than no-one else would want him. Am I right?'

Nelson may have softened the question with his quip at the end but that didn't stop Ruby feeling uncomfortable. It wasn't just the public rejection that bothered her, especially as, judging by Christie's reaction to her earlier comment, people were only likely to see it as a lucky escape on her part.

'You know me, guv,' Jenkins growled. 'I'm as easy as they come.'

Ruby ignored the smattering of laughter this comment provoked. Much as her initial text to Danny had done on Saturday night, Jenkins had put the ball in her court, as confirmed by everyone now staring at her. But she didn't find her discomfort deepen. That they had already decided what her decision was likely to be, and her belief that being initially placed with Jenkins had been a test by Nelson, paled into comparison against her true feelings. With

Jenkins she had only begun to scratch the surface and she had already seen that they made an effective team.

'I want to stay with DI Jenkins,' she said firmly, and refusing to alter her expression at the unwitting gasps and even the odd *ooh* that met her answer.

'Ah, shit Cooper, I guess you should have brought Steve back a bigger souvenir,' joked Nelson, diffusing the tension.

'No offence, love,' Cooper called from the back in a strong Essex accent. 'But you're welcome to that cranky old bastard.' It was affection rather than bitterness that dominated his tone.

'Okay, okay,' Nelson said, trying to re-establish a semblance of order. 'So, a few new things came in over the weekend which I'll talk to individuals about shortly but the only other thing to make you aware of is that we'll have a visit from the top brass later in the week.' This news was met by groans. 'You should count yourselves lucky, normally DSI Robson only comes over if there is something he is concerned about, so him deciding to bring the top brass with him is a compliment.'

'Yeah, but that means Jones will need to wash his clothes,' someone shouted from Ruby's side, provoking more uproar.

'Part of me wishes I hadn't told you but, seriously, we do need to put on a good impression because if Robson chews my arse then…'

'You chew ours,' came the chorus back.

'Exactly. So, if that means Jones needs to go to the laundrette and Smithy has to spend some time sorting out his mess of a desk, then so be it. Oh, and Steve?'

'Don't drink all the coffee,' Jenkins mimicked back, much to everyone's amusement.

'Right then, off you go everybody.'

Ruby felt much happier than after last week's briefing, but she still experienced a similar anxiety when walking up to Jenkins. She felt a little awkward about what had happened and considered whether she should explain why she had elected to stay his partner.

'Looks like we're stuck with each other for a little while yet,' Jenkins said, causing her to abandon the idea.

'You could have warned me Cooper was due back.'

'To be honest, what with everything that went on last week I hadn't given it a second thought,' he replied. Ruby decided she would take the positives out of that because it implied he hadn't spent their time together praying for when it would end.

'So, er, what now?' Ruby asked as they exited the conference room.

'In terms of a new investigation?' Jenkins responded.

'Exactly. Brutal acid attack for my first case so what's this one going to be? International espionage?'

Jenkins laughed. 'It's not quite as simple as that. We're still on the acid case.'

'You what?'

'Just because we've got the guy who did it doesn't mean we don't have a million and one other things to do. We may have got enough evidence to charge him…'

'He confessed for fuck's sake!'

'…but that doesn't mean we have everything we need to ensure a conviction.'

'Didn't you hear what I just said? He confessed and Samie said it was him too.'

'I get that, Ruby, but the number of times they go on to retract their confession… What we need to do is to make sure we have enough compelling evidence to ensure he goes down for it, regardless of whether he subsequently chooses to fight it.' Jenkins' tone was calm, almost paternalistic, but not in any way patronising.

'You just called me Ruby,' she said with a beaming smile.

'That's your name isn't it?' he replied evenly.

'But you never called me Ruby. In fact, the only time you did was when you were shouting down for me to–'

'I could go back to calling you DC Knight if you like,' he interrupted, and Ruby thought she could detect a certain awkwardness in his tone.

'No, Ruby's fine,' she said, waving her hand dismissively. 'As you said, it's my name after all.' She paused for a moment. 'Does that mean I should call you Steve, then?' she asked, with an impish twinkle in her eyes.

'Jenkins will do just fine,' he replied gruffly and turned to head over to his desk. Ruby was about to do the same but decided to visit DCI Nelson instead.

* * *

'Have you got a moment, guv?' she asked, after her confident knock had been met with a request to enter.

'Sure, take a seat,' he replied, shuffling the papers he was looking through into a neat pile. 'Not changed your mind about DI Jenkins already, have you?'

'No, guv, quite the opposite actually. I was hoping you might be able to give me more of an insight into him.'

'Oh really? Like what?' It was clear from the way Nelson leaned forward that Ruby had piqued his interest.

'Whatever you think might be useful,' she replied coyly. 'Perhaps why you put me with him in the first place?'

'As you know, his usual partner Cooper was on holiday,' Nelson offered.

Ruby decided she would not answer and merely raised her eyebrow to indicate that she doubted this was the sum total of the reason.

'And some of it was to see how you two would get on,' he eventually conceded.

'Why did you think that might be an issue and why was everyone surprised when I wanted to stay with him?' Ruby was trying to keep her tone light, conversational. DCI Nelson didn't need to explain his decision to her and the last thing she wanted, having made some ground with the arrest over the weekend, was for him to be offended by any apparent insubordination.

'Ah, come on, I'm sure you know exactly why,' Nelson responded with a fox-like grin. 'What you really want to ask is why I think you two have got on better than expected.'

'Not at all,' Ruby protested. 'I just wanted your advice on how I might be able to keep up the momentum.'

'Okay, sure,' he replied, with an open-handed gesture that suggested he remained unconvinced but was happy to play along with whatever game this was. 'Steve and I have worked together for many years and in a number of different guises. We've learned a lot about each other along the way. Because of his... demeanour, many of the other detectives fail to appreciate his capabilities, not that I'm suggesting it's their fault. Jenkins has a certain way of appearing... how can I put this... disinterested. Let's just say he's a complex character and has grown far more complex over the years. Cooper was livid when I first partnered the two of them up, but I stuck to my guns and, as you saw back there, they have formed something of a bond. As I'm guessing you've found out, and hence why you are willing to carry on partnering him, is that, beneath that bluff exterior, lies a good detective.'

'So, you thought he might be good for my development,' Ruby stated.

'Yes, but it's not as simple as that. I'll admit I put you with him to test your character, but I knew that the ultimate reward for you wouldn't be proving me wrong or however you felt about it, but gaining yourself a decent mentor. If I had partnered you with Christie or Smithy or any of the other younger detectives I would essentially be breeding more of the same. I wanted you to work for what you would learn and, similarly, I wanted to expose you to a different kind of investigative work. If I were to say to you that he's old school, I wouldn't be referring to his age or the way he comes across. Absolutely, he relies on evidence, but he trusts his instinct; his gut. Back when we used to work more closely together the way he could read a situation used to amaze me.'

'So, what happened then?'

'Ah well, that's a complicated business and it would not be fair for me to speak out of turn.' His expression was sincere rather than coy and Ruby guessed that there would be little point in trying to delve any deeper than Nelson was willing to offer. 'But when I said before that it wasn't quite as simple as it being good for your development, I thought it might be good for him too. Whilst I'm sure you rub him up the wrong way in all manner of respects, I wondered whether your enthusiasm may start to rub off on him. You see, Cooper is a bit of an old cynic like Jenkins and so, although they work well together, they are a bit too alike.'

'So, you're hoping I might be able to bring out of Jenkins whatever you think he has hidden over the years, and for reasons you can't tell me?'

'That's about the size of it. I bet you're pleased you came to see me,' he said, standing in a clear indication of wishing to end their conversation.

'Yeah, great, guv,' she replied but, much as she had gained little about Jenkins, she had appreciated a chance to talk to DCI Nelson without him chewing her out for not making enough progress on a case.

She was about to close the door behind her when something from across the room caused her to stop. 'You didn't, did you?'

'What's that?' Nelson enquired, his head already buried in paperwork.

'Never mind, it doesn't matter,' Ruby replied. Much as Nelson might not be quite the douchebag he had presented himself as last week, she doubted he had decided to reward her brilliance in cracking the acid case by sending her a bunch of flowers. As Ruby tentatively approached her desk she could see the rest of the office watching her, whilst trying not to appear like they were doing so. Feeling her cheeks begin to flush she decided that she would meet this head on.

'Ah, Steve, you shouldn't have,' she called across the office, and causing all the faces to swing in his direction, like people watching a tennis match. But he didn't seem willing to play along, so she swept up the bouquet in her arms and sniffed them theatrically. 'Lilies, my favourite. I thought I only made that comment in passing…' She smiled at the *oohs* this triggered. However, she didn't want to risk overplaying it and cause a rift between her and Jenkins. As Nelson had alluded to, although she had begun to scratch the surface, there was still much for her to learn about her partner.

Anyway, she was anxious to sit down and read the small card attached to the flowers. She believed she knew the true identity of their sender but her heart was racing at the thought all the same.

> *I hope these brighten up your day like you did for me yesterday. Danny xxx*

Ruby inhaled the scent once more and replayed in her mind the kiss they had shared.

Chapter Nineteen

It wasn't just that the next time Danny had arranged to see her was Friday evening that had caused the week to drag. As Jenkins had warned, there was much they still needed to piece together about the acid case. Ruby found most of it interesting, but seeing as they already had their man, there was none of the thrill of the chase. She may have spent her entire time in uniform yearning to join CID but at least when she had been a PC, there was the excitement of knowing anything could happen at any moment. What she was coming to understand about her new career as a detective was that the highs might be much higher, but they were interspersed with lows.

As if to emphasise the lack of urgency with what they were doing, Ruby and Jenkins were often interrupted by having to attend to other crimes. The irony of petty theft being the sort of thing that she had originally expected to monopolise her time, didn't escape Ruby; not that it was quite as low-level as her friend had made out with her text on her first morning. However, much as she hoped to get onto some high-profile incidents in the future, she welcomed the relative calm after such a tumultuous start.

Jenkins was also treating her as an equal. After a couple of days, Ruby decided to comment on it, in a subtle way that didn't make it seem like she was fishing for compliments, but she received his typical shrug. She guessed it was a mixture of her having proved her capability with the acid case, and that giving her more freedom in what they were doing now was far less risky.

Nevertheless, the more relaxed nature of her week didn't allow her mind to become anxious about seeing Danny again. If confirmation had been needed of his keenness beyond the flowers, his subsequent texts provided it. Given they'd already kissed, Ruby knew there was a chance he would be hoping for more following their next date. It wasn't that she was terribly conservative, and it certainly wasn't that she found the idea of a physical relationship with him unappealing, but she feared that it might spoil what had developed between them in such a short space of time. Ruby knew it was wrong to judge Danny based on her past experiences, and he certainly hadn't shown himself to be pursuing her in order for her to be just another notch on his bedpost, but if this relationship had the potential she believed it did, she didn't want to rush things.

In the end she resolved that there was no point worrying about it. It would only serve to ruin her anticipation of their date, something she had been looking forward to since the moment it had been arranged, and she should trust that she could make the necessary adaptions to whatever situation she found herself in.

But by Friday afternoon she started to feel sick through the cocktail of excitement and anxiety. Part of her wished for something to come through that would require her to stay at work late but, if anything, it proved to be the quietest part of her week. Having said goodbye to Jenkins, and after all her attempts to find out what he had planned for the weekend had failed, she went home to get ready.

'And when are we going to meet this boy?' her mother asked the moment Ruby came back downstairs.

'You look lovely, by the way,' her father said in an effort to deflect things, and earning a look of reproach from his wife.

'It's just our…' Ruby paused, trying to remember how much she had told them about her change of plans last Friday and therefore what number date they would think her on. 'It's just early days,' she corrected herself.

'Good, you don't want to rush into anything too quickly,' her mother responded in that Irish Catholic way she managed to adopt when the subject of intimacy was even hinted at.

Ruby opened her mouth to point out that her mother couldn't have it both ways; on the one hand wanting to meet the person she was dating, whilst also encouraging her to take things slowly. 'I'd better get going,' she said instead, rushing out of the house far earlier than was necessary.

Danny walked into the bar on the stroke of 8pm and the single most comforting thing Ruby found about his demeanour was that he seemed apprehensive too. His eyes drank in her appearance before he realised he was doing so and his mumbled apology caused Ruby to laugh. Moreover, the speed at which he consumed his first beer suggested a person who required a certain amount of Dutch courage.

Yet as the evening progressed, and the drink flowed, it wasn't long until they settled down into the sort of easy conversation that had been a feature of both their previous meetings. But it was somehow deeper, more meaningful than before. By the time they had left The Waffle House on Sunday, they had exhausted most of the typical *getting to know you* chatter and Ruby took it as a sign of their compatibility that they kept finding more things to discuss. That some of them were important, like views on current affairs, and others contained nothing more than observations on what was currently in the music charts, only added to the pleasant mix of the evening.

But just as Ruby thought they might seek to wind things up where they currently were, and move onto a club, Danny's consumption dropped rapidly. There was nothing about his behaviour that suggested he was any more intoxicated than what she would describe as *tipsy*, and she found herself unable to fully concentrate on their conversation, as preoccupied as she was with contemplating the implications of this. With him also appearing similarly distracted, and their discussions becoming stunted as a result, Ruby narrowed down the possible causes to two.

That one of them was the thing she had been worried about all week wasn't her primary concern because the alternative was far worse. He was building up to telling her he had made a mistake and he wanted them to just be mates. It suddenly made sense to Ruby. Whereas others would have told her via a text message, Danny was a decent person who believed that the right way to handle things was face to face. Whilst one could argue that the apparent good time they'd been having was an indication otherwise, Ruby knew that it could also be seen that they made a better proposition as friends.

'Ruby, there's something I've been wanting to tell you,' Danny said after an especially awkward silence.

Oh, here goes, she thought, already trying to work out what expression to adopt that might convey only mild disappointment.

'I really want to sleep with you,' he said.

Any sense of controlling her reaction went straight out of the window and she simply regarded him with shock, far more so than if he'd said it an hour ago. But she wouldn't reply, at least not yet, because it was clear he hadn't finished getting everything that had been bothering him off his chest. 'I just wanted you to know in case you thought…'

'Thought what?' Ruby asked, now confused.

'But the thing is,' he continued, ignoring her prompt. 'I really think you're special, so I want to wait to prove that I'm worth it.'

Ruby looked into Danny's eyes and found herself believing every word he'd said. More than that, she found it the most romantic statement she'd ever heard and, knowing that any words by her would dilute its potency, she leaned forward and kissed him.

Chapter Twenty

'Seriously, though, can't uniform do it?' Ruby said huffily, turning the police radio down in the hope Jenkins might be more inclined to ignore the request that had come through.

'Well, yes but we're not exactly busy at the moment, are we?' he replied patiently.

Ruby couldn't deny the truth in his statement, especially since they had tied up all the loose ends in the acid case, but that didn't mean she had to like it. 'We already know what we're going to find though, don't we?'

'Or, more to the point, what we're not going to find,' Jenkins responded, correcting her.

'Exactly! He'll point to a gap in the shelves and claim that there was stock of some expensive item on there. Even if he has a receipt that proves he purchased it in the first place, that's not to say he isn't hiding it in the back of his van instead and is just using us to help with his bogus insurance claim.'

'When did you become such a cynic?' Jenkins responded. Ruby wanted to tell him that she had learned from the best but could see from his faint smile that he was expecting that exact retort.

She refused to give him the satisfaction. 'Well, at least that should take us through to knocking off time.'

'That's the spirit,' he said in a tone she knew was intended to be deliberately patronising.

'What's got into you?'

'How do you mean?' he replied innocently.

'No, seriously. It might only be Monday, but you've been… different since last week. In a good way I mean.'

'Maybe it's the later start on this shift pattern.'

'Fine, play it your way, Jenkins, but don't think I haven't noticed how you seem brighter and less… less grumpy, especially at the start of the shift.'

'Perhaps I have just learned to accept your incessant chatter,' he responded lightly, but, even from side on and with Jenkins continuing to look at the road ahead, she could see a serious look to his face – not that for one moment she believed his answer. 'We're nearly there now,' he added, ending the conversation.

* * *

Under Ruby's intense scrutiny, the shop owner may not have actually confessed to the scam but he might as well have, given the way he apologised for being hasty. He claimed that he would need to speak to his brother first, just in case he had decided to take the items without informing him. But, as Jenkins had said, it was close to knocking-off time so she decided not to take it any further and let him off with a stern lecture about wasting police time.

'I'm tired,' Ruby admitted as they headed back to the car. Easy workload or not, she had struggled with this slight change to her working hours. Returning home at close to 10pm meant that it was well past midnight before she had wound down sufficiently to go to bed, but she was still awake at 7am. What had been more frustrating was having to kick her heels, making conversation with her parents before it was time to go into the station. Whilst the experience with the acid attack had somewhat put her off estate agents, she resolved that she would spend some of her free time tomorrow morning flat hunting. As expensive as rental in St. Albans might prove, she reasoned that not having to travel back and forth from Hemel so often would make it worthwhile.

'At your age I was never tired,' Jenkins said vacantly. This was the closest Ruby had ever been to learning more about him than what she was presented with each day. She opened the car door, fully intent on finding a way to have him open up more.

'Possible break-in on the Ridgeway. Alarm triggered, shouts heard and two vehicles leaving at speed.'

It had taken a while, and a number of requests, for Jenkins to finally acquiesce to Ruby's desire to have the general police radio on when they were out of the office. She knew that they would be contacted directly if there was anything that required their attention, but she liked to know what was going on out there. She suspected that Jenkins' eventual acceptance had less been about agreeing with the sentiment, and more in the hope that it would distract her from her endless stream of inane small talk.

'No,' Jenkins said firmly.

Him already knowing what she was going to say didn't put her off. 'Ah, come on. It's practically on the way back to the station and, it might give us something decent to do tomorrow.'

'Let someone on the night shift do it.'

Ruby smiled at this. Not only was it not a flat refusal but Jenkins had chosen not to question her dubious geographical claim. 'Where's your sense of adventure?'

'I should have stuck with Cooper,' he sighed, and in that moment Ruby knew that she had won.

'Great, I'll call it in,' she replied enthusiastically, all feeling of tiredness having now gone. A simple break-in it might turn out to be, but the address alone – in St. Albans' equivalent of Beverly Hills – promised something much more interesting than what they had been dealing with over the past week or so.

* * *

'What kind of people do you imagine live along here?' Ruby asked as they drove past the first large properties with their wrought iron gates and expensive cars on the driveways.

'I don't,' Jenkins replied flatly. Before they could see the marked police cars, the correct direction of travel was indicated by the steady pulse of the blue lights from around the bend in the road.

That what they were attending was more serious than it initially appeared had been implied by the subsequent radio chatter. 'Tell me what you've got,' she asked the first officer she saw upon getting out the car.

'There's a woman dead in the hallway,' he replied grimly.

Ruby tried to disguise the impact of the massive dump of adrenaline this news prompted. She had seen dead bodies before in London, but this would be her first as a detective. 'Cause of death?'

'Er… murder I guess,' said the officer uncertainly.

'Carry on, officer,' she said, shaking her head and walking past. With forensics yet to arrive and erect the bright floodlights they used when attending a scene at night, it was only the orange glow that lit their way, but it was enough to corroborate some of what they had been told on the radio.

'See the skid marks there,' Jenkins said, pointing to two patches where the gravel had been displaced to the extent that the aggregate underneath, topped by a layer of weed blocking membrane, was visible.

Already the scene outside was clear, a pair of marks belonged to the car that had entered, and the other had come from one taken out of the large detached garage to the side of the property. 'At least two men then,' she said, knowing that she didn't need to be careful about being gender neutral around Jenkins. 'Judging by the skid patterns I'd say what they arrived in was four-wheel drive whereas the one they took was rear wheel only.' She took the grunt that followed as one of agreement. 'Are the gates electric?'

'No, why? Jenkins asked in a tone she recognised as being one to test her powers of investigation.

'Well, it would imply the attackers were known to her... unless they hacked the frequency of the gates that is,' she said, shaking her head. 'Not that it matters anyway because they're not electric and so it could have been anyone.'

'Looks like it. Let's go inside, shall we?'

Although uniform had been through the house to check for intruders, the place was now empty, save for the body lying in the large expanse of the entrance hall. The two paramedics who had attended her were standing outside; one of whom was visibly shaken.

'Blunt trauma,' Jenkins said calmly. 'She was probably dead before she felt it.'

'Do you think they meant to kill her?' Ruby asked, captivated by the small pool of blood surrounding her head. Whereas some of her colleagues had struggled with the sight of blood, she had always found the way it changed appearance under different forms of light fascinating. In the dark it had an inky blackness, almost like night itself, whilst in bright daylight it could be a vivid red. Here, underneath the chandelier style arrangement, it fell somewhere in the middle. If it wasn't for it, and the blank eyes staring towards the ceiling, Ruby could almost believe that the woman wasn't dead. She was wearing a simple top and skirt, unhelpful in the sense that it didn't help establish what she'd been doing that evening. Even splayed across the floor, Ruby could tell that the woman went to an expensive hairdresser – the blonde dye appeared almost natural. Her eyebrows had recently been threaded, she had eyelash extensions and her nails were pristine acrylic. As a consequence, Ruby doubted that this woman ever went outside the house without looking her best.

'Why not just threaten her if they had come to get the car keys?' Jenkins replied, assuming as Ruby did that the purpose of the home invasion was for what had been taken out of the garage.

'Perhaps they did, but she must have turned and ran.'

'Because the blow was to the back of her head? Possibly, although she triggered the personal alarm on the keypad here,' he said, pointing to a command module by the front door.

'Shall we take a look in the garage then?' Ruby said, stepping outside. She didn't wait whilst Jenkins spoke to the ambulance crew to explain to them that they would need to hold back until forensics gave them the all clear.

'Two-man job then,' Jenkins said when he caught up to her.

'Unless there was something special about the particular model,' she countered, knowing that his assumption was based on their being another car, a top spec current-plate Range Rover, still inside. 'Most high-end motors are stolen to order.'

'Fair enough,' he replied mildly. 'Hey, has anyone got hold of the husband yet?' he shouted across to a nearby officer.

'Apparently he's on his way, guv,' came the reply. It prompted both Ruby and Jenkins to head back out to the road, ready to intercept him. As bad as having to deal with the wives of Michael and Jake had been, this had the potential to be much worse.

'Shall we tell one of the officers to make sure he doesn't get to the house?' she whispered.

'No, we can handle it,' Jenkins replied confidently.

Ruby supposed that if, between them, they had managed to take down a vicious acid attacker, one distraught husband should not be beyond their capabilities.

'I bet that's him now,' Ruby said, hearing the sound of a high-powered engine approaching at speed. She had barely said it when they found themselves doused with the crisp bright white light of a vehicle that was attempting to pull into the drive, despite the marked police cars doing a fine job of mostly blocking it off.

Ruby approached the driver's side and, out of the glare of the xenons she noticed the distinctive side vents of a Maserati before the door opened.

'Jesus Christ what happened?' a man in a dark suit cried, as he hauled himself out of the seat with a speed and grace that defied his bulk.

'Mr Hamilton?' Ruby said, trying to use her body to shepherd him away from the direction of the house.

'What happened?' he repeated – more of a demand now that he had an individual to focus his attention on.

'Sir, I need you to confirm that you are Mr Hamilton,' Ruby insisted.

'Yes, yes I am. Where's Kelly?' He was already making a move to push past her.

'Sir, please step this way,' Jenkins' gravelly tone intervened, and he grabbed the man's arm and started leading him to the Mondeo. 'I need you to tell me what you have already been told.'

Ruby had been stood beside Jenkins when it had been explained to him exactly what had been said to Mr Hamilton over the phone, and understood that this was her partner's way of trying to keep the man occupied until he was safely sat down in the back of their car.

'I…I… not much,' he said, shaking his head. 'Where's Kelly? Is she okay?'

They hadn't made it quite as far as the Mondeo, but Jenkins must have decided that it was sufficient because he turned to face Mr Hamilton. Most people would describe

Jenkins as grim-faced at the best of times but there was a certain foreboding quality to it that even Ruby found chilling. Mr Hamilton knew it too because he was already attempting to shove him out of the way.

'Kelly!' he called at the top of his voice and, although he managed to repeat it, he cracked on his third attempt. Jenkins grabbed his shoulders as he collapsed to the floor and bent to speak quietly into his ear whilst the man sobbed.

'I'm sorry, Mr Hamilton, but she was injured in the attack and died.' Ruby noticed the way Jenkins' voice unwittingly went up an octave. Even though she had got to know that there was more that lay underneath his hard appearance, it was comforting to find that he couldn't dish out bad news as cool and calmly as it first seemed. 'I know you want to see her, but we need to preserve the integrity of the crime scene.'

Ruby could see Mr Hamilton visibly baulk at this but, thankfully, he did not try and regain his feet.

I promise that you will see her soon,' Jenkins continued in as kindly a voice as she had ever heard him use. 'For now, you need to let us do our job in finding out who did this.'

Jenkins must have taken the nod that followed this as an indication he had said enough because he stood up, his knees popping in the process which, under other circumstances Ruby would have chosen to make a remark about. 'Do you want me to watch over him?' she asked.

'No, I'll get one of the officers whilst we continue our primary enquiries.' Ruby noticed him turn in the direction of the nearest uniform, raise his hand, and then think better of it before signalling to a bigger guy talking to a member of the public.

Jenkins motioned at her to walk with him back up to the house, but she gave her head a brief shake and bent down next to Mr Hamilton. 'Your car has been taken,' she added.

He looked up at her and the sobbing stopped. 'Why… why are you telling me this? You think I give a shit about some fucking car?!'

'Hey,' the officer whom Jenkins had beckoned shouted, but Ruby raised a hand to tell him it was okay.

'No, sir, but I need to know the registration number, so we can trace it.'

He looked up at her blankly. 'I… I don't know it.'

'What?' She knew shock could do all manner of things to people's minds, but this seemed ridiculous.

'I'm… I'm a car dealer. I take different stock home all the time,' he said. 'I… I can't remember which one I had in the garage tonight.'

Ruby stood up without responding and Jenkins leaned in towards her.

'Thanks, I completely forgot…' he said.

'That's what partners are for,' she said, raising a hand dismissively before taking on a more serious tone. 'Not that it has got us anywhere. What did you make of that?'

Jenkins shrugged, seemingly back to his normal self. 'I guess being a car dealer explains all the flash motors.'

* * *

'There's nothing more we can do now until the morning,' Jenkins said a couple of hours later. Although there was a squad car still there, and it had been joined by a forensics van, the place had taken on an eerie quality. Kelly Hamilton's body had been taken away and Mr Hamilton had gone to the station to give a preliminary statement, seemingly the point at which the bystanders took their cue to leave.

'Can we just go through it one more time, guv?' Ruby said, ignoring the roll of Jenkins' eyes this request provoked. 'Consider it my equivalent of you writing in your notebook. Speaking of which, when we get back to the station, you're not going to head up to CID just so you can lock it away as part of that work separation crap?'

'No.'

'So, it was a load of crap?' she asked, confused and assuming that it wasn't just her tiredness that was leading to her failure to grasp his meaning, but was also making her ponder something so inconsequential.

'No, but, if I don't finish back at the office, then I leave it in the glovebox.'

'I guess that does the same job,' she responded evenly.

'Look, shall we just get on with this?' he said.

'Sure,' she replied quickly, somewhat grateful for the gee up. 'Based on what we have so far we think the intruders let themselves in through the gate. They made no effort to hide their presence as they drove onto the gravel. This implies they looked respectable and fits the idea that they were few in number, possibly just two. One or more of them approached the door and, although Mrs Hamilton answered, she decided to trigger the alarm and run, at which point she was hit over the head. Blunt trauma. Her attacker or attackers then went and retrieved the key to a car we haven't yet identified and the two vehicles, one being the original, then sped away. I haven't left anything out, have I?'

'Only that one of the neighbours thinks she saw an Audi estate. It would make sense for that to be the second vehicle to leave the premises, but seems inconsistent with the notion they were stealing to order.'

'Unless it was something like an RS6. They can be very expensive, especially with lots of options added.'

'Okay fine, you're a car geek, I get that,' he replied with a smile.

'So, home to bed then whilst all this is being looked into?' she asked, her body reacting to the suggestion by increasing her awareness of her aching feet.

'Yep, it's a bit like going to sleep on a flight. We may wake up to find we're already there with this one.'

'I never knew you were so positive,' Ruby remarked, heading back to the Mondeo.

'Me neither,' he said, following her.

Chapter Twenty-one

As enchanting as Jenkins' claim that the case might be solved before she returned to the office in the morning, and as exhausted as she felt when she rolled into her bed just after 1.30am, Ruby found herself unable to switch off. It wasn't so much the details of the case that were troubling her, more the ease with which a person can be killed. It seemed such a needless waste that a single blow to the head, in an effort to subdue Kelly Hamilton, had ended up killing her. And for what? Some car that her husband didn't even know he had in the garage.

Whilst still remaining on the same thread of consciousness, her mind began to drift at tangents before finally settling on Danny. If this evening was a perfect illustration of life being too short and how quickly it can be snatched away, then why was she so hesitant in taking things to the next level with him? It didn't even matter that he seemed to want to take his time too because she was sure that he was only saying the right thing, perhaps having already sensed the way the wind was blowing. If anything, it was just adding more pressure to the situation where, in an effort to make their first time seem perfect, they would spend the whole act wondering how the other person was feeling rather than enjoying it.

But now wasn't the time to be sending Danny a message pertaining to things of a physical nature. He was likely to assume she was drunk, or perhaps just a bunny boiler, and besides, she would still find herself unable to sleep, waiting in fear for what he might send in response.

So instead of focusing on what she was missing out on and getting herself more wound up, she tried to think of all the things she had to be thankful for. Yet all it did was take her down the road of wondering what it must be like to be Mr Hamilton, possibly still at the police station, and realising over the course of the evening that your whole world has collapsed. Her job was meant to do good for people, to help protect them against the evils in society but, apart from when she was investigating things of a trivial nature, all she seemed to be doing was sharing in people's own tragedy.

When sleep finally did come, it was filled with haunting dreams of how Michael Robins' children might react when they first see him without his bandages.

* * *

'You look like shit,' Nelson said as Ruby walked into his office the next morning. 'And you, Steve, don't look much better. Rough night was it?'

'Something like that,' she replied, seemingly on both their behalves.

'Anyway, I think I'm up to date on last night's break-in. I assume you two are going to want to stay on this?'

'Yes, guv,' Ruby said, against Jenkins' advice from when they had first arrived at work. With no new leads overnight, and no DNA or prints coming through from forensics, he had warned her that this had the potential to prove as frustrating as the acid case. She had gone on to remind him that they'd got a result on that one, when really it was the memory of Kelly Hamilton's sightless eyes that made her want to see this one through.

'Okay then, but I won't hold my breath,' Nelson responded and, from his change in expression, she guessed he had read the curiosity in her reaction. 'I'm not saying it's not equally as important but, this time, we don't have a crazed attacker on the loose. To me this has the whiff of organized crime which, not only makes it difficult in itself, but is less of a… how can I put this tactfully, a public concern.'

'You mean people won't care as much because they won't think it could happen to them.' It was a statement rather than a question, but lacking any bitterness. She may not like hearing it verbalised so simply, but she couldn't deny seeing Nelson's point in this.

'I don't mean that it's any less important,' he countered. 'In actual fact, without the pressure from above and outside on this one, it might make things easier for us.'

Ruby figured that this was as close to an admission from Nelson that he could have behaved more appropriately in her first week, and she didn't see the need to push him any further.

'Right then,' Jenkins said, standing and perhaps also sensing that it was better to draw things to a close. 'We'll get to it.'

'Where to first?' he enquired once they had left Nelson's office.

'I think I would like to start off with speaking to Mr Hamilton again.'

'I thought you might say that,' he said with a mock sigh. 'Tell you what, I'll dig out where he's supposed to be staying and you make us a couple of coffees for the journey. You look like you could do with one as much as I could.'

With her task as simple as filling up two Styrofoam cups from the percolator, she read through the statement taken from Mr Hamilton last night. Not that it took long either. She was frustrated by its lack of detail and knew that she would have done a better job when in uniform, always looking for clarification or expansion when answers seemed vague. It barely told them any more than they had learned in their own brief exchange with Mr Hamilton. He had been out for the evening with some friends when he had received the call about an incident back at his house. The officer had done nothing to flesh out the details of Mr Hamilton's whereabouts; something she and Jenkins would have to begin with addressing if they were to establish an effective alibi.

* * *

'Thank you for coming in to see us, Mr Hamilton,' Ruby said uncertainly, after the officer on the main desk called up to inform them he had arrived. Jenkins confirmed that his keenness to come and see them rather than have them go to him was definitely unusual, if convenient from their perspective.

'Call me, Gary,' he responded, devoid of any feeling.

'Thank you, Gary,' Ruby responded brightly. 'I would ask you how you were doing today if it were not a stupid question, and I'm grateful for you sparing the time to speak to us when you must be busy with… arrangements.'

'Do you mind if we record our discussion?' Jenkins enquired as they sat down.

'No, all this was explained to me last night,' Gary replied, his voice flat, which Ruby could understand given the circumstances.

'Yes, and thank you for the information you provided our colleagues,' Jenkins continued, in a professional manner honed over the decades. 'We would like to explore these in more detail.'

'I see.'

'It says here that you were out with friends when you received the call regarding what had happened at your house.'

Jenkins was looking down at the paper in front of him, as though he was checking through the notes. Ruby knew this to be a strategy to make the question appear more casual than it really was.

'Yes, that's right.'

'And where was that exactly?'

'Oh, it was just some pub in town.'

'Which pub was that?' Jenkins was still looking down and his tone remained conversational.

'I'm not sure which one, just, you know, one of the ones on London Road.' Gary was sat up straight and showed no signs of appreciating how vague his responses were.

'Left or right-hand side?'

'I'm sorry?'

'If you were to enter London Road from the centre of town, by the traffic lights at the top of Holywell Hill, would the place be on your left or right?'

'Oh, I see,' Gary replied and put on a thoughtful expression. By this point Ruby could feel herself becoming restless. She knew Jenkins was managing the situation but that didn't stop her wanting to reach over the table and shake Gary until he achieved a better handle on what was happening. 'Left,' he said eventually, before adding, 'I think.'

'How far down would you say?' Although he had stopped regarding the piece of paper, Jenkins' tone remained calm and patient.

'Oh, not far.'

'What are the names of the people you were with?'

'I'm sorry?'

'The friends you went to the pub with.'

'Oh, I see. I'm not sure of the names of all of them, they're more acquaintances you see…'

'Let's start with the ones you do know, shall we?'

'Erm, well there was Harry and I believe…'

'Harry who?' Jenkins interrupted gently.

'Oh, his last name?' Gary asked, his voice sounding helpful. 'I'm not sure I know it. I think it might be Collins, but that might be another guy altogether.'

It wasn't so much a sigh, but Jenkins didn't respond immediately, and Ruby guessed that even he was now struggling to keep his cool. 'I assume you have his phone number. You know, so you can arrange when and where to meet.'

'Yes, I do,' Gary nodded.

'Can you show it to us please?'

'Yes of course,' he responded, theatrically tapping his pockets. 'Oh, I don't think I brought it with me.'

'What?' Jenkins made no attempt to hide his incredulity.

'I must have left it behind, or perhaps it's still in the central console of my car. I could go and check if you like?' Gary began standing.

This time it wasn't so much a sigh, more a deep exhalation, purging Jenkins of all the bullshit he had been forced to ingest. Ruby could feel a prickle of anticipation of what might follow but he didn't speak to Gary again, instead he turned towards her and gave her a simple nod.

She was being let off the leash and to Ruby's lips, freedom had never tasted so good.

'Sit… down,' she hissed, adding to the menace of her tone by the emphasis she placed on these two simple words by virtue of the gap between uttering them. Gary didn't so much oblige as drop into his chair like he had been struck round the head. Ruby didn't have time to contemplate the irony of this observation. 'I'm sure I need not remind you of the seriousness of the situation…' Another pause, but this time to allow his mind to comprehend what she was referring to. 'But we have wasted the last ten minutes going around in circles trying to find an answer to one basic question. Now I don't know you, Mr Hamilton, so I'm going to give you the benefit of the doubt that, somewhat inexplicably, you don't know the name of the place where you went to, aside from an unconvincing description of its general whereabouts, nor do you know whom you were meeting up with, save for some random first names. However, know this: we will find out where it was, either because you decide to start cooperating with us now or we track you on the city centre's CCTV cameras.

'It's all the same to us,' she continued. 'But, Mr Hamilton, what you have to ask yourself is two things. Firstly, how do you think your apparent unwillingness to share your whereabouts last night looks, especially as I point out to you that it would similarly act as your alibi.'

Even if she knew that she hadn't already been getting through to him before, her last point about needing to clear his name from the possible list of suspects caused his concerned expression to turn into one of horror. He opened his mouth to speak but a single raised finger stopped him.

'I'm not finished Mr Hamilton,' she chided. 'The other question you need to ask yourself is whether you want us wasting all this time when our priority,' she made a circling motion to emphasise it related to all three of them, 'is capturing whoever did this to your wife.'

'What, you think I don't…?'

Raising that finger again caused his voice to die in his throat. In that moment, Ruby felt certain of one thing. If a few home truths were enough to make him so obedient that he responded to a simple hand gesture, in the same way a dog could be trained to sit, she doubted he was the sort of cold blooded killer that would off his wife under the guise of a break-in.

'Before you respond, Mr Hamilton, DI Jenkins and I are going to step out of this room for a moment. When we come back in the first words out of your mouth are going to be something more useful. Otherwise, I am going to consider arresting you on suspicion of murder.' Ruby stood up to walk out.

'Map!' Gary cried out, causing Ruby to turn back. 'If you show me a map of London Road, I'm sure I could pick out for you which pub it was.'

'Fine, we'll get you one,' she said, her exasperation not entirely disingenuous. Gary had thought of a good way of appearing not to admit that he had been acting dumb, whilst at the same time being able to provide them with the answers they were now insisting upon. 'Although if you had the common sense to bring your phone…' she added, her voice dripping with sarcasm.

'So, you think he may be our suspect then?' Jenkins asked once the door was closed. Ruby couldn't tell whether the smile that had accompanied his question was because he had enjoyed her little display in there, or he was truly curious as to the answer.

'Nope,' she said, keen to find out which it was.

'I see, playing it coy,' he responded, still clearly amused.

She should have known he would avoid playing her games, but she wouldn't let that prevent her showing off her acumen.

'Fine then,' she sighed, the glint in her eyes betraying her false modesty. 'Aside from the fact I don't think he'd have the balls to do it, surely he would have come up with a more effective alibi than that shambles. And on a more serious note, his distress last night seemed genuine.'

'Yes, but he does seem much calmer today,' he added thoughtfully.

'Too calm,' Ruby said. 'I can't wait to find out what he's hiding. Can we just cut him loose as soon as he gives us the location?'

'Might as well, I can't stand the thought of having to go through the same pantomime with each question. We'll then see him again as soon as we know more about his supposed alibi. Shall we?' Jenkins asked, gesturing to the door.

It didn't take Gary long to select a venue from the Google map Ruby brought up on her phone. Moreover, there weren't that many to choose from, with at least three places she remembered from her younger years now having transformed into restaurants instead. She had never been into the Honey Bee, it had always seemed a bit of an old man's pub, but she'd walked past it a few times. Just to be certain he wasn't still messing them about she brought up some interior pictures and had him describe the layout to her.

'He seemed far more nervous leaving, than he did when he arrived,' Ruby commented as they watched Gary pull out of the car park in his Maserati. London Road was only the other side of Victoria Street and they figured they would be just as quick walking as driving.

'Yes, there's definitely more to Mr Hamilton than meets the eye.'

'Do you ever get bored of this? I mean, after so many cases, do they begin to lose their potency?'

'I suppose there's a certain novelty that wears off after a while,' he conceded. 'But each case is different. For example, when you woke up this morning did you think you would be having to threaten the victim's husband like you did?'

Ruby paused for a moment to consider whether there was any implied criticism in Jenkins' voice but, as usual, it seemed merely observational. 'I guess not.'

It felt quite strange walking unnoticed among the other pedestrians, none of them apparently suspecting she was a police officer. She gestured at a man in front of them talking loudly into his mobile phone. 'What would you do if what he was saying sounded like he was up to something illegal?'

Jenkins shrugged. 'I suppose that would depend on what it was. The thing is,' he continued, picking up on the train of thought that had brought Ruby to this question, 'what we're doing is different to an officer walking their beat. We have a specific purpose in mind that we should only become distracted from if there is something serious.

Just like a police car attending an emergency wouldn't trouble itself with a motorist using their phone whilst driving.'

Ruby knew their conversation was mundane, simplistic even, but in the absence of being able to engage Jenkins in discussing matters outside of work she had become used to making small talk under the guise of learning more about the job.

'You ever drink in here?' she asked as the pub came into view.

'Once or twice.'

'Nice is it?'

'Much like any other.'

Ruby sighed. Jenkins was back to offering short answers to her questions and not looking to promote any dialogue. Although open, it was not yet lunch and empty save for a couple of lone souls having a quiet pint whilst reading the newspaper, the bar staff were still in the process of setting up.

Having got the attention of one of them Jenkins flashed his warrant card. 'I'm DI Jenkins and this is DC Knight, can we see the manager please?'

'Er, sure,' the young man replied. 'She's just out the back, I'll go and get her.'

'Shame we're on duty, there's a nice garden behind,' Ruby commented.

'Huh,' scoffed Jenkins but she noticed him taking a lingering look at the beer pumps running most of the length of the bar.

'Can I help you?' asked a middle-aged woman, with intricate tattoos visible under her vest top.

'Yes, we're trying to confirm the whereabouts of a gentleman who claims to have been in here last night at approximately 10pm.'

'Okay,' she replied, taking the enlarged driving license photo from Jenkins.

'He would have been wearing a suit and was here with some friends,' he continued.

'Hmmm, I'm not sure. We tend to get a few of the city types in here mid-week,' she offered.

'Perhaps we could ask your staff if they remember serving him. Were they on shift last night?' Jenkins enquired, cocking his head at the other two who were trying to look busy whilst remaining in earshot.

'I suppose,' she replied evenly. 'Although I do think I vaguely remember him.'

'I notice you have CCTV outside,' Jenkins continued, which was news to Ruby. She hadn't even thought to look as they were approaching. 'Do you have any in here too we might be able to look at?'

'There's a couple of cameras in the main areas but it's an old system and we tend to record over them if there haven't been any incidents the night before.'

'I see,' Jenkins said mildly. 'Well, it's still early so perhaps we might still be able to find something on them.'

'Look, is he in any kind of trouble?' The woman placed her hands on her hips, adopting a more confrontational tone.

'Why do you ask?' Jenkins appeared oblivious to her stance.

'Yeah right,' she scoffed. 'You lot come here asking your questions but whenever we need help, if a fight breaks out or something, it's ages before anyone arrives.'

'I'm sorry, I can't really comment on that. If you'd like to lodge a complaint, then I could give you the–'

'Fat lot of good that would do,' she snorted, interrupting Jenkins' offer. 'Look, can we make this quick? I've still got a lot to sort out before the lunchtime rush and, no offence, nothing puts the punters off their pints more than Old Bill hanging around.'

'You were telling us about this gentleman,' he prompted her, pointing back at the photo.

'Like I told you, he was in last night. Around the time you mentioned.'

'You seem far more sure now…'

'Yeah, well I've had more of a chance to think about it.'

'Did you serve him or was it one of the others?' Jenkins was now leaving barely a breath between the end of her answers and his next question.

'One of the others, I think.'

'Did you see him at the bar buying a round or was he sat somewhere?'

'Oh, er… sat down I think.'

'Where exactly?'

'I'm sorry?' She had now crossed her arms in the classic defensive gesture, her pose now defiant.

'If you didn't see him at the bar but you're certain he was in here, then where was it you saw him?' Jenkins made an arcing gesture across the mostly empty tables for emphasis.

'I, er… I think he might have been there,' she replied, indicating a small table in the corner.

'He told us he was with more than three friends,' Jenkins countered, leaving the implication hanging even though Ruby didn't recall Gary being anything like as specific. She wondered whether they would have been more accepting of the woman's unhelpful responses had it not been for the suspicion that Gary had aroused from their earlier discussion. Regardless, she was itching for Jenkins to let her have a go.

'Oh yeah,' the landlady said, shaking her head in confusion in far too exaggerated a motion. 'It must have been over there, then.' She was now pointing at a rectangular table.

There was no nod from Jenkins this time. Instead he turned to her and spoke. 'What do you make of it, DC Knight?'

'Well, it's bullshit isn't it, guv?' she replied, thinking it was clever that he was having her address him rather than

158

the landlady herself. With so many prying eyes it would be better if she didn't seem so directly confrontational. Not that she couldn't see out of the corner of her vision that the bar staff had suddenly stopped whatever they were pretending to do as soon as she had delivered her assessment of the situation. 'One minute we're being told that she doesn't recognise the guy and the next she's certain that he was here. Then when asked where exactly she had seen him, she doesn't know and then starts making up places where his group might have been sat. And that's before we get into being told that we're unable to check the cameras because, in this day and age of massive data storage, they have to record over the previous day's footage.'

Jenkins was nodding slowly as though taking all these points into consideration. He was playing the role of good cop rather effectively. He then turned and leaned over the bar conspiratorially. 'Perhaps you might prefer if we continue this conversation in private.'

The landlady seemed only too pleased with the suggestion. 'Yes, come through to the back,' she responded in a welcoming tone, lifting up the lid of the bar in the corner, and leading them through to a small kitchen area. 'Paco, take five will you?' she said to the chef who was in the middle of cutting up salad items.

'Look, we're not doing anything illegal here,' she said as soon as they were alone, her voice hushed. 'It's a private function room so, aside from serving them some drinks, what they do in there I consider… well…'

'Private?' Ruby offered, feeling a tingle of excitement. Recalling what Jenkins had said earlier about remembering their priorities when encountering potential wrongdoing she added: 'Whilst we can't give you the details of what we are investigating, I can assure you our primary concern isn't what your pub is used for.' Ruby knew this was a slight lie until they could establish that this had nothing to do with Kelly Hamilton's murder, but she could see no harm in trying to get this woman on side.

'Gary and his friends rent the room out to play poker.' *Gary now, is it?* Ruby thought disdainfully. 'I know it involves money and we haven't the requisite license but, seeing as we don't make anything out of it ourselves, I figured what's the harm?' The last bit was close to being a plea.

'And you can confirm that Mr Hamilton was here between 9pm and 10pm last night?' Ruby enquired, ignoring the landlady's request for reassurance.

'Oh yes,' she replied, her helpful tone a distinct contrast to earlier. 'He arrived here shortly after 8pm and I saw him dash out after he received a phone call.'

'Can you describe his demeanour at that point?' Jenkins asked

'He'd gone white as a sheet. I was certain there was something wrong. I would have done something myself but his friend was trying to calm him down.'

'Which friend was that?'

'I don't know; some foreign guy. Eastern European, I think. I only see him when its poker night. Chased after Gary as he came marching through the bar; didn't seem happy with him leaving.'

'Oh really?' Ruby enquired.

'Yeah, I don't know much about poker but I wondered whether he was losing or something and wanted a chance to win his money back. Anyway, the guy let Gary go after whispering something in his ear.'

Jenkins gave Ruby a look to check whether there was anything more she wanted to say. She offered him a brief shake of her head. 'We'll be seeing you,' he said to the landlady and started making his way back through to the bar.

'What does he mean *seeing you*?' she asked Ruby, causing her to smile. So much for her being the bad cop. She'd bet any money that he'd chosen his words very carefully in order to put the wind up her. Ruby gave her an enigmatic shrug and followed her partner.

'Still think he didn't have anything to do with it?' Jenkins asked when they were back on the pavement.

'I'd be starting to have my doubts were it not for the fact his alibi is even worse than it was before,' she replied.

'Maybe that's what makes it so good. How better to make a cast-iron alibi appear even more convincing than to make it one that you wouldn't appear to want to reveal to the police.'

Ruby spent the next few minutes considering this line of argument and Jenkins seemed satisfied not to disturb her. They were most of the way back to the station when she spoke again. 'I still don't buy it. Even if we find that he's got into some serious debt through his gambling or whatever else and he was looking to get the insurance money from his wife dying, he'd be stupid not to keep his alibi separate from all that. Only a fool would flash that in front of our noses.'

'But he was rather keen to avoid us finding out.' Despite usually keeping his own cards closer to his chest, Jenkins didn't sound convinced by this claim. 'Unless,' he said with more enthusiasm, 'it was those he was in debt with seeking payment by stealing his car. What happened to his wife was as it presented itself: just a case of them being over-zealous with their efforts to silence her.' Ordinarily Ruby might have been minded to suggest that *over-zealous* was an unfortunate way to describe the killing of a woman, but she was more interested in considering the thrust of Jenkins' point.

Unconsciously their pace quickened. 'I can't see a way this doesn't fit,' she said excitedly. 'Like I told you, his distress at what had happened to his wife had seemed genuine. And you heard what he was like when I mentioned that his car was stolen. Perhaps that's why he hasn't been at all helpful with helping us identify which car it was because he doesn't want us to be able to track it back to them. He must be in debt with some serious people here.'

'You're not kidding,' Jenkins responded. 'Which would also fit why he didn't want us knowing what he was doing whilst all this was happening,' he added.

'And also why they knew it would be a good time to steal the car.' All sense of tiredness following their late night yesterday had now gone. She was buzzing and couldn't wait to get this wrapped up. 'Holy shit, Jenkins, when Nelson spoke about organized crime earlier even he couldn't have imagined it would be like this. In finding out Kelly Hamilton's killer we might blow the lid on some huge network. Do you think we should tell the DCI as soon as we get back?'

'Woah, hold your horses there,' Jenkins said, stopping walking and forcing Ruby to reluctantly do the same. 'Let's not start getting carried away. First we need to establish *if* there is a connection between his penchant for poker and what happened to his wife.'

'But…' Ruby started to protest before accepting that Jenkins was making a fair point. She couldn't help but smile at what he would have made of all her assumptions on the Friday evening of the acid case, when she had been running around CID in her bare feet, even if many of them had turned out to be correct. 'So, where do we start then?' she asked, pleased that her question had prompted Jenkins to recommence walking.

'Well, everything really: credit cards, bank accounts, his business finances, mortgage records; anything that might show him getting into financial trouble.'

'What are we waiting for?' she called over her shoulder and jogged the remaining few yards back to the station. What had started the day as a case that might not be solved could be done and dusted before they were due to knock off.

Chapter Twenty-two

'I still can't believe it,' Ruby said as Jenkins gently tried to escort her to the stairs. 'I mean, are you sure there isn't something we've missed here?'

'Like what?' he replied impatiently, and Ruby could see he was as frustrated as she was at them not finding a single shred of evidence to suggest the Hamiltons' finances were in anything but rude health. 'To be honest, I guessed as much as soon as we saw that the business was doing well.'

'Doing well? Judging by the figures, we're in completely the wrong game!' Ruby said bitterly. On a normal evening she was sure that Gary would have long gone home to his massive house by now, having made enough money to ensure that he and Kelly could continue to live the life of which they had become accustomed. 'But I agree; that's where I would have looked to hide my losses. That way he could try and keep it from his wife and carry on driving around in a Maserati and have a brand-new Range Rover still sat in the garage.'

'Just make sure you try and park it for tonight,' Jenkins said awkwardly, and Ruby realised that he was trying to be humorous in an attempt to make light of his concerns for her.

'I'll try,' she said, hoping he wouldn't detect that her accompanying laughter was forced. 'Although I might teach myself the rules of poker. If that prick we spoke to this morning seems to be doing well at it then I don't see why I shouldn't!'

'That's the spirit,' Jenkins replied, now at his car. 'See you in the morning!'

'Whatever,' she replied with mock grumpiness, before flashing him a bright smile and getting in her Up! GTI. She couldn't help but feel touched at his efforts to cheer her up. Yet she doubted any of it would do any good and, if she didn't fall asleep pretty much as soon as she went home, she was liable to spend the evening churning over everything in her head.

Before she even realised what she was doing she had her phone out.

> *I know it's short notice but do you fancy going for a drink tonight? R x*

As well as being prepared to take things slowly in terms of their physical relationship, Danny had proven willing to accept that her shift pattern this week would see her stick to her unofficial rule of not dating on a weeknight. She hit send before she could start to second-guess his likely response. Not that it stopped her staring at the phone afterwards, wondering what he was going to type. If it was her, she would play it casually and demonstrate that she wasn't just available at the drop of a hat. She would give herself a taste of her own medicine.

> *TBH it's been a long day, and I've not long got back from work myself. D x.*

There it was, not an outright refusal but as good as one, and exactly what she had ended up expecting. Yet any credit she gave him for showing a bit of backbone was outweighed by the disappointment she felt. If he had agreed, perhaps she might have convinced him to go to the

Honey Bee with her. Not that she would tell him the reason why, but Ruby would have derived a certain satisfaction from watching the nervous behaviour of the landlady the whole time they were there. But enough of that; she had wasted too much time already not thinking of an appropriate response and she didn't want him to believe that she was sat there feeling upset; more out of a sense of pride than any fear it might make him feel guilty.

No worries, I could probably do with an early…

Ruby didn't get to finish what she was typing because a second message came through.

You could always come round here and I could cook us something? D x.

Her initial reaction was an irrational concern that he must have thought this was what she'd been hinting at from the start. But how would he have read that into her message and, more to the point, why would he have been compelled to make the offer if he hadn't wanted to?

She went back to the reply she had been typing and deleted all the text. *I appreciate the offer but I guess I should probably just…* She stopped. What was she doing? She was declining his offer, not as a result of having truly considered it, but as some automated response, similar to an email out of office reply. When had she become so risk averse? It wasn't as though she was showing any signs of it in her work; Jenkins seemed to have even found a way to nurture her tendency to jump in at the deep end with the way he used her to put pressure on Gary and the landlady today.

She knew it was a defence mechanism to avoid getting hurt but similarly understood that continuing with this behaviour was likely to drive Danny away.

What's your address? I'll come straight round. Ruby x

Sending this felt like more of a statement of intent than Danny could ever fathom. So much for not taking her work away with her as Jenkins' constantly preached; she would ensure that the tenacious, fearless Ruby that was as liable to get her into trouble as to see her become a successful detective, got into the car with her each evening. Yes, she would go around to Danny's house and no, she wouldn't be nervous that he may take this as an indication that she wanted to sleep with him. If it seemed like they were building towards that moment, then she would deal with it at the appropriate time depending on how she was feeling.

Decision made, Ruby welcomed the speed with which Danny sent her his address because it prevented any more procrastination. The whole purpose of her contacting him this evening was about trying to wind down after a testing day rather than swap one set of anxieties for another.

* * *

'Nice place you've got here,' she said, after being buzzed up to his apartment and walking into the large open-plan living space. 'It must be only a couple of minutes' walk from the train station too.'

'I got a good deal because I bought it off plan,' he replied modestly, taking her jacket. 'Can I offer you some wine?'

'Yes please,' she responded eagerly, having decided she would worry about how she would get home if and when it became an issue. Following him into the kitchen area, the inviting smells that had greeted her at the door were now causing her to salivate.

'It's nothing much, just a simple pasta dish made from some bits I had knocking around,' he said, pouring her a generous glass of white wine. She was willing to accept that chardonnay being her favourite grape variety was just coincidence, but had it not been for the short time between his offer and her arrival she would swear he had gone out and bought the fresh ingredients especially.

Not that the confident way he moved around the kitchen and swiftly put together their supper hinted that he was anything but an accomplished cook. But perhaps in an effort to reduce the formality of it, he suggested he pop the home-made pesto topped chicken and chorizo dish in bowls which they could enjoy in front of the television.

The time passed swiftly and Ruby accepted a second glass of wine, but drunk it slowly to ensure her options remained open. It would be far more awkward to have to wait for a taxi to arrive to take her home than to jump into her own car.

It was her body that betrayed both the hour and the long day at work. Finding herself unable to stifle a yawn, Ruby wasn't surprised when Danny reached for the remote control and muted whatever political chat show they had stumbled across. 'It's getting late,' he said, with Ruby unable to determine anything more from his infuriatingly even tone.

'I guess I should…' she started to respond, already leaning forward to get up from the sofa.

'Wait,' he said, placing a gentle hand on her arm and causing her to turn back to face him. 'I don't want you to feel like you should go.' Danny shook his head in frustration. 'I didn't mean it like that,' he continued, trying to compose himself but still a world away from the relaxed but confident man Ruby had spent the last couple of hours chatting to. 'What I meant to say is that I don't want you to go.' Finally getting the words out as he'd wanted to, seemed to help settle him. 'It's fine if you do; like I said the other evening, I see no need to rush things and I wouldn't want you to think that I only asked you round tonight because I…'

Not for the first time that day Ruby marvelled how a single finger gesture had the power to silence a man. But this time it wasn't held aloft in a threatening motion to warn of the danger of speaking out of turn. It was on Danny's soft lips, telling him that it was fine, she knew what he wanted, and she wanted it too. With him quiet but his eyes positively screaming with desire, she removed her finger, but only so she could replace it with her own lips.

Chapter Twenty-three

'Won't your parents be worried where you got to last night?' he asked, kissing the top of her head as they lay together in the bed, enjoying the warmth of the sun's early rays pouring in through a gap in the curtains.

Part of her wanted to respond that she was a grown woman and she didn't need permission to stay out, but she knew that it would only serve to make her sound childish. 'I texted them whilst you were in the shower.'

'Did you tell them where you were?' His question was delivered casually but Ruby was becoming attuned to even the slightest change of tone in people.

'More or less,' she replied, keen to avoid offering a downright lie.

'Didn't want to commit to telling them about me until you have made up your mind?' His voice was still playful but there was definitely something more serious underneath.

The belligerent side of Ruby didn't like the idea of being tricked into revealing her feelings, especially when she had seen through the ruse so easily. And yet she could understand his desire for some reassurance, not least because she had felt the same way. But that had changed last night and the way he had made love to her showed a tenderness that she had never experienced before.

'You can come and meet them whenever you like,' she said, having decided that giving such a positive response was likely to put an end to the matter.

'How about tonight?'

'What?'

'You said I could meet them whenever I wanted, so what about this evening then?'

Ruby considered Danny's question carefully, trying to work out whether he was merely bluffing. The truth her apprehension was based on the high probability of her parents, specifically her mother, saying something embarrassing; a concern that would remain no matter how long she delayed their eventual meeting. 'Fine, leave it with me,' she said before adopting a less serious tone. 'Although this is a big step and I need one more opportunity to check that we are genuinely compatible.'

'Oh really?' Danny responded. 'What exactly did you have in mind?'

'This,' she said, rolling over to face him, whilst reaching down beneath the sheets.

* * *

'Forget what time we were meant to be starting?' Jenkins said as Ruby crossed in front of his desk nearly two hours later.

'Hardly,' she replied. 'I figured that there's little point being here until you've had chance to pour a jug full of coffee down your throat.' She paused, suddenly not so sure Jenkins had been joking. 'Why, Nelson hasn't been looking for me, has he?'

'Nah, you're alright. I told him I thought you were downstairs looking through some records. Fancy getting out of here?' Jenkins said, standing up.

'Sure, where are we going?' Ruby asked, content that she wasn't going to be asked what had delayed her, not that she would have dreamed of telling him anything even approaching the truth.

'Let's go and meet our mate Gary,' Jenkins replied, as cheerfully as Ruby could remember him sounding.

'Where is he?' she asked, stepping out of CID barely two minutes after she'd first entered.

'Not a clue,' he said breezily, 'and that's why you're going to phone him and find out.'

'Great,' she responded, knowing there was little point in trying to protest.

'No, we'll come to you,' she repeated for the second time, a couple of minutes later. 'Honestly, Mr Hamilton, we can go round in circles all day if you like but the outcome will still be the same.'

Ruby listened carefully as he finally revealed his address. 'We'll be there shortly,' she said, trying to hide her surprise, and not doing a great job of it by Jenkins' reaction as soon as she ended the call.

'What's the matter?'

'You'll never guess where he is…'

'Erm, let's see… I reckon he is probably at the dealership,' Jenkins replied thoughtfully.

'Oh my God, how did you know that? Was it because you still think he's in some form of financial trouble and he's had to go back to work so soon because he–'

'I could hear him speaking on the other end of the line,' Jenkins said, finally interrupting her. 'And I guess now I don't need to ask you what you made of that.'

'Being smug doesn't suit you,' she responded, but, hard as she tried to make her words sound, she couldn't prevent a wide smile breaking across her face.

'Seems like the lie-in did you good,' he muttered.

You don't know the half of it, she thought to herself, her smile now turning into a grin.

Chapter Twenty-four

'I never would have guessed it was this place, even after we saw the sort of flash motor Gary was driving,' Ruby said.

'You like your cars then?' Jenkins commented.

'Definitely. The thought of finally being able to buy my own was one of the very few reasons why I decided to move back out here. No offence,' she added hastily.

'None taken. So why did you go for that dinky little toy car you're currently peddling?'

'It's not a toy car,' she replied huffily. 'And it would kick this Mondeo's arse any day of the week, especially if the roads got twisty. I'm guessing you're not much of a petrol head then?'

'Not really. As nice as these are,' he said, pointing to the selection of Ferraris, Bentleys and high-end Mercedes on the forecourt, 'they just simply look like a sizable deposit on a house wasted to me. It saddens me when I pass some pokey or run-down property with a smart motor on the drive. To me it seems to highlight where people's priorities have gone wrong.'

'You mean someone like me? I'm driving round in a brand-new car and still living with my parents.' There was no bitterness to Ruby's tone, just a genuine curiosity to find out Jenkins' thoughts on the subject.

'But you said that was only a temporary measure because of the speed at which the job came up.'

'So, you do listen to me,' she beamed, sure that 99% of what she spoke to him about, unless directly related to a case, went in one ear and out the other. What she wouldn't want to admit was that she was starting to have second thoughts about her original plan. She still wanted to get out from under her parents' feet but was now thinking it might be mad to be committing to a twelve-month rental when things were progressing so nicely with Danny.

'Only because you have a captive audience. Now, shall we discuss how we're going to play this?'

'Nah, I like it organic,' she replied dismissively.

'Fair enough,' he said, crossing the road. He was walking with intent and Ruby struggled to keep up, especially once they hit the forecourt and she had so much beautiful metal to admire. Given the nature of the business she guessed the only sort of drop-ins they received were dreamers and those guys who could afford to make a six-figure purchase on a whim. She and Jenkins constituted neither group and they were quickly spotted by one of the sales staff who, rather than approach them with that trained smile all decent salesmen had learned to adopt, headed towards the back of the showroom.

They had barely made it halfway across the floor when a flustered Gary emerged from a small office. 'Ashamed to be found back at work so soon,' Ruby whispered to Jenkins.

'Play nicely; at least for the time being,' Jenkins said in response, his lips barely moving.

'So, have you figured out which car...' Ruby called out by way of greeting but was interrupted by a man in an expensive suit stepping through the door from which Gary had come. 'Perhaps you would like to go back inside whilst we have a quick word with Mr Hamilton.'

An awkward silence descended whilst the man continued standing there. Ruby wondered for a moment whether she had been too subtle in her request to be able to speak to Gary in private but there was something about the way he regarded her that suggested he had understood perfectly.

'I guess customers at this end of the market don't like being made to wait,' she said to Jenkins, just loudly enough so her voice would carry across the showroom.

Gary gave a nervous laugh. 'Oh no, Mr Petrov isn't a client, he's an old associate of mine,' he said before turning to the man in question. 'Would you mind giving us a moment?'

Petrov regarded Gary with the same look of defiance he had shown Ruby. Eventually he turned around and walked slowly back into the office.

'I hope it wasn't something important,' Jenkins added once Gary had scuttled over, showing more consideration than was normal for him.

'Oh no,' Gary replied, waving a hand dismissively. 'I assume you are here about the stolen car.' He reached inside his jacket pocket and began moving towards the front entrance.

Jenkins began to follow but Ruby remained rooted to the spot. 'Are you trying to get rid of us?' she asked coldly. What she really wanted to say was that making assumptions was dangerous and they might have been here to say they had discovered the identity of his wife's murderer, but she knew such a comment would be inappropriate, bordering on cruel.

'Of course not.' He laughed shrilly, turning back to face her. 'It's just that a business such as this relies on its clientele having the utmost confidence in our integrity. The mere presence of police could give the impression of impropriety.'

'I thought you said Mr Petrov wasn't a customer and, unless I'm mistaken…' Ruby decided that a long lingering look around the showroom, which was deserted save for the salesman who had first alerted Gary to their arrival, and was now busying himself over by one of the filing cabinets, would suffice to finish her sentence.

'Fine,' Jenkins said, breaking the tension with a sigh. 'We can take a walk around the back. I'm sure DC Knight would appreciate the chance to view the rest of your stock in any case.'

'Wait!' Gary cried, grabbing Jenkins' shoulder and stopping him in his tracks. The look he received in return was one of pure menace and Gary quickly withdrew his hand. 'No, it's fine to talk here,' he added placatingly, thrusting the piece of paper he had retrieved from his pocket at Jenkins.

The rest of their conversation was as Ruby might have predicted. When challenged about his poker playing, he claimed that his failure to be open about it yesterday had been fear of getting into trouble, whilst at the same time trying to play down the amount of money involved. Ruby saw no question to challenge him on it; if circumstances had been different and they remained suspicious that it might be linked to his wife's murder, then they would have insisted on speaking to each person who had been there that evening.

He continued not to appear concerned about the loss of a car, which they now understood to be a Mercedes AMG GTR and worth in excess of £100,000. Claiming that was why he had to pay extortionate insurance premiums, Ruby detected a certain triumphalism in the way he added that no amount of money could compensate him for the loss of his wife, as though he was attempting to point score, especially with the way he was directly looking at Jenkins as he delivered the claim.

Nevertheless, she had persisted with the sorts of questions she needed to ask, even if Gary's answers were entirely predictable. Why that particular model – these things tend to get stolen to order. Do you expect to get it back – it's probably long left the country by now. Why steal it from your home – the security at the dealership is state of the art. Ruby would almost consider him cold were it not for the way he had been upon first hearing about his wife. Numb, lifeless was probably a more accurate description and in keeping with the sort of loss he had experienced. What's more, she was starting to understand why he was at work today. She guessed it was an unconscious attempt to hang onto a constant whilst the rest of his life was in turmoil. Similarly, it could be something of a defence mechanism; he had already lost something dear to him and was determined he wasn't going to lose any more if he could help it. As healthy as the books looked, he would have a huge amount of capital tied up in the dealership's stock and even a quiet couple of weeks could impact the overall health of the business.

'What did you make of that?' Ruby asked as she and Jenkins headed back to their car, so bland and mundane by comparison to what they'd just seen.

'Hmmm,' came the simplistic response, but Ruby could tell it was more than Jenkins reverting back to his old trick of trying to avoid being engaged in a conversation. Even if the fury of earlier had left his expression, his eyes retained a particular intensity, which now seemed to be mixed with uncertainty.

'Well, I guess it's back to the station unless you can think of another angle,' she said wistfully.

'I guess,' was all she received in return.

*　*　*

Ruby tried not to allow Jenkins' mood to bring her down that afternoon. Whilst she was sure they had developed a bond over the few short weeks of working together, she knew she was still far from understanding him and dismissed his sullenness as just being the reverse of his usual pattern, where he typically started the day in such a way, only to brighten up in the afternoon. Besides, she had much more important things on her mind, and it wasn't the stack of paperwork associated with the case, nor the various loose ends they needed to tie up surrounding neighbours' statements now that they had the details of the stolen car.

What had started out as a fairly casual conversation that morning, if in tone more than actual meaning, had led to Danny calling Ruby's bluff about meeting her parents. The reason for her being late to work hadn't been so much because of her extended lie-in with Danny, but needing to return to Hemel to get changed before coming all the way back to the police station again. That her ability to silence her mother's seemingly endless questions about the man with whom she had spent the night, by claiming she could find out for herself within a matter of hours, was a hollow victory. Ruby had to go through the charade of answering her mother's claims that it was far too short notice for her to arrange something like this, by saying that she would cancel Danny, only to find out that, miraculously, something could be cobbled together in time.

Ruby was under no illusion what he would face when he sat down at the dinner table. Fiona might have left Ireland as soon as she reached adulthood, and expanded her cultural references further by marrying a man from the Caribbean, but the Irish need to feed their guests was so ingrained as to be part of her DNA. Ruby had to withstand a myriad of questions regarding what Danny liked to eat, not that she knew the answer or, much less, cared because Fiona would provide such a comprehensive spread as to cover all bases regardless.

Knowing that Danny's food-related needs would be catered for did not deal with her primary concern. It may have been his idea, but the fact remained that bringing him to her childhood home was a big deal and one that would not have escaped her parents. Even setting aside her mother's propensity for being over-dramatic, Ruby had kept previous boyfriends away until she was fairly certain they represented a long-term proposition. Whereas in the case of Danny, much as she liked him, they hadn't been dating long enough to even have the chat about whether they were *going out* or merely just seeing each other.

One upshot of Ruby's anxiety that Danny was likely to run a mile after tonight was that it made the afternoon speed by far quicker than it ordinarily would have done, and she would need to leave on the button if she were to get home and changed before Danny was due to arrive.

'You coming then?' she called across to Jenkins as she was putting on her coat. Normally it was him trying to usher her out of the door, but he remained in the same position he had adopted all afternoon, head down and writing endless notes, and not just in his little book.

'Not quite yet,' he replied without looking up.

If Ruby hadn't bothered to try and get to the bottom of his mood during the hours back at the office, now wasn't the time. She would just have to hope that he would go home and do whatever it was he did of an evening and come back with a different outlook tomorrow. She hated to admit it, even to herself, but the only thing that kept her going during the grind of a case that didn't want to reveal itself, aside from on days when the man she liked was meeting her parents for the first time, was chatting to Jenkins. She resolved that if he didn't seem more himself in the morning, whatever that was, she would cajole and coerce him into giving up what was keeping him in a mood.

'Fine, well I'm off to enjoy the life side of my work/life balance,' she said, as a final attempt to provoke a reaction.

'Okay, good,' he replied, but in a tone devoid of any true meaning, still apparently distracted by whatever was going through his head.

Chapter Twenty-five

It was nice to wake for once without still feeling tired. The length might have only been a fairly standard seven hours, but the stiffness of her limbs confirmed she must have slept like the dead. Not only had the evening gone far better than she could possibly have hoped for, but it seemed to remove all her anxieties about her blossoming relationship with Danny. It was still early days, but she knew now that he had the potential to be *the one* and, rather than it scare her, she had drawn a certain comfort in it. And that serenity, combined with there being little about the Kelly Hamilton case that still intrigued her, conspired to give her the kind of sleep that had eluded her since she had moved home.

Danny had got off to an excellent start immediately on his arrival. Ruby had heard him pull up and had assumed that the length of time he took to get out of his car was due to him having second thoughts or, at the very least, trying to bring his nerves under control. What he was really doing was wrestling with the two bunches of flowers he had brought, of equal size and stature, but containing different flowers so as not to appear a lazy duplication, as well as a bottle of single malt whisky. In some respects it was the latter that impressed Ruby the most. Knowing her heritage, he could have gone for the more obvious choice of rum, which indeed was Frank's usual tipple, but she took it as a sign that he didn't want to conform to stereotypes.

Then there was Danny's attire. It was smart enough to suggest he was taking the evening seriously, but without looking like he had simply come straight from work. As much as he had set the bar high for his conduct over the rest of the evening, he proceeded to build on his excellent start.

Having charmed her parents, answering all their questions with both clarity and modesty, and making all the right noises about the mountain of food Fiona had prepared, the only thing that worried Ruby was whether he had actually enjoyed the evening. Stealing a few moments to talk to him as he went back to his car, and with her parents having said their farewells on the doorstep, she asked the dreaded question. His response was as enthusiastic as it appeared genuine, and he even said the magic words regarding having her meet his family.

The entire journey into work the following morning had been consumed with thoughts of her living arrangements. Her parents' behaviour the previous night had been as good as she hoped, even if she was under no illusion that most of it had been a response to Danny's magnificence, and she figured that staying there a while longer might not be the worst thing in the world. Certainly she felt more comfortable presenting it to herself this way, rather than as buying herself enough time until Danny invited her to move in with him.

'So much for playing it cool,' she muttered as she waited for the barrier to the station's secure car park to retract. Not that she was overly concerned that she may be getting ahead of herself. If nothing else, what the past few weeks had shown her was that it was important to live in the moment, because you never knew what was around the corner.

Walking into CID she wasn't surprised to see Jenkins' desk empty. As she headed into the kitchenette she found herself ever so slightly looking forward to spending some time with him. His unwillingness to talk about anything other than their investigations would provide a welcome refocus on her immediate priorities. Dreams about waking up to Danny each day, and what would precede it the night before, would now have to wait until tonight. As unlikely as she thought it was that they would discover the identity of Kelly Hamilton's killer, they still had a job to do, and she would not admit they had failed to Nelson or anyone else until all possible avenues had been explored to the full.

'Feeling better today?' she asked as she swung around the corner, only to be met with an empty room. As if to confirm Jenkins' absence, the percolator was full of liquid. A quick glance at the time on her phone confirmed that it was still a couple of minutes until they were due to start work but Ruby could already feel a sense of unease building. She had never known him to be anything other than punctual; he had even arrived early at the estate agents on the Saturday they were supposed to be off work.

Ruby trudged to her desk and spent the next half hour watching the door. First, she sent a text and then she tried phoning him, only to end up with the same automated voicemail message that had thwarted her attempts to get hold of him the last time. When it approached an hour after she had expected him to start, she went to check the rotas; surmising that if he hadn't told her about Cooper returning from his holidays, perhaps he had also failed to mention that he had booked some time off.

'Come in,' Nelson barked when she knocked on his door a short while later. 'Ah, DC Knight, good to see you. How's that murder case coming along?' His tone was more conversational than expectant.

'Yeah, it's about that, guv,' she replied. 'I can't find Jenkins.' She felt uncomfortable enough going to the DCI about this and couldn't bring herself to be more exact and see her partner get into trouble.

'Oh, perhaps he's downstairs getting some files,' Nelson responded with a sly grin. 'You two really should learn to synchronise your time better.'

'No seriously, guv, this isn't at all like him. I sent him a text and have also tried to phone him.'

The laughter that her expression of concern received was unexpected, but Nelson didn't appear to be behaving cruelly. 'Listen, Ruby, I don't want to sound unkind but, as I've explained before, I have worked with Steve for many years. As I said, he is a complex fellow, and I can assure you that I have come to accept the odd… unexplained absence from him. Let's just say that we're likely to hear from him when it gets closer to lunchtime and, based on past experience, I'm sure he will have a thoroughly spectacular but entirely plausible excuse for his errant behaviour.'

Ruby stood there regarding Nelson carefully. Not only did she know exactly what he was alluding to, but it hadn't taken long working with Jenkins to come up with her own theory for his demeanour most mornings.

'Look, if it would ease your mind,' Nelson continued, no doubt sensing that she remained dissatisfied, 'you could always pop round there and pick him up on your way to whatever people you need to visit today. Just make sure you leave in plenty of time to allow him a chance to pull himself together. Understand?'

Ruby merely nodded. However phlegmatic Nelson seemed to be about all this, she still felt a certain loyalty towards her partner, as complex an individual as he might be. Yet she would take up Nelson's suggestion, not so much because, without Jenkins, she was unsure what to do next with the Kelly Hamilton case, but it would help to ease the concern that had been building up inside her so far that morning.

She tried Jenkins' phone number again before getting into her car and it was only when it went through to voicemail once more that she started to consider how she would handle the situation when she arrived at his house. The thing that worried her the most was how he would react to her being there. After spending a month avoiding talking about anything personal, disturbing him was bound to cause an issue between them. She could cope with anger; it could be met head on and always had the tendency to lose its potency over a relatively short period of time. What she didn't want him to feel was humiliation, because that could signal a shift in the balance of their relationship and, no matter how hard she sought to reassure him that it would never be mentioned again, it would remain at the back of both of their minds.

However, as uncomfortable as she felt, Ruby found her curiosity building as she pulled into Jenkins' street in the King Harry housing development. Viewed in isolation these properties wouldn't seem anything special, their '70s design not dissimilar to the Robins' but she knew that to afford one these days would be difficult for anyone on less than a very handsome salary, with it only being a short walk down into Verulamium Park and then on to the cathedral and the city centre.

Just discovering the location, never mind seeing the property itself, revealed more to Ruby about Jenkins than the combined total of her prior knowledge. It certainly suggested that, unless left to him by a relative, he must have lived in St. Albans for many years and, most likely, had a family at some stage.

And judging by what Ruby saw as she pulled up, that stage must have long since passed, with the overgrown front garden matched by dreary, dated curtains pulled across each window, except one of the rooms downstairs. But there was the unmistakable sight of the unmarked

Ford Mondeo, confirming that, as well as this being the right house, Jenkins was highly likely to be inside.

Taking a deep breath, as she dodged the stinging nettles reaching out to her on the short path up to the doorway, she decided that, in the absence of a doorbell, she would begin knocking quietly, and build from there until she finally heard movement from within.

'Jesus, how much of a state must you be in,' she muttered when she found herself hammering on the door. She was contemplating seeing if she could fight her way around to the back when she was disturbed by one of Jenkins' neighbours.

'Can I help you?' The round lady in her early sixties enquired suspiciously, folding her arms across her ample chest.

'I'm looking for my colleague,' Ruby replied, trying to remove any hint of defensiveness from her tone.

'Steve, you mean? Nah, I often see him come and go but rarely does he stop outside long enough to speak to anyone. Nice enough fellow, even if we'd all benefit if he decided to take a bit more care of things.' The woman nodded at her neighbour's front garden, as if any indication were needed as to what she was referring to. 'But, then again, it was terribly sad what happened to his wife. Tragedy like that can change a man.'

'His wife?' Ruby exclaimed, instantly knowing that she had made an error.

Jenkins' neighbour's eyes narrowed. 'A colleague you say? Have you got some form of identification then?'

'Yes I do,' she replied tersely, crossing her own arms to indicate that she didn't intend producing anything of the sort. 'When did you last see Mr Jenkins?'

'Like I said, I rarely see him these days, but I often hear his car pull in and out.'

'And?'

'And I think I heard him come back yesterday evening. Look, what's this all about?'

'Nothing that concerns you,' Ruby replied, turning away despite knowing full well that this was unlikely to see the woman retreat into the confines of her own home. Fearing that resuming her banging on the front door would only lead to a resumption of the questions, she waded through the overgrown grass to the downstairs window. The first thing she noticed as she peered through was the dated sofa, and she widened her angle to get a more comprehensive view of the living room. Ruby half expected to find Jenkins slumped in an adjacent armchair, empty bottles strewn around him, but when she did spot him, the sight that greeted her presented her with an altogether different shock.

'Holy shit!' she roared, the instant dumping of adrenaline in her system ordering her to move but she fought against it just to make sure she wasn't mistaking what she could see through the door and into the hallway beyond. The lower half of a body was dangling in front of the open staircase, its feet half a metre or so suspended above the floor.

'What is it?' demanded the neighbour, the insistence in her voice mixed with fear.

'Call an ambulance!' Ruby shouted back, rushing towards the front door. The house may have been dilapidated, but the frames of the windows and doors seemed to be the modern UPV type and she didn't hold out much hope of being able to bust her way in. But she had to try, she needed to see if those legs belonged to the person she thought they did.

Ruby first aimed a hard kick, which in reality was more of a stamp where the sole of her foot met the door just below the handle. It did cause it to flex slightly in the middle but that only served to highlight there were further anchor points, top and bottom. Next she barged it, trying to distribute the contact more evenly over the surface of the door. Again there was a modicum of movement but all it really did was send a jarring sensation through Ruby's shoulder and down her torso.

She was about to go again, despite knowing that applying more pressure was likely to see herself injured. As she stepped back a few paces to take more of a run at it she was halted by a shout from next door. 'Wait, I think I have a key!' The woman was still holding her telephone and Ruby could see doubt in her eyes.

'Lou gave it to me, you know, just in case of emergencies. That was back when they first moved in and long before she–'

'Just fucking get it then!' Ruby roared at her, not interested in the history surrounding how she came to be in possession of it. She would just have to hope, as this woman was beginning to allude to, that the locks hadn't been changed in the meantime.

'Perhaps I should be the one…' The woman was saying as she came stumbling back out of her house a few moments later but Ruby was not interested in conducting this discussion either. Snatching it from her, and causing the woman to recoil in shock, she was back at the lock in the blink of an eye.

'Just hold on,' she called through the door as she thrust the key in the lock, despite knowing how pointless the words were. Just as she turned the handle, she thought she could hear the faint sound of a siren but gave it no more consideration because she was in.

The light that streamed around her into the hallway illuminated enough of Jenkins that she could see his skin was deathly pale and bloodless, except for the bruising that surrounded the electrical cable tied around his neck. Blinking back tears, and not giving a damn about preserving the integrity of the scene or whatever such shit, she bounded up the stairs to untie him. 'Grab his legs,' she yelled in response to the gasp of horror she heard from the doorway. She desperately fought to untie the rudimentary knot that had secured the flex to the post at the top of the stairs. Even though she understood the reality of the situation, she couldn't bear the thought of Jenkins' body slamming against the ground. And yet, ruin as she did the fingernails she usually took such care of, its weight was preventing her getting any real purchase on the cord.

'Have you got him?' she barked, though the grunts she could hear from below provided her with the answer. 'I need you to lift him up, so I can untie him, but be prepared for when I do.'

But whatever effort Jenkins' neighbour was exerting wasn't enough and the tears of fear that were silently coursing down Ruby's face soon turned into sobs of frustration. She didn't know how long she remained like this, desperately scrabbling until the tips of her fingers were bloodied and raw, and it wasn't until she heard the rush of footsteps outside that she regained her senses.

Moments later a female paramedic was trying to ease her away from where she was crouched. Part of Ruby wanted to fight back; she was meant to do this for her colleague, her partner, and she had failed. Instead she allowed herself to be led back down the stairs and out into the front garden where the neighbour was now waiting.

'Do you think he's…?' she asked, seemingly unable to bring herself to complete the question. Ruby didn't even look at the woman, much less answer her and sat down on the grass, pulling her knees in to make herself into a ball. And she waited like this, refusing requests from the paramedics for them to tend to her injuries, until DCI Nelson arrived.

Chapter Twenty-six

'You're not driving like this,' Nelson said, his voice serious enough to convey that the matter wasn't up for discussion. 'You'll ride with me and I'll have someone else bring your car back to the station.'

Ruby spent the short journey trying to avoid Nelson's attempts to engage her in conversation but once there, she knew she couldn't survive unless she tried to express some of the mix of emotions that were flooding her mind.

'Look, I can be the one to take the statement from you and that way we can also try and figure out how we cope with this,' Nelson said after considering her visible anguish for a few moments.

Ruby knew in this instance that he was the right person to be speaking to. Not only did he have a duty of care towards her, but he understood Jenkins better than she did. Whilst the rest of the team were largely friendly to her, and she knew she could offload onto someone like DC Christie, with the exception of Cooper, whom she had barely said two words to, no-one seemed to appreciate Jenkins' qualities.

'Okay, run me through what happened from the point you decided to take up my suggestion of going round to his house,' Nelson said when they were sat in the easy chairs Ruby had never previously occupied.

Ruby sipped at the cup of water that had been placed on the coffee table between them, in an attempt to compose herself before having to run through the horror of the past hour. Emotion and feelings would come later; for the moment she needed to concentrate on as dispassionate a chronology of events as she could muster.

Nelson maintained his silence throughout, regarding her with fierce concentration. It was only when she finished her statement at the point when she was escorted outside the house, where she remained until Nelson arrived, that he put aside his sense of professionalism, indicating to Ruby that, with the formalities out of the way, she could do the same.

'I can't imagine how awful it must have been for you,' he said, unable to avoid glancing down at her still-bloodied hands. 'I'm so sorry I put you in that situation.'

'You weren't to know,' she said with her head dropped, before lifting it so her eyes could meet his. Ruby didn't know why she was worried about his feelings when hers were so painful, but she needed him to know that she didn't blame him for what she had been forced to endure. 'Why... why do you think he did it?' This was the question that kept swirling around her mind and just voicing it was ever so slightly soothing.

'I... I told you he was a complex individual,' Nelson began, snapping the whole of Ruby's attention towards him. 'I know I alluded to it before, but it wasn't my place to say anything. I guess I owe it to you now to be a bit more specific to avoid you thinking you might have been, in some small way, responsible.' Until this point Ruby had not even considered that she may have some culpability but, in Nelson saying so, she was convinced that her thoughts would have headed down this dark path at some point. 'When I said we had worked together for many years that was true. When I first started out in CID in

Watford he had recently become a DI. We weren't partnered up or anything, but I still saw him as my mentor. I had made it as a detective early in my career, much as you have, and Steve was the man I wanted to become after a few years in the job.'

Although Nelson had started to become absorbed by his own recollections, he paused at this point and Ruby could feel he was studying her expression to see if this claim required qualifying.

'I guess you must have seen some of that person in him,' he said, 'otherwise I doubt you would have been so keen to remain his partner. You see, there was an effortlessness to the way he conducted an investigation. Not the dispassionate and, dare I say, disinterested way others here would describe him, more an assurance that he knew what he was doing. In the beginning I even thought it was just arrogance until I saw him pump out result after result. The best way I can describe it is as intuition, you know?'

Ruby nodded, believing that she did; if nothing else but for the way Jenkins had learned where to trust her qualities early on, resulting in the effective way he had read the situation in Samie's house that Saturday morning.

'The change in him was subtle at first, almost imperceptible. The outcomes of his investigations remained strong, but he lost some of that sparkle, that swagger that had defined my perception of him in my first few years in CID. It was only when our DCI moved on and he resisted all calls for him to apply for the position that I found out what had gone wrong. His wife had been diagnosed with cervical cancer. They had only been married a few years and she could only have been in her mid-thirties,' he said, shaking his head as though he could barely believe it even now. 'Only a couple of the people in the department knew about it and they decided to tell me to stop me going on about the promotion he should have been going for.

'To be fair to him, his work didn't really slip throughout the whole time she was being treated, during which I moved up to DI. By all accounts the chemo had gone well but, and it must have been five or six years after she was first diagnosed, they found that the cancer had spread. IVB I think they called it, where it had begun attacking her liver as well as her bones.

'She… she didn't last much longer after that,' Nelson concluded quickly, cuffing at the tears that had formed in the corners of his eyes.

Ruby didn't know what to say, so she reached across and put, what she hoped would be seen as, a reassuring hand on his shoulder. She recoiled when it elicited a laugh, but she quickly realised that it was bitterness rather than amusement that had prompted it.

'I… I never even met the woman, you know, and here I am ten years later still crying about her death,' he continued.

'It's okay,' Ruby said, her own tears forming once more. 'You didn't have to know her to be affected by her passing; you could see the impact on your… your friend.'

'Huh,' Nelson snorted. 'Some friend I was. Within about six months I had secured myself another promotion and moved here.'

'It's alright,' said Ruby, not usually one for indulging people in their self-pity. 'So how did he end up with you here, then?'

'Well, as you know, Watford's only just up the road and I started to hear… things.'

'About his drinking?'

'Yes. The people who knew him like I did had either moved on themselves or had remained in fairly junior positions. He was never caught drinking on the job, but his time-keeping became erratic along with his moods.'

'So, what, you had him transferred over here?'

'More or less,' Nelson shrugged. 'Given everything he was and everything he'd been through I thought a little time in a different, quieter, environment might see him straight. I also thought that the shorter journey into work would help him,' he added, but his smile soon faded.

'And did it?' Ruby asked, instantly regretting the question, given where Jenkins was now.

'Well, not as much as I'd hoped,' he replied evenly. 'He might never have returned to the person I had looked up to with such admiration, but we found a… certain equilibrium. I guess you could say he repaid my faith in him by not displaying the sort of characteristics that were getting him into trouble back in Watford. Plus, I knew I could trust him with certain investigations, perhaps not to do a stellar job, but a solid one.'

'So why now, all these years later?' Ruby enquired, getting back to her original question. 'If anything, wouldn't you say he'd improved recently?'

'Like I said the other week, I knew putting you two together was a bit of a gamble but, and you know this probably better than I do, it seemed to be paying off.'

'I liked him,' she responded; those simple words causing fresh tears to fall. 'I didn't know him, I get that, but I had started to enjoy working with him and that… that makes this all the harder for me to understand. He had even started to seem a little brighter in the mornings which I thought meant he…' She paused, thinking. 'I didn't smell any alcohol on him,' she continued, reflecting back on those awful minutes in the house.

'We'll have to wait for the toxicology report but Jenkins, like many addicts, was adept at hiding things. Of course people suspected it, but he never gave anyone cause to blow the whistle on it. But what you say might be true, often it is when people start to clean up their act that they start to fully appreciate how messed up their life has become.'

'So, you do think I might have had something to do with it,' Ruby said quietly.

Now it was Nelson's turn to try and offer some kind of physical reassurance, and he moved to the seat next to her. 'If you did, it was only because you managed what I hadn't in all the years he had been here with me. You saw the way he was when you first arrived, and you saw the state of his house; the family home he had purchased with his wife when the future had seemed so full of promise. You couldn't call what he had now a life; he was merely existing. Perhaps he finally realised that.'

It wasn't the continued implication that she was somehow responsible, however delicately put, that was causing the anger to rise in Ruby; it was how quickly Nelson seemed willing to come to terms with what had happened. 'You told me you never would have sent me round there if you had even suspected that was something I might find.' She didn't know whether it was the words themselves or the bitter way she delivered them that caused him to recoil as though slapped.

'I… I didn't,' he stammered. 'How could you even think such a thing?'

'Then why are you finding it so easy now to explain all this away?' Although her attack remained vicious, she didn't really believe there was anything suspicious about his suggestion to go to his house. 'I just think you're too willing to accept that this was suicide,' she added, a little more calmly.

'But what else could it be?' Nelson countered, his voice shrill. 'From what I saw, and what you told me, I can't expect the evidence to come back as suggesting anything else.'

Ruby opened her mouth to protest some more but knew she had nothing on which to base a counter-argument. She might still not be able to accept that Jenkins would have sought to end his own life, in spite of what Nelson had just told her about the extent of his problems, but that didn't mean it wasn't true. What's more, she was conscious that she was attempting to rationalise what was inherently a deeply irrational act. Her Catholic upbringing may have tried to teach her that humans were different to animals but all her time in the police had shown her was that the only difference was that animals weren't cruel. Sure, they were often single-minded, and the animal kingdom could be a violent place, but that violence was only ever to serve a purpose, an instinct for survival, and never as a source of entertainment. Who was she to try and understand what would drive someone to take their own life when she, for all her own anxieties, had never experienced tragedy nor mental health issues.

'It's okay,' Nelson soothed, perhaps sensing some of her inner turmoil. 'And I promise you that we'll look into anything that comes back as suspicious but if you're going to stand any hope of coming to terms with this, you need to accept things for how they currently are.'

'Yes, guv,' she said, her voice devoid of any real feeling.

'I think it might be wise if you considered taking some time off.' As delicately as it was put, Ruby detected that it was more of an instruction than a request.

'I'm not sure I've accrued any holidays yet,' she said, knowing that Nelson was likely to tell her that this was not what he had meant. 'I don't want to,' she added, hoping honesty would prove more effective.

Nelson sighed, rubbing his head. 'Well you're not staying today, that's for certain. You're still in shock and you need to go home and be around those you love. If you still feel the same way tomorrow then we can chat, but I need you to understand that if you wanting to be here is through a sense of duty, or somehow because you're new to the job, then you need to forget that. You're a promising detective, Ruby, but you need some time to heal.'

'And what about you, guv?' she asked, preferring not to respond directly to his claim. 'Don't you deserve some time to come to terms with things? For all the pain I'm feeling, I've only known Jenkins a few weeks whereas you…'

'It's not as simple as that,' Nelson interrupted firmly. 'I have a department to run and I have to put its needs above my own.'

Ruby didn't have the energy to combat such stubbornness, especially as any claims to the contrary would undermine her own resolve that she would be better burying her head in work than moping around at home. Fixing him with what she hoped was a reassuring smile she said, whilst standing up, 'I know that you're my boss and everything, but you can always talk to me if you need to.'

She didn't wait for a reply and her swift departure from his office was matched by the speed with which she crossed CID and descended the stairs. She had struggled to maintain some semblance of control of her emotions whilst she had been in with Nelson, and knew that one look at the pitying faces of her colleagues would cause her to crack.

It was only once she was safely back in her car, parked in a spot she never would have selected and a further reminder of how different this morning had been to any other, that she allowed the sobs to wrack her body.

Chapter Twenty-seven

Driving off, with her vision still blurred, she only activated the car's Bluetooth connection to her phone because she wanted to ring ahead to warn her parents. If they saw her getting out of the car only a few hours into her shift, and looking the state that she undoubtedly was, they would be beset with worry. Even though it would only last a few moments, she wished to spare them that and would call to explain that she was coming home. But as she swiped through her contacts list on the car's touchscreen she found herself settling on Danny's number instead. She wasn't sure she had made anything more than a passing reference to Jenkins when speaking to him, but it was his voice she wanted to hear. He would be at work and unable to meet her but perhaps it was a reminder of what she had in her own life, in stark contrast to the barren existence of Jenkins', that may start the process of her recovery.

'Ruby, what is it?' he asked by way of greeting, the concern in his voice reverberating around the car's speaker system.

'I'm sorry, Danny, I haven't disturbed you, have I?'

'No, it was a boring meeting and I was glad of an excuse to step out of it,' he said jovially before taking on a serious tone once more. 'You've never called me during the day before. Is something the matter?'

Such a simple question but she didn't know where to begin, and she instantly regretted putting Danny in this position. Standing in a corridor somewhere was not the ideal situation for him to have to deal with this. 'Something happened at work today.' She heard the sharp intake of breath on the other end of the line. 'But I'm okay by the way,' she added hurriedly. 'Well, I guess I'm not, but I mean that I haven't been injured or anything... I just needed to hear your voice.'

'Oh, Jesus, I'm so sorry babe,' he replied, those simple words causing any doubt Ruby held about the wisdom of calling him to evaporate. 'What can I do to help?'

Ruby smiled, despite herself. 'Like I said, I just needed to hear your voice.'

'Look I can knock off early once I have finished up here,' he said, seemingly ignoring her claim. 'If you can do so too, come and meet me at my flat and I can look after you.'

'I'm on my way home already,' she said.

'That's fine,' he responded but his voice sounded conflicted. 'Of course it is but... if you wanted some space or anything in the meantime you could just head round to mine. You could help yourself to whatever and, you know, watch some TV or something until I get back.' He stopped talking but Ruby sensed this was just a pause, rather than him waiting for her answer. 'That's if... if you want to...'

'I do,' she replied truthfully, 'but how will I get in?'

'Oh shit, yeah, sorry,' he said, sounding genuinely disappointed. 'Tell you what, I was going to ask my PA to go out and get me some lunch. I'll have her come round to give you the keys instead. I reckon I could get her there in under half an hour. That okay?'

'Yes, and thanks,' Ruby said, hanging up before she could think of a reason to change her mind or contemplate how important Danny's job must really be if, not only did he have a PA, but also one he could send on personal errands.

Parking up in one of the allocated bays within ten minutes of finishing the call, Ruby decided she wouldn't bother her parents with her news until later. Instead, she got out and wandered to the mini-market, which looked little more than a glorified newsagents, opposite the block of apartments. The selection of produce on offer might have been limited but it all appeared fresh and she decided to pick up some items with which she could put dinner together. Even before Danny's latest act of kindness, she still had much to thank him for, and she hoped that being able to prepare a nice meal would go some way to rewarding him. She would also use it as a way of reassurance that today's awful event hadn't completely wrecked her. Ruby was conscious that it was still very early days in her relationship and, as much as she would need to lean on him this evening, especially when deciding what to do about work tomorrow, she didn't want to sow any seeds of doubt in his mind regarding her resilience.

Neither her mother's competency nor her father's flamboyance in the kitchen had rubbed off on Ruby and she decided that it would be dangerous to over-stretch her limited capabilities in an effort to impress Danny. Ordinarily when called on to cook, she would select a pasta dish but elected to try something different because she didn't want it to stand in comparison to Danny's excellent meal the other evening. Instead she settled on something that wouldn't require a flurry of last-minute activity – she would use her spare time alone in the flat to get everything prepared.

Danny had been true to his word and it was early afternoon that she heard him buzz up to be allowed in. If he felt awkward at having to request access to his own flat, he didn't show it as he held up a bottle of wine for her to see through the small video monitor.

'I guess you could probably do with a drink,' he said, when she finally greeted him at the door.

'I hope you don't mind but I already helped myself to one,' she responded guiltily, indicating to the largely empty wine glass perched on the kitchen worktop. Deciding what to cook had consumed all her thoughts in the mini-mart and she had relied on rummaging through his cupboards to find something alcoholic.

'Me casa es tu casa,' he replied in a mock Mexican accent, instantly removing any concern that he might have found her behaviour presumptuous. Not that helping herself to wine in his absence was anything like as bad as what she had got up to once the casserole had been left to bubble away slowly.

Convincing herself that it was better to remain occupied, Ruby had eschewed switching on the television in favour of checking out the daytime view from the balcony. However, seeing everyone going about their business was only a reminder that she ordinarily would have been doing something similar; soon causing her to retreat back inside. Wandering around the living area and having a closer look at Danny's stuff had seen her quickly drawn to the bedroom. Mere sight of it caused her to rekindle fond memories and, for the first time since this morning, she could feel a positive emotion truly begin to compete with the pain inside her. More than that it felt naughty, wrong even, to be somewhere so personal without Danny's permission but the thought that he could return home any time soon only made her more reluctant to leave. As she looked in his wardrobe and carefully went through his drawers, she didn't know what she expected to find, though until then Danny had only ever come across as the perfect gentlemen. That she found nothing that might suggest otherwise, was as disappointing as it had been reassuring.

'I hope you also don't mind but I have begun preparing dinner,' she responded. 'It won't be ready for a couple of hours and I've tried not to make too much of a mess.'

'Smells wonderful,' he said, sweeping her up into his arms. A few moments later, as he began to pull away, she could see the seriousness in his expression. It wasn't so much that she wasn't ready to reveal the reason for her unexpected visit, she just knew that she didn't want to get caught up in all that until she had made the most of only the second opportunity she'd had to be alone with him. She led him into the bedroom with a confidence that she trusted he wouldn't mistake as familiarity with the room.

Chapter Twenty-eight

'Are you sure about this?' Danny asked her the next day. 'I could shift a couple of meetings back to this afternoon and we could spend the morning together.'

'As much as I could think of nothing better, I really need to do this,' she said with a reassuring smile.

'Okay,' he replied, with just the right amount of disappointment in his tone. 'But will you come back round tonight, you know, it's the weekend and everything?'

Ruby shifted position in the bed to better look into his eyes. His expression matched the sincerity of his tone. 'I'm not sure,' she replied. 'Again, I could think of nothing I want more but I really should see my parents. I haven't even told them about…'

'Seriously, there's no pressure from here, I just want you to know that you're always welcome.' He paused for a moment before offering her a shy smile. 'But it would be nice to see you at some point this weekend.'

'Agreed,' she said, rolling away to sit on the edge of the bed. 'However, on my next visit I really must bring more than just what I'm wearing.' On this occasion she didn't plan on going back to Hemel; using the extra time to pick up some cheap underwear and a new shirt from the supermarket on the way into the station.

* * *

It wasn't just her new clothes that made her feel uncomfortable as she ascended the stairs up to CID. She knew that Nelson would want to interrogate her over her decision to return to work so soon. The truth was she wasn't sure that it was a good idea and, in the absence of a compelling justification, she would need him to trust her instincts.

Like Jenkins had.

That she had slept reasonably well last night, she believed was more because she was still in shock, rather than the combined effects of Danny's company and the couple of bottles of wine they had worked through.

As soon as she punched in the code to gain entry she marched over to Nelson's office. If she went to her desk and tried to act like everything was normal, he was more likely to be suspicious. 'Good morning, guv,' she said, whilst giving a light rap on the open door.

'Hello, Ruby,' he said in a voice that suggested he wasn't in the least bit surprised to see her arrive at work today. 'Come and sit down.' He indicated at the chair in front of his desk rather than the more relaxed area they had used yesterday. 'I can see this playing out one of two ways. You're going to try and convince me you're fine and your argument will either be based on you having only worked with Steve for a month, or that you're as tough as nails and you're more than capable of coping with what you witnessed yesterday. Am I right?'

'No,' she replied, satisfied that her response wasn't a lie given she hadn't decided how she was going to approach this conversation. 'I just don't see how moping around at home is going to help things.'

'I guess I can see where you're coming from with that one,' Nelson said.

'And we still have an investigation to complete,' she added.

He nodded slowly. 'Do you require any help with that?'

Ruby knew exactly what Nelson getting at, and although she clearly would need a new partner at some point, that was certainly not something she was ready to face today. 'In all honesty, I think we might be about done with it. At one stage we thought we might be on to something, but it didn't seem to check out.'

'It happens,' he said agreeably. 'Seeing as it's Friday, why don't you just concentrate on that today and see where you are by the close of play. If you need to go anywhere and could do with someone with you, just get the duty sergeant downstairs to allocate you someone from uniform.'

'Okay, guv,' she said, standing up and doubting that she would do any such thing.

'And if you need to talk…' Nelson added as she started walking out.

There was something in his tone that caused Ruby to stop. She had been so consumed by her own thoughts that she hadn't considered how hard he might be taking it. Certainly the dark circles under his eyes suggested he had got little sleep last night. 'And the same goes for you,' she said with a weak smile.

Keen to keep herself busy, if for no other reason than to make the others in the office less likely to approach her, Ruby buried herself in her work. She went through everything associated with the murder of Kelly Hamilton with a fine-tooth comb and, whilst it kept her occupied for the best part of the day, it hadn't taken her long to accept that it wasn't going to lead her anywhere.

She wasn't hungry at lunchtime but took a walk into town all the same. As she sat on a bench picking at a fairly tasteless pre-packed sandwich, she brought out her phone to text Danny. As she punched in the overly-cheerful message, she realised that it was a poor substitute for what she really wanted to do – speak to him.

Today the phone call was better timed and he was able to take his lunchbreak in order to speak to her at length. Ruby figured that Nelson was unlikely to complain if she took a little longer for her own break than was strictly appropriate.

What had started off as a pleasant conversation in which they avoided discussing whether she would come over again that night, in favour of planning an activity for Sunday, soon moved on to how Ruby was finding things at work. She didn't really want to discuss it, partly through wishing to go back to talking about more enjoyable things and also because she knew that Danny would be thinking she had made the wrong decision by going in today. Yet, she soon found herself offloading about how stuck she was with the investigation and that it felt like she was only treading water until she got shifted onto something else next week.

'I just… I just don't want to let it go,' she sniffed.

'Because it's the last connection you have with Jenkins?' Danny enquired.

'Kind of. I feel I owe it to him to finish what we started, but without him, I don't know where to look.'

'Remember how you told me last night that you felt you were getting close to him because he could predict what you were going to do and vice versa?'

'Yes?' she replied, pawing at a silent tear rolling down her cheek.

'Well I hope this doesn't sound stupid or anything, but if you knew what he was going to say, why not imagine he was still there to bounce some ideas off.'

'What, like consider how he would react to any theories I have?' Ruby tried to hide the scepticism she felt at this suggestion because she knew that Danny was only trying to be helpful.

'Why not? What have you got to lose?' he replied evenly.

* * *

Having said goodbye to Danny and thrown away the remains of her lunch, Ruby wandered back to the station considering the advice she'd been offered. It still sounded a little too much like something one would do in the movies but, at the very least, it may give her a little more focus for the rest of the afternoon. She knew she would be able to enjoy the weekend better if she had something to tell Nelson before she left, and a thread to follow up on Monday morning.

Back at her desk, and having been unable to resist getting a coffee from the kitchenette, she began to look through everything associated with the case again. On the face of it, all was exactly as it had been presented. The home invasion had been committed to steal a very particular car. The delay in finding out the specific vehicle hadn't prevented them being able to run the plates through the country's vast network of Automatic Number Plate Recognition cameras. The car's failure to trigger a single ANPR was hardly a surprise, given any professional criminal worth his salt would switch the registration plates as soon as they were out of the immediate vicinity.

Kelly Hamilton's death might seem to some like an unnecessary over-exuberance on the part of the robbers but suggested the brutal realties of organized crime, which relies on ensuring there are no witnesses to blow the whistle on their activities. In so many respects it was a cut and dried case that, with no leads, was bound to be wrapped up by Nelson following her discussion with him that afternoon.

Ruby was conscious that she was probably only thinking this because the acid case had turned out to be different to how it first appeared, but she remained troubled by Gary Hamilton. Even though each of his individual behaviours could be explained away, combined, she found them hard to ignore. Yes, his disinterest in the car being stolen was perfectly understandable given what had happened to his wife and, sure, his unhelpfulness the next morning could be explained by fear that the illicit poker tournament could get people into trouble. But then there was his swift return to work and his unwillingness to discuss the details, despite there being no customers in sight. Again, all attributable with reasons, but in combination…

'Hold on,' she muttered, sifting through the various financial statements that had been pulled whilst they had been investigating the gambling angle. They had been so fixed on seeing whether it had got him into any difficulties that they hadn't considered the other element associated with it. Apparently they only got together to play poker once a month, hardly frequent enough to constitute an addiction. But the car-jackers had chosen that very night to rob his house. Surely that was one coincidence too many?

Taking Danny's advice from earlier she first considered what she would suggest they do with that information and then imagined Jenkins' response. She would be desperate to go and confront Gary about it, but Jenkins would try and temper her by asking what she expected the likely response to be. He might even go as far as to say she would be making a fool of herself, barging into the dealership and asking him to explain why he thought they had picked the one night when he would definitely have been out.

And what would she do when met with such a claim by Jenkins? Aside from getting the hump she would know that she needed more than just a wild theory if she were to convince him they should act on it. In the absence of any genuine evidence she knew her chances of winning him round would be based on the extent he believed that Gary was a potential suspect.

'This is no use,' she said out loud, feeling the frustration bubbling up within her. What she had told Danny about her blossoming partnership with Jenkins may have been true, but it was more lop-sided than she had made out. They were working more effectively because he had learned where her thoughts and talents lay, undoubtedly helped by the way she wore her heart on her sleeve. But if any confirmation had been needed that Jenkins remained largely a closed book, then yesterday morning surely proved it. She may have noticed him become more withdrawn as the day before wore on, but she hadn't for one moment considered it was leading him to anything like that. She had merely put it down to his confrontation with Gary at the dealership reversing the good mood he had started the day in.

Certainly the barely veiled hostility Jenkins had shown was curious. Ruby tended to be the one to make snap judgements on others whilst Jenkins remained more objective but, by that stage, she had even started to feel guilty for the dislike she had developed for a man who had just lost his wife. Surely, given what Jenkins had been through in his own life, he was likely to be even more sympathetic towards Gary.

Ruby could perhaps begin to understand how it might have related to his decision to commit suicide if it had come the night after they had discovered what had happened to Kelly Hamilton. But a couple of days later and when Gary was hardly an emotional wreck? It just didn't make sense.

'DC Knight, can we have that chat now?' Nelson called across CID to her.

'Can you give me five minutes please, guv?' Ruby took his retreat back into his office as acceptance of her request. She couldn't go and speak to him like this. Even if she managed not to blurt everything out, he was liable to then just see her apparent lack of progress as a sign to put this case to bed.

She needed more time to think things through.

Now she recalled Jenkins' odd behaviour at the dealership, she was hard pressed to move on from it, much less accept that it may have something to do with what happened later. If only he had opened up to her about what he had been thinking rather than spending all afternoon silently writing at his desk.

'Oh. My. God.' Ruby declared, not bothered in the slightest about the odd looks this provoked from those around her. As she strode across the office she saw Nelson coming to his door again. 'Not now, guv,' she said, holding a finger up to emphasise that it was not a good time.

A quick shuffle through what was on Jenkins' desk confirmed that it wasn't there. 'Keys,' she called out. 'Who would have a key to his drawers?'

'Ruby, what is it?' Nelson hissed at her in a low voice, with an expression that suggested he was finding her behaviour worryingly erratic.

'It's fine, guv,' she whispered back, trying to fix her face with a reassuring smile. 'Did you know that Jenkins always filled in a little notebook each day? Perhaps there is something in there that might…' She paused, looking into Nelson's eyes. Was she really going to claim there could be a clue in there as to what tipped him over the edge? '…might help me with the investigation.'

'Er, okay,' he replied uncertainly, pulling a small ring of keys out of his trouser pocket. 'I think one of these should do it.'

'Great,' she said, grabbing them and trying to calm herself down before finding the correct one. Despite her efforts to retain a semblance of normality she couldn't help but give a little cry of delight when the fourth turned the lock.

But the drawer had nothing more than some random stationary and an empty crisp packet. The other two drawers yielded a similarly unsatisfactory bounty.

'But he always…' Ruby began to protest. Now was definitely not the time to get into Jenkins' insistence that he complete his notes and lock them away before finishing each night. 'It'll be in his glovebox then. Guv, do you mind if I go back to his house to collect it?'

'If you think it might be useful, then sure,' Nelson replied a little too enthusiastically, signalling to Ruby that he would be only too happy to have her out of the office for a while; perhaps hoping that if she took her time it would be the end of the day and she would have the weekend to get a grip on things before having to start again on Monday.

'Great, I won't be long,' she said, already heading for the door. 'Oh wait!' She turned back. 'I'm going to need a key to get into the car. Do you have a spare one of those?'

'His personal effects are probably still downstairs, why don't you grab his key on the way out?'

Ruby attempted to compose herself as she entered the duty area. It was one thing for Nelson to see her erratic behaviour, but it wouldn't aid the situation if she seemed all crazed in front of uniform. 'Hey, Sarge,' she said casually to the guy filling out his logbook at the desk. Things were quiet down there; a situation that was likely to change once the public hit the pubs as a start to their weekend.

'Good afternoon,' he responded without any real warmth, and barely offering her a glance before continuing with his writing. Under other circumstances she might have found the link between this and Jenkins' near obsession with his own notes amusing. Yet she would not react to his passive hostility; although her intention had always been to go into CID, she had worked with plenty of officers who had viewed plain clothes as having a superiority complex.

'I understand the personal effects of DI Jenkins might be stored down here.'

This elicited a far more positive response than her cheery greeting had. The duty sergeant put down his pen and looked up at Ruby as though seeing her for the first time. Although he remained business-like, the change in demeanour could only have been due to him knowing Jenkins, at least on some level.

He called over a young officer and had him lead her to evidence storage. It took Ruby a few moments to find what she had come for. Opening the first box with Jenkins' name on it she saw the set of Ford keys shining under the harsh sodium light. Judging by how few other items were in there, they had only taken those on his person and, had he hung them up on his arrival home, she would have needed to look elsewhere.

She gave a small humourless chuckle as she remembered the first time she had regarded Jenkins in his baggy, cheap suit. Not that she suspected anything at the time, but it always amazed her how many alcoholics, or alcohol dependents, whatever the distinction was, happened to be skinny. Ruby had always been fortunate with her physique but a night on the town inevitably seemed to make her put on a pound or two. It appeared that the benefit of still wearing the same suits from his healthier days had been the amount of storage space it afforded him, if the contents of the box was anything to go by. As well as a wallet bulging with cards and receipts, but with no sign of any actual money, there was his mobile phone, four biros, three pay slips, a couple of letters and, underneath them…

His small black notebook.

'Are you okay in there, ma'am?' the young officer called in.

'Yes,' she said pushing past him, hoping that her mock irritation with his impatience would do a sufficient job to cover up her shocked expression.

DCI Nelson was still in the open-plan CID area, talking to another detective, when Ruby burst back through the door. His look of displeasure at seeing her again was soon replaced by one of concern as he took in the manner of her appearance.

'Got a minute, guv?' she said, striding towards his office.

'I knew I shouldn't have left it to you to decide when to return to work,' he hissed at her after jogging to catch up.

'Look, I get that you think I have been acting strangely this afternoon but you're going to want to see this,' Ruby said triumphantly as he closed the door.

'What is it?' he asked, not bothering to have either of them sit down.

'It's Jenkins' notebook,' she said, holding it aloft. 'It was in with his personal items.' All this did was generate a blank look from Nelson. 'Only those things he actually had on him when he… he died.'

Nelson sighed and moved to one of the easy chairs. 'Sit down Ruby.'

'Guv, don't you see what this means?'

'No,' he replied flatly; no hint that he was even remotely interested in being enlightened.

'This notebook was found on his body,' she said, trying to mask her impatience. 'Jenkins never took it home with him. He always locked it in his desk here or, if he was out, in the glovebox. He was very insistent about ensuring he didn't take his work home with him.'

Nelson let out a snort which Ruby knew she would need to ignore, despite finding it sounding to her more cruel than ironic.

'When it wasn't in his drawers I assumed it must have been in his car, hence why I asked you for the keys but I forgot that we were here at knocking off time and so it wouldn't be the kind of situation where he'd need to leave it in his glovebox. Also, he was usually the one to try and convince me to go home but that night I left before him. He said he was nearly done but he was still filling this in, and I needed to be somewhere and I–'

'Hold on!' Nelson said, raising his hand. 'You're making even less sense now. What exactly is it that you're trying to tell me?'

Ruby took a deep breath, sensing she only had one more shot at this. She needed him to see the significance, rather than continue to view her discovery as trivial. More than that, she would have to go beyond stating how out of character it was for Jenkins, and offer Nelson some form of explanation as to what this all meant.

But Nelson beat her to it. 'Have you checked what he was writing in there? You said he was busy filling it in when you left. Perhaps there might be some clue…'

Ruby cursed herself for charging back up to CID so hastily. The whole initial purpose of finding the book was so she could follow Jenkins' train of thought. It was meant to have been about the case itself, but it made sense that it could also contain an indication of where his personal thoughts were heading. So much for trying to convince Nelson that she was on to something; now she just appeared to be acting irrationally.

She opened up the notebook and flicked through to the last page of writing. It was as she had expected when she had first tried to find it. Just a series of seemingly random jottings about the case they were working on.

'So, no suicide note then,' Nelson said, crossing his arms.

'No, but don't you see that proves my point,' she countered with as much confidence as she could muster. 'Not only does this show he was acting normally that afternoon, it also makes his hanging on to it suspicious.'

'Are you telling me that you don't think he killed himself?'

This was it. This was the real question that lay behind everything. And the truth was Ruby didn't know the answer, much less whether any doubts over Jenkins' apparent suicide were not just her mind's way of showing that it was struggling to cope with what had happened.

'I... I don't know,' she said, hating that her body had sought to betray her by producing more tears.

Today there was to be no switching of chairs for Nelson so that he could physically comfort her. However, there was a softening of his tone to accompany the unfolding of his arms. 'Look, I don't want to admit it either,' he added calmly. 'I was up most of last night thinking of all the ways I could have supported him more; and whether there were any tell-tale signs that he was slipping I had failed to recognise.' He shook his head in acknowledgement that he still hadn't made his mind up about either of these. 'But the fact is we will probably never know what finally triggered it and, worse, we could drive ourselves mad trying to read into every word and gesture made.'

'Trying to rationalise the irrational,' Ruby mumbled, verbalising her thoughts from yesterday.

'Indeed,' he said, seemingly satisfied that she was finally starting on the right path. 'I meant what I said a few moments ago about it being wrong of me to have allowed you back to work so soon. I really should have insisted that you take some time off and use some of that time to engage with our counselling services.'

Ruby didn't like the notion that she couldn't cope with this on her own but knew that to visibly baulk at this would only confirm to Nelson that she was still in a state of denial. 'Do you just want me to go home now, guv?' Perhaps if she made a tactical retreat he might allow himself to be convinced of her recovery on Monday morning.

'It's not quite as simple as that,' he replied, his tone now serious. 'Your... theatrics out there didn't go unnoticed. Although you not being here for a while is probably the best thing all round, I worry what it would do to your reputation longer term. As harsh as this may sound, if they see you being sent home now, I can't guarantee how convinced they'll be of your ability to cope under pressure.'

Ruby supposed that she should feel grateful that he was looking out for her in this way, but shining a spotlight on her behaviour was difficult to take. 'So, what then?'

'In a moment we're going to go to the door together. We'll stand outside and I'm going to say something to you that we both laugh at. Then you are going to wander back to your desk where you will remain there, under the guise of working, until it's time to knock off in about an hour. Understood?'

Ruby offered a simple nod.

'Good, and then you are going to spend the weekend doing whatever it is you do outside of here. On Sunday evening I'm going to call you and we're going to have an honest discussion about how you are feeling, and we'll decide what's next from there.' He stood up, motioning for Ruby to do the same.

With the door now open he pretended that he was concluding their conversation. 'So, I said to the instructor, if you think that's impressive, you should see my other one.' Ruby found it easier than she had expected to offer a short burst of laughter in response, such was the bizarreness of Nelson's comment.

Once back at her seat and with the rest of the team having returned their attention to whatever it was they were doing, Ruby started to flick through Jenkins' notebook again, despite all thoughts of doing anything more today with their case having now gone. With still a third of the pages remaining blank, she was surprised how far his notes went back, and she skipped to the first page addressing the acid attack.

Not that anything about Jenkins' scrawling was of much interest. It wasn't just that it gave no hint as to his downward personal spiral, his train of thought about their cases was hard to follow, even with those, like the acid attack, which had led to an outcome. Ruby knew that she shouldn't be surprised; they were not designed for anything other than Jenkins' personal consumption, but that didn't stop her feeling a little disappointed to find no references to her in there. She would have liked to have seen some indication of the way their working relationship had developed.

It wasn't long before she was back at the final few pages. Unlike on many occasions, he hadn't left himself any questions from the night before, no doubt a reflection on them having tied up all the loose ends on Gary Hamilton's gambling and his financial records before clocking off. However, his very last entry was different. With the events of their final day together still fresh in her mind, it was easier to follow Jenkins' train of thought. She could see how his initial notes tied in with their visit to the dealership but his comments for the afternoon were more speculative. Even were it not for the single word question, by way of a conclusion, she could see that he hadn't yet ruled out Kelly Hamilton's murder having something to do with her husband.

Scam? The blank space below it only served to emphasise its potency. But they had already considered whether Gary had been looking for a life-insurance pay-out, or some other reason why he might benefit from his wife's death. Putting aside the matter of him initially providing the least convincing alibi Ruby could imagine, there was the simple truth that his finances were healthy. Even if it weren't for Gary's burgeoning personal accounts, cash-flow within the business must be sound if he hadn't been in the least concerned about needing to wait the inevitable months it would take the insurance company to pay out on the stolen car.

But that wasn't the thing that was really troubling Ruby. She understood where Nelson was coming from in saying that they were unlikely to ever know what had finally tipped Jenkins over the edge, but rather than accept the notion that her doubts were centred around her failure to come to terms with what had happened, she kept finding more ways to question what appeared to be the accepted version of events. First, she had struggled to believe that Jenkins would do that without giving her the slightest indication, even if it was just with her using the benefit of hindsight. Now, not only was there the fact that he had his notebook on him when he never took it home, but he had ended his writing with a question that he would never go on to answer.

But as much as this all disturbed her, she knew now more than ever, that she would have to keep her concerns to herself. One more misplaced comment to DCI Nelson was likely to see her hauled up in front of Occupational Health and liable to result in her being signed off work for the foreseeable future.

She would have to figure this out on her own.

Ruby couldn't change what had happened to Jenkins, nor did she think Nelson could be convinced it was anything but suicide. Similarly, she might never understand the reason why Jenkins had abandoned his strict habit of not taking his notebook home with him, especially when it gave no hint as to what he intended doing that evening. However, what she could change was her failure to understand his final question. If nothing else, she might be able to find an answer to it and, in the same way she was loath to give up the case, and leave Jenkins' last investigation unfinished, this might provide some form of resolution, no matter how small.

Perhaps Jenkins had been looking at Gary's financial situation from a different perspective. Rather than taking it as a sign that his poker playing wasn't a problem, it was conceivable Jenkins had been considering whether things were too healthy. She hadn't thought to check their sales figures and, although she imagined margins to be high at the top end of the used car market, the fact remained it was a relatively small business that would require most of its clients to travel out to visit. Certainly, there hadn't been anyone there when they had visited and every day a car remained on the forecourt it would be continuing to depreciate.

But *Scam* was quite a conclusion to jump to, especially for someone as reserved as Jenkins. She replayed their time at the dealership in her mind to see where he might have got that impression, but all she found herself focusing on was his hostility towards Gary, a stark contrast with his enduring patience when they had been questioning him on his alibi the day before.

Ruby looked up from her desk and was surprised to see that most of the hour until she was due to finish had now passed. But, rather than find it a sense of relief, she knew that she would be unable to deposit her thoughts behind her when she left in a few minutes, and staying late would be out of the question with Nelson now watching her like a hawk.

'Fine,' she muttered, whilst starting the process of making it look like she was packing up. She would leave on time but that didn't mean she had to stop her work just yet. She would visit the dealership on her way home. Perhaps just being there would give her a greater insight into what was going through Jenkins' mind. She was more into cars than the average person, and certainly Jenkins, so it shouldn't take too much to figure out what the potential fiddle was there. That they would be closed for the evening was also a good thing in Ruby's mind. She would be able to have a potter around the outside undisturbed and wouldn't have to answer any awkward questions from Gary as to why she was there without her partner.

Chapter Twenty-nine

After a truly challenging day in the office, and one where she hadn't exactly covered herself in glory, it felt good to be out and back in her car. But before starting the engine she wanted to get something out of the way first. She was tired, but more than ever she wanted to see Danny tonight and wished to respond to his request that morning before he made alternate plans for the evening.

> *If the offer still stands, I would love to come over this evening. I'll need to go home first and collect some things but should be over by 8pm. R x*

She felt satisfied with the message. He would take the gap between her finishing work and going around to his place as meaning she needed a chance to talk to her parents about what had happened to Jenkins, when in reality it bought her plenty of time to continue her musings on potential scams at the dealership itself. Besides, she knew that she wouldn't be able to enjoy her weekend if she hadn't at least given some thought to what she was going to say to Nelson when he called on Sunday evening. It was going to be a challenge to tread that fine balance between sounding like she was coping too well, and consequently appearing unconvincing, and providing him with ammunition that he would use against her claim that she was fit to return to work the next day.

Pulling up at the dealership felt odd. Viewing it from exactly the same angle as she had in Jenkins' car only served to reopen the wounds of his passing. Mixed in with all the emotions from before was a new one – anger. Ruby had spent the past two days contemplating why she was unable to see Jenkins' action coming, to the extent that she had begun to question her skills as a detective. But there was every chance he had sat here with her, discussing the cars on the forecourt knowing what he was going to do later that day. It trivialised their relationship to the point of irrelevance, which hurt but also made her angry for caring so much and allowing herself to be so affected. Moreover, she wouldn't be here now if it were not for some sense of loyalty towards him, to conclude a case he had decided to turn his back on; a sense of loyalty that was clearly not reciprocated, otherwise he would not have sat here debating the relative merits of the different marques, pretending that the day was the same as any other.

Ruby stepped out of the car into the chill of the evening air, the gloom of dusk from when she had left the station now replaced by the inky black of night. It wasn't so much the bright light that bathed the forecourt that bothered her, more that none of the models had been moved to a secure carpark whilst the business was closed. Even if their high-end security systems meant that they couldn't be stolen, they surely would be a target for vandals unless…

Unless a security guard was employed. Ruby instantly slowed her walking and, for the second time, regretted making her way out here. Proving to the security guard that she was here on police business would be as simple as flashing her warrant card, but it added another unwelcome complication and would make her feel uncomfortable about poking around with them watching.

Ruby returned to her car and took a deep sigh as she pulled out Jenkins' notebook. What had she been thinking when she decided to come here? That the answer to his riddle would just reveal itself? Not that she believed it was some kind of cryptic clue anymore. Like Nelson had said, who knows what is going on in the head of a suicidal man? Besides, all the car scams she could think of seemed inappropriate in this context. Modern digital dashes had virtually eliminated the old practice of clocking, whereby an unscrupulous dealer would make it appear the car had done fewer miles, so he could command more money for it. The notion of a *cut and shut*, where two crash damaged vehicles are joined together to make one seemingly perfect, but otherwise thoroughly dangerous, example didn't fit this end of the market either.

Ruby had to concede that the cloning of vehicles by altering their identifying marks, perhaps to mask stolen cars, was more suited to motors such as these because of the profit margins involved but this realisation didn't excite her either. Plausible as it may be, she couldn't see how it would fit with what had happened to Kelly Hamilton.

She put her head in her hands and started massaging her temples to try and sooth her tired mind. This was pointless and worse than being grilled at home about her partner's suicide. Similarly she wondered whether it was wise to be spending the evening with Danny. Sure, being with him could provide the welcome relief she was hoping for but, equally, there was a chance he might grow tired of her malaise.

As Ruby raised her head once more, this time absolutely determined that she would end this poor excuse for an investigation, she noticed some movement to the far left of the forecourt. Before the man stepped into the light, he had been visible by virtue of the tip of his cigarette. Ruby didn't think it was especially professional for a security guard to be wandering around smoking, but she figured that he probably had little else to do and it was better than him being asleep somewhere.

It certainly was keeping him lively, judging by the way he was pacing around and moving his arms. A moment later Ruby understood the real reason for his behaviour. He was talking animatedly to someone else; a person who had now stepped into the light himself. From what she could make out, the new man was trying to calm the first guy down, and Ruby was interested in finding out the nature of their disagreement.

She didn't want to risk turning on the ignition so she could operate her electric windows, in case it automatically switched on her headlights and alerted them to her presence. Instead she slowly opened her door and winced at how it triggered the illumination of the interior. But the two men were too caught up in their argument to notice and she strained to try and understand what it was they were saying.

But the first man was already chucking away the remains of his cigarette and heading back around the side of the building. Whatever the second guy had said to placate him had only done a half-job because he was still waving his arms around and making noises she couldn't quite make out.

A few moments later, Ruby was back with the scene that had initially greeted her. Everything looked exactly as it had been before, and had she arrived now, she was sure her sense that this was all pointless would have been the same. But things were different. Absolutely, the likelihood was that she had witnessed two security guards squabbling but there were a number of things that didn't sit easily with her. Unless this was the point at which they swapped shifts, which it was surely too early for that, having more than one guard on at any time seemed overkill, expensive metal on display or not. And regardless of whether he was upset, she didn't feel comfortable with the casual way the man had flicked his cigarette butt onto the forecourt. If

Gary Hamilton was so concerned about the perception of his discerning clients, he would not want to arrive tomorrow morning, probably their busiest day in terms of sales, to find the place strewn with litter.

People behave irrationally when they're in a state of high emotion, a voice in Ruby's head reminded her; the undercurrent to the claim being that she should know this as well as anyone.

'So what?!' she mumbled to herself, getting out of the car once more. It didn't matter what the root of their unprofessionalism was, Ruby was a detective constable and thoroughly entitled to question something that concerned her. It wasn't a similar situation to what she had discussed with Jenkins as they had walked to the Honey Bee, where they talked about letting something go because they had other priorities to deal with – her very reason for being here was because there was something amiss.

Stepping between the closely spaced bollards and onto the forecourt, Ruby already had formed the semblance of a plan. She would not mention any concerns she had to the security guards. Moreover, she would seek to befriend them by talking to them in a fraternal way, implying that the nature of their jobs was ostensibly the same. Certainly, she felt far more comfortable doing that than the alternative which was playing the hapless female.

'Fellas,' she called confidently as she rounded the building, instantly regretting her hastiness. The back was nearly as well illuminated as the front but she could have almost believed that the hive of activity going on in the small, detached, workshop was innocent, had it not been for her shout causing the six people to immediately cease what they were doing and look in her direction.

Never before in her life had Ruby felt such a need to make a decision and yet so powerless to do so. The voice in her mind from earlier was imploring her to turn tail and run, but then what? Not only could she imagine how ridiculous this would sound when she called it into the station. When her back-up arrived, what would she expect them to find? What she would need to do is to continue with her plan to front this out. Why wouldn't people be surprised to find her approaching when the business had been closed for a couple of hours? Hadn't she just been thinking about how tomorrow was their busiest day; making it only natural that some of the staff would have to do a little overtime.

With her shaking legs not helped by the anxious glances the six men shot each other, Ruby continued forwards. 'Sorry to disturb you. Is Mr Hamilton still around?' Her voice may have sounded a little too shrill in her ears, but she was satisfied that this was a plausible reason for her being here. If she was told he had already gone home, she would thank them and leave, perhaps adding weight to her story by asking them to pass on a message. Alternatively, if he was here then he would surely vouch for her.

'Hold on,' barked the guy whom she had believed to be the security guard earlier, now walking steadily towards her. She began to back away but something in her peripheral vision caused her to stop. From the back of the workshop stepped Gary Hamilton, but the sight of him didn't provide the reassurance she had been hoping for. Even if it were not for his frightened expression, the man shoving him forwards would have been enough to cause alarm.

Whatever was going on here; it was too late for Ruby to run. There was only ten yards between her and her potential assailant, and he could be on her before she had even turned around. 'I'm DC Ruby Knight,' she boomed, reaching into her inside pocket to retrieve her warrant card.

'Don't.' It wasn't so much the word itself but the confident and dispassionate way it was delivered that made Ruby freeze. The man from behind Gary emerged, and smiled at the look of recognition on her face.

'Mr Petrov?' she stammered.

'Er, no,' he replied with a small laugh. 'Petrov is a Russian name, but I would expect nothing less from our ignorant host. My name is Zamir and I am from Albania.' His English was excellent but delivered with a soft Eastern European accent.

She ignored his introduction, instead choosing to focus on Gary. 'What's going on?' she asked him, regretting the pleading tone to her question.

'What are you doing here? Why can't you just stay away?!'

'Not another word from you,' Zamir said, jabbing Gary in the ribs, before turning back to Ruby. 'Miss Knight, I think it would be better for everyone if you allowed us to escort you home. We're just about done with our business venture here and you need see nor hear from any of us again.'

In that moment Ruby would have liked nothing more than to leave and, had it not been for the look of pure anguish on Gary's face she might have accepted Zamir's invitation. 'No,' she mumbled before clearing her throat. 'No, I am a detective constable in the Hertfordshire Constabulary and I am here as part of an ongoing investigation. I have reason to believe there is illegal activity going on here and I am going to submit everybody to a search.' Ruby had performed countless stop and search procedures whilst in uniform in London and turned around to look at each of the men gathered there. But the confidence of following a familiar procedure drained away as soon as she regarded their fixed expressions. She reached into her pocket, 'But first I am going to call for assistance and meanwhile I want all of you to line–'

'Don't,' Zamir instructed in the same firm tone he had used when he had first made his presence known. 'I'm going to give you one last chance to walk away. Like I said before, it would probably be best all round.'

'And if I don't agree?' The defiance in Ruby's question was undermined by the nerves she was unable to keep from her tone.

'Well,' replied Zamir, shrugging. 'Then we will have to deal with matters in a similar way to before.'

'No, you can't, you…' But Gary's protests were cut short by a lightening quick punch to his kidney that saw him collapse to his knees.

Zamir was in the process of making his suit look immaculate again but Ruby was no longer paying full attention. Instead her mind was racing with the possible implications of what had just been said. She opened her mouth to query what he had meant by *before* but the mirth she now witnessed in his eyes caused the question to die in her throat.

'Jenkins,' was what she muttered instead.

'Yes,' he replied mildly. 'Two evenings ago he marched round here with the same contemptible arrogance you just did. It's fortunate for Gary here, that you seemed utterly surprised to see us.'

'What?' Ruby was still struggling to comprehend the situation she found herself in.

'I did consider whether Gary had sought to tip your colleague off, even if the evidence of him arriving here alone suggested otherwise. But I had no way of finding out for sure, if we were going to make his death look like suicide. Tell me, what was your reaction when you first heard what had happened to him?'

Ruby was stunned. What Zamir was saying sounded unbelievable, but at the same time she knew it to be true.

'Please, you don't need to do this,' Gary implored from his still crouched position.

'Don't you put this on me, you pathetic little shit,' Zamir spat, leaning over him menacingly. 'If you had sought to keep to our arrangement, an arrangement that had made you fucking rich by the way, none of this would have happened. She's only here because of you!'

'But you killed my wife,' he cried, cowering even more in anticipation of another blow.

That it wasn't forthcoming was almost as surprising as the comment Zamir chose to make instead. 'I've already told you that wasn't my intention. If she had followed the instructions given to her…'

As mesmerising as the scene was, and as much the revelation came as a shock, Ruby didn't watch it without conscious thought. She had already begun to back away but Zamir returned his attention to her before she had chance to make a break for it. For the second time that evening she was frozen but this time it wasn't with indecision. She knew exactly what she had to do but she didn't know whether she had more time to improve her chances of escape.

As Ruby stood there regarding Zamir's expression, she hoped she would get at least one more chance to put some more distance between them before he decided to chase, but the cruel smile forming on his lips told her that her time had run out.

Ruby took a gamble and dashed for the other side of the building from which she had come. She had been unable to gauge the current position of half of Zamir's men, and her managing to get up to speed without feeling any hands grabbing her, suggested her decision had been the correct one. Running faster than she ever thought possible, it was mere seconds before she was back on the forecourt again. The thumping of her pulse and her deep breathing was masking the exact distance of the footsteps behind her, but she knew that indecision was the only thing likely to now see her caught. Whilst the choice of running up the road was fraught with variables, if she could get back to her car she may be able to speed off to safety.

Ruby only needed to slow her pace slightly as she reached into her pocket for the key fob and managed to swing the door open and catapult herself inside in one fluid motion. With the clutch depressed, a quick prod of the starter button caused the engine to fire with the programmed flare of revs that had caused her to giggle when she first test drove the model. She slammed the gear stick into first, simultaneously releasing the clutch whilst pushing down on the accelerator, when her door was flung open and an arm hoisted her out of her seat.

That the car lurched forward before the engine conked out was of no concern to Ruby, because she was outside the vehicle and being thrown to the ground. Even were it not for the sickening crunch as her head slammed against the hard tarmac beneath, she wouldn't have tried to get up. This had been her one chance to escape and she had blown it.

'Well that's it, decision made, you heavy-handed moron,' Zamir said, jogging over. 'Someone get me her phone and, for fuck's sake, get her off this road.' Moments later Ruby had been hefted to her feet and was being half-walked, half-dragged back across the forecourt. 'Get her a chair,' he barked at someone before switching his attention to another of his employees. 'And you should be watching Gary like a hawk,' he chided.

The thumping in her head and the abject terror she now felt was combining to make Ruby nauseous. Her fight to prevent herself throwing up, at least served to slow down the rate of conscious thought. Not that her predicament required much in the way of comprehension. Gary's business was either a front for Zamir's organization or had been propped up by its money. For whatever reason, perhaps merely because he no longer needed them and wanted to go legit, Gary had sought to break their ties, something Zamir had clearly been unwilling to let happen. Ruby didn't know the extent of the truth in the claim that killing Kelly Hamilton had been accidental, a bungled attempt to put the frighteners on Gary, but if they had been responsible for Jenkins' death then they were every bit as dangerous as they now appeared.

'So, what's the scam then?' Ruby croaked, unable to summon any of her earlier false confidence. She might never know what had alerted Jenkins to it but at least she could know what *it* was.

Zamir laughed. 'Ever the detective, eh? Well it's simple really. Despite what you British may think of us, there is quite a bit of wealth in Eastern Europe. Did you know that Bratislava is the sixth richest region in the EU? No, I didn't think so, but with any new money, those that have it like to show it off. Fortunately for us, some of the bureaucratic practices in these countries have yet to catch up. Besides, who really is bothered about where their supercar came from as long as the price is right?'

'So, Gary sells stolen cars?' Ruby couldn't quite believe what she was hearing. If just one of his customers discovered their purchase's true provenance the game was up.

'No, no, you misunderstand. The reputation of this business has to be beyond reproach. All we do, is rent out a little space here. If you like, we hide our cars in plain sight. We just pop a different number plate on them for a while, until the dust settles, and then ship them over to the continent, after making any adjustments that are required to the cars' identifying marks. If we happen to be a little low on stock we know someone who can give us the location of specific cars.' Zamir turned to give a cruel wink at Gary.

'Is that it?' She could barely believe she was having the conversation in the circumstances but her inquisitive mind wouldn't stop her from wanting to find out more.

'As simple as that,' Zamir replied with a grin. 'But don't underestimate the transformation it's had on our enterprise. Whereas once our chances of getting a car out of the country was about 75%, now it's more like 95%. And don't just think of it in terms of the reduction of lost revenue. The expense there is a drop in the ocean compared to the hassle of having to bribe the driver to keep their mouth shut or…'

'…or ensuring there is enough threat to their family to achieve the same result,' Ruby said, bitterly.

'Exactly,' Zamir replied with a shrug that implied he only did what circumstance forced him to. 'So, what we give Gary in return for his hospitality is a price worth paying.'

'What are you going to do with me?' Ruby had learned enough of the operation here and hoped that the surprise of her question would elicit a more truthful answer than she might otherwise expect.

'I'm afraid you've left us with little choice. Stolen cars are one thing but… well, let's just say that I think the time for walking away has passed. If it's any consolation then I do regret it having to be this way. I may have found you arrogant and rude the first time we met but there's a certain spark about you I like. Much more so than that other guy…'

'Jenkins,' she hissed. 'His name was Jenkins.'

'Of course,' he nodded solemnly. 'But I think you've just illustrated my point right there. Even if it were not that two suicides would look too much of a coincidence, I doubt people would believe you to be the type to do it.'

For the first time Ruby could feel the tears starting to well up, but she wasn't about to weep for her own fate. The way Zamir spoke of Jenkins was as though he had sensed more about what troubled him than Ruby had ever worked out. But rather than use that knowledge to help him, as she surely would have, he had exploited it to create a situation where Jenkins' death had appeared unsuspicious. What must it have been like for her partner, having fought off the demons for so many years, to have to fake his suicide? How did they do it? What sort of leverage had they exerted?

'You'd better just kill me now then, because I'm not playing along with whatever you've got planned for me.'

Zamir laughed; it was full and hearty and echoed around the workshop. 'He sure was right about you being a feisty one. I assure you that it does pain me to have to break my promise to him not to go for you, but I'm sure he would see us as having been left with little choice.' He paused, all trace of humour leaving his face, then lunged forward to grab Ruby's wrist. She gasped in shock and only understood what he was doing when he pressed her thumb against her mobile phone's homescreen. He released his grip, smiling thinly. 'And yes, you are going to cooperate, otherwise I won't just be killing you but also…' He hesitated whilst he swiped through the screen, the irony of it being similar to what she had done with Samie's phone not escaping Ruby. 'Oh yes, here we are. Obviously there's Mummy and Daddy,' he mocked. 'Is Gemma your sister? Oh, wait, who's this? Danny…'

'Don't you fucking dare!' she spat.

Zamir gave an irascible sigh. 'Someone shut her up for me, will you?' As Ruby quickly swung her head from side to side, she could see three of his men closing in on her. She only had time to ponder whether their keenness to answer his command was out of a sense of loyalty or merely to put themselves in his good books. It was the guy who'd dragged her out of the car that got to her first, the *heavy-handed moron*. As she turned away from the impending blow, the wince she saw on Gary's face made her believe that this was probably the guy who had killed his wife with one strike.

Chapter Thirty

It was movement that first stirred Ruby towards consciousness. Not her own, as such, but around her. It was when they lurched forwards that she began to understand where she was. Realising that she was in a vehicle of some sort served to allow the associated sounds to penetrate whatever protective bubble her mind was sitting in.

'Take it easy, will you?!'

The request caused her eyes to snap open before the irritated response came from the driver. 'Fuck off, you dumb prick, or would you rather explain to Zamir why we got left behind?'

Even within the gloom of the car's interior Ruby knew the fat neck and broad shoulders diagonally opposite her belonged to the man who had assaulted her twice. *Kelly's likely killer*, her brain sought to remind her. She didn't know which of Zamir's men was the driver directly in front where she sat, but was surprised to see Gary next to her.

If he was pleased that she was awake, his face didn't show it as she turned towards him. *Where are we going?* Ruby mouthed, exaggerating her facial movements to convey as much meaning as possible. He shook his head, initially causing her to believe that he hadn't understood her, but when he turned away she guessed it was more that he didn't want to speak to her.

'Fucking coward,' she mumbled, judging that he had understood that by the way his back stiffened, before turning to face her with his finger on his lips in the universal sign to be quiet.

'Where are we going?' she called loudly, enjoying, despite herself, the jolt of shock her demand provoked from the men up front.

'We're taking you home,' the driver replied, causing a snigger to come from the passenger seat; their earlier squabble seemingly forgotten.

'Home? But how…?' Her question was answered before she'd even said it by her attacker holding up a small card. Unable to see what it was in the light, she leaned forward and a passing streetlamp obliged by briefly illuminating her driver's license.

'What? Why?' she asked, regretting her efficiency at getting her details updated as soon as she had moved back in with her parents.

'We thought you might like to introduce us to your boyfriend,' the driver sniggered.

'But… but he doesn't…'

'We know,' he replied in mock exasperation. 'We saw your little message to him and we simply sent him another one asking if he would come around to yours instead.'

'No!' she called out involuntarily but regained enough composure to prevent her blurting out anymore. Her mind was flooded with what would await Danny when he got there and, in the absence of any clue as to how to try and get out of this, she knew that saying more could only make the situation worse.

'Ah, don't be like that,' the *heavy-handed moron* pleaded sarcastically. 'It's all the same to him whether he bones you at his place or yours.'

'Excepts he's the one who's fucked now!' the driver added, quick as a flash, and causing them both to hoot with cruel laughter.

As appalled as Ruby was, she didn't let the moment pass. 'Are you going to let this happen?' she hissed at Gary whilst her two kidnappers were still giggling. She didn't wait for an answer; the look of sheer impotence written across his face was enough. 'You're going to stand by and let them kill me, like they killed Jenkins, and like they killed Kelly?'

A flash of anger completely altered Gary's expression and she knew what he was going to say before he shouted: 'I didn't let them kill my wife!'

'Shut the fuck up back there!'

But Ruby barely heard the order, let alone paid attention to whom it came from. This was progress. Next to her was the man whom she had met outside his house, the man who was rendered distraught by what had happened to his wife and who had shouted at her that he didn't give a shit about a stolen car. Yet whatever the depth of his emotion, it was nothing compared to hers. It was one thing to think that she was going to die but another entirely if the ones she loved were going to be dragged into this. And even if it weren't for them, she couldn't allow Jenkins' death to be seen as the pathetic last action of an alcoholic who had lost anything of meaning in his life.

'You're going to let them kill me, are you?' she roared, her face mere inches from Gary's. 'And you're going to let them kill my boyfriend too and then stand around whilst they set it up so it looks like he did it?' The pause that followed was only momentary but enough for Ruby to make two crucial, linked decisions. She would not reveal that her parents would also be there; it would neither add weight to her argument with Gary, nor would it cause a change of destination. And in coming to this conclusion she realised that, no matter how intolerable their plans for

Danny were, she could not allow her parents to come to any harm. That it only left one option was a crumb of comfort, even though it was still likely to result in her own death. 'Please don't try and stop me,' she said to Gary softly, hoping he would choose to continue the path of least resistance and not fight to spare his own wretched existence.

Ruby leaned forward, reaching beyond the headrest in front of her and clawed at the eyes of the driver. His initial screams were more through shock than pain, and were matched by her own as she reopened the wounds that she had caused when attempting to free Jenkins from the chord that had strangled the life from him. But the knowledge that the absence of her usually long nails were preventing her from popping his eyeballs only caused her shouts to increase in volume and intensity as she tried to push them back into their sockets. She could feel his hands pawing at hers, matched by the slewing of the car, but she would not release her grip; pulling herself tighter against the seatback that separated them.

But then a punch to her face almost caused her to falter. It was more the unexpected shock of it, rather than the glancing blow itself that nearly made her release her grip on the driver. As she turned in the direction from which it had come, she could see the man who had knocked her out once already repositioning himself in the passenger seat so he could take better aim this time. Any move to try and protect herself would only provide a brief respite because the driver would be released and her plan would have failed. She would still be taken home and there would still be the inevitable harm to those she loved.

So, in contrast to back at the dealership, she turned to face the full force of the impact. She hoped that the effects of this, combined with her already damaged skull would see her killed outright. Perhaps then the others would be spared and her body would simply be dumped at the side of the road.

If anything the fist looked even larger than it did before, illuminated by the colour of the large media screen in the centre of the car's dashboard. As it burst forward to meet her, she fought her body's natural instinct to close her eyes, for if this was the last thing she was ever going to see, she wouldn't allow herself to shy away from it.

And the blackness did come to replace the gloom of the vehicle's interior, but not as Ruby had expected it. From her left Gary had launched himself between the two front seats, taking the full force of the blow in his chest, and knocking her forward in the process. With her face planted against the headrest in front of her she had released her grip on the driver; her left arm crushed under Gary's weight. But her right was free and she was going to set about doing what little damage she could achieve with that again when her hand brushed something familiar. She moved it back in the direction from which it had come, to check that she could get enough of a purchase on it, not just to grab hold of it, but to be able to move it. With the pressure on her left arm being released she knew that Gary had either slunk back to his seat or was being hoisted up by her intended attacker. But either way it was too late. With a final thrust forward, that did little to move the seat in front, she yanked the steering wheel as hard as she could to the right.

The following moments were surreal as Ruby tried to interpret the change of movement her body was experiencing. The car lurched into the oncoming lane and it seemed as though her input was going to do nothing more. But then she could feel the outer tyres dig into the surface rather than continue to rotate freely. The car stopped turning right and, instead, pitched violently to the left and began to roll over. There was a brief moment of weightlessness as Ruby was lifted off her seat, before crashing down onto Gary and finding herself tossed in the air again as the car entered its second barrel roll.

Ruby lost all sense of direction but even that was momentary as her head eventually met the hard surface of one of the rear windows and all thought disappeared.

Chapter Thirty-one

Waking up in an unfamiliar place was unusual to Ruby. She hadn't opened her eyes yet but she knew she wasn't in her own bed. When she had been dating a guy long enough to be considering sleeping with him, she liked it to be on her terms. But then she remembered that it had been different with Danny. She had gone around to his place feeling confident that she was equipped to deal with whatever situation arose and, in the end, she had been the one to make the first move. She had been back since and she recalled intending to go there again. Perhaps she was there now, and when she opened her eyes, she would see him lying next to her.

It was with thoughts of Danny that Ruby finally regained consciousness. But even before she grasped a true sense of where she was, she knew it wasn't him she was looking at.

'Take it easy,' soothed DCI Nelson, reaching for the button to alert the nurses.

'Wait,' Ruby croaked, trying and failing to get her arm to respond in an effort to stop him.

'What is it?' he whispered, smiling but unable to hide the concern in his eyes.

Already Ruby could feel exhaustion trying to pull her back under but she needed to understand what had happened. 'My family? Danny?'

'They're all here. I offered to sit with you whilst they went and got something to eat. They've been with you since you were brought in.' It was only then that Ruby noticed that it was daylight that was allowing her to see her boss.

She opened her mouth to ask another question but was stopped by a nurse bursting in. 'You were meant to keep her company, not try and wake her,' she scolded as she approached the series of monitors beside the bed, before moving to the small bag of clear liquid running from a tube next to the IV drip. 'Let's see if we can make you a little more comfortable,' she continued in a far softer voice.

'Hold on,' Ruby implored, willing the nurse not to pump whatever painkiller she intended into her system. At least not yet. 'The car?'

The nurse turned to look quizzically at DCI Nelson who smiled and nodded. 'It's okay, Ruby, we know. It was found in the bushes by a passing motorist. Gary Hamilton was conscious you were all dragged out. He told them what had happened.'

'Where is he?'

'I'm afraid he died on the way here and the two other occupants were pronounced dead at the scene.' He paused to clear his throat. 'I can't tell you how lucky you are to be alive.'

Ruby's eyes closed. She did feel lucky but that wasn't what convinced her to give in to her need to rest. When she next woke, she would be greeted by those people she had fought to save. More than that, she would be able to tell everyone that Jenkins had died whilst in the line of duty.

If you enjoyed this book, please let others know by leaving a quick review on Amazon. Also, if you spot anything untoward in the paperback, get in touch. We strive for the best quality and appreciate reader feedback.

editor@thebookfolks.com

www.thebookfolks.com

MORE FICTION BY DENVER MURPHY

If you enjoyed THE DEEP END, you'll love the other books in the series, available on Kindle and in paperback from Amazon.

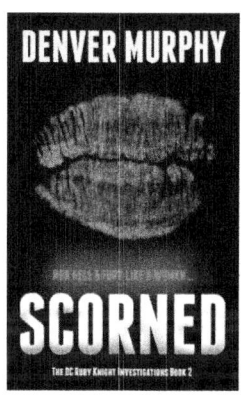

SCORNED – Book 2

Having made an impression with her first case, DC Ruby Knight begins an investigation into a spate of burglaries in St. Albans. However, as they become increasingly violent, she is put under more and more pressure to bring the culprits in. But her efforts are scuppered when the unexpected happens and she has a murder on her hands.

BENEATH THE SURFACE – Book 3

When a teenaged boy is found hanging from a tree in a park, DC Ruby Knight suspects it is not the suicide her colleagues presume it to be. But alienated from her team and under pressure from her chief, she'll have a hard time convincing them they are dealing with murder. Can she follow her instincts and catch the killer, or will her maverick antics get her the boot?

BORDERLINE – Book 4

When a girl is attacked on her way home after a night out, DC Ruby Knight is determined to prevent another incident. But the community quickly take matters into their own hands. The young detective is forced to question her own sense of right and wrong when revenge tries to trump justice.

THE DCI BRANDT SERIAL KILLER TRILOGY

Book I, ONE STEP AHEAD

Someone is on a killing spree, targeting young women. But they always seem one step ahead of the police investigation. Why? Could it be that detectives are looking for one of their own?

A thrilling game of cat and mouse.
Get the whole series on Kindle or paperback now!

Printed in Great Britain
by Amazon